ADAM
AND THE
ARKONAUTS

Also by Dominic Barker

Blart: The Boy Who Didn't Want to Save the World

Blart 2: The Boy Who Was Wanted Dead Or Alive –
Or Both

Blart 3: The Boy Who Set Sail on a Questionable Quest

To Alice, my mother

ADAM
AND THE
ARKONAUTS

DOMINIC BARKER

BLOOMSBURY

LONDON BERLIN NEW YORK

583339

*I would like to thank Talya Baker, Ele Fountain,
Caroline Hill-Trevor, Ian Lamb, Nancy Miles, Susannah
Nuckey, Helen Szirtes and Carol Walter*

Bloomsbury Publishing, London, Berlin and New York

First published in Great Britain in May 2010 by Bloomsbury Publishing Plc
36 Soho Square, London, W1D 3QY

A CIP catalogue record of this book is available from the British Library

ISBN 978-1-4088-0025-6

FSC
Mixed Sources
Product group from well-managed
forests and other controlled sources
Cert no. SGS - COC - 2061
www.fsc.org
© 1996 Forest Stewardship Council

Typeset by Dorchester Typesetting Group Ltd
Printed in Great Britain by Clays Ltd, St Ives Plc, Bungay, Suffolk

1 3 5 7 9 10 8 6 4 2

www.bloomsbury.com

www.dominicbarker.com

PROLOGUE

Deep, deep in the Amazon rainforest, two days' paddle by canoe from the nearest human habitation, Doctor Will Forest hacked his way through the dark jungle. Sweat dripped from his brow, his clothes were clammy against his skin and he itched unbearably from the bites of swarms of insects. In spite of this, his determination didn't waver. He attacked the undergrowth with his axe, chopping his way through vines thicker than his arm while trying to avoid the stabs of thorns sharp as daggers. Above him the jungle canopy was alive with the sounds of birds and monkeys, their cries mixing together into a shrieking cacophony that swelled and intensified as the Doctor forced his way deeper into the forest. Strangely, the harder the battle became, the more the Doctor seemed to relish it. For this was the land he had come so far to find, undiscovered, unspoilt, unknown by man since the beginning of time: a place that might hold the answer to a mystery that had consumed him for many years.

Unexpectedly a shaft of light pierced the thick canopy.

A great tree had been struck by lightning and had fallen, cutting a swathe through the surrounding vegetation – its blackened stump was still ever so slightly smouldering.

'This will do,' said Doctor Forest softly. 'This is where I will try for the last time . . .'

A lifetime's quest had brought him here. As a boy, he had seen a dog and a cat on the brink of a fight. They had barked and hissed at each other, making their bodies as big and scary-looking as they could. At any moment, a tangle of fur and biting teeth seemed certain to ensue. But then . . . then, somehow, the hisses and barks had become less angry, their bodies had shrunk back to their normal sizes, and the two creatures parted without hurting one another. Watching on, it was obvious to young Will Forest they had argued, threatened but ultimately decided that it was better for both of them not to fight. They had communicated.

And it was then he had asked himself the question that would dominate the next twenty years of his life: if animals can communicate with each other, shouldn't humans be able communicate with them too?

He had grown into a man trying to answer this question, studying a variety of species, how they interacted with their own kind and with others, and trying himself to establish some sort of contact, but always with limited success. He had got married, had a son, and still he felt compelled to search for the answer.

He decided to focus his efforts on man's closest evolutionary ancestors: the monkeys. If he could crack the code with them, he felt sure it would lead to success with other species. The trouble was gaining the trust of these animals. They had learnt, justifiably, to fear mankind. Perhaps only in a place where man had never before set foot would an animal allow him to discover the answer to his question.

So now, after years of tireless research, Doctor Will Forest crouched motionless near a smouldering tree stump in a clearing in the remotest part of the world, and waited.

A golden spider monkey spindled down the trunk of a nearby tree, her long thin arms and legs expertly reaching from one branch to another – her hands moulding odd knobs of wood into secure handholds. Dropping easily to the ground, the monkey scanned the clearing. Nuts and fruit, dislodged by the tree that had fallen in last night's storm, were strewn temptingly across the rainforest floor. She moved towards them, her eyes ever watchful for predators, for she was far more vulnerable when away from the safety of the green canopy.

She picked up a nut, cleverly broke open the shell and then swallowed the kernel. Then, chattering a little to herself, she found a piece of fruit, then another nut. Convinced there were no predators nearby, she seemed confident, able to relax and enjoy her meal.

It is now or never, thought the Doctor. And he moved.

Immediately the monkey's head swung round towards him, the half-eaten nut in her hand, ready to dash for the trees in an instant. But she had never seen a human before. Was this strange furless white beast really a predator? The monkey gave herself a fraction of a second to decide. And in that fraction of a second the Doctor made a noise – the noise that, after so much study, he had concluded meant to monkeys: hello.

The monkey did not flee.

Fifteen minutes later, she was still there. And she was chattering warily to the Doctor.

Thirty minutes later, the monkey and the Doctor had moved closer to one another. The Doctor's arms mimicked the movements of the monkey and he was copying the cries she made.

An hour later, the monkey and the Doctor were crouched opposite each other. The monkey stretched out an arm towards the Doctor, palm outward in a display of friendliness. Slowly, he moved his own arm towards hers. This was no circus trick achieved after hour upon hour of tedious repetition and a system of rewards and punishments. This was it: genuine voluntary communication between species, based on equality and mutual cooperation. The Doctor felt a surge of pride. The door to a whole new world of understanding between men and animals was opening. The monkey pressed her palm against the Doctor's.

As they touched, a creeper was swept aside on the far side of the clearing, another one behind the Doctor, a third to his left. Four Amazon tribesmen, naked except for loincloths, emerged from the undergrowth, each carrying a wooden blowpipe. Doctor and monkey froze.

Then into the clearing strode a man wearing an immaculately pressed expensive brown suit, sporting a monocle and carrying an ivory cane.

Surprised, the monkey pulled her hand from the Doctor's and scampered away, leaping into the nearest tree. The Doctor couldn't believe it – his moment of triumph dashed.

'Why did you frighten her away?' he demanded angrily.

'You are a very clever man, Doctor Forest,' the monocled man observed, stepping firmly and deliberately on a blue beetle which was scuttling innocently across the clearing.

'How did you know –' began the Doctor.

'Silence,' interrupted the well-dressed intruder, stroking his chin. 'You are evidently confused as to who will be asking the questions in our conversation. Let me enlighten you. It is going to be me. You will notice the blowpipes in the hands of my companions. You may also notice the darts they carry. Be assured that they are tipped with the most deadly poison known to mankind. One word from me and four darts will fly towards you, simultaneously piercing your skin. Their marksmanship is unrivalled. Death will be instantaneous.'

This time Doctor Forest said nothing.

Shocking the Doctor into silence seemed to cheer up the monocled intruder. He adopted a friendlier manner as he strode towards him, pausing only to stab a spider with his cane.

'My name is Professor Scabellax. I am intrigued by the

same area of scientific exploration as you. Five years ago my own research stalled. Can you imagine the frustration? A man such as myself, who has never failed at anything, waking up in the morning without an idea in his head. Or at least a scientific idea . . .'

The Doctor was only half listening to the Professor. He was trying to calculate if there was any direction in which he might run that would give him a chance of reaching the haven of the forest before a dart could fell him. Instinct told him he was too far away.

'I hired some discreet people to monitor the work of the others in the field. It quickly became apparent, Doctor, that you were the only serious scientist. So I had you followed, I had your computer files copied, your lectures observed and your travel monitored.'

'That is outrageous,' cried the Doctor. 'That is –'

'I thought it was rather clever!' observed Professor Scabellax, swatting dead a bright red butterfly that alighted briefly on his arm. 'But then, suddenly, you and your nice young family set off for the rainforest. It was most inconvenient of you. My investigators, excellent though they are, could find no information to explain your sudden departure. Yet I sensed it was important. So there was nothing for it. I had to follow you myself.'

How much does he know? the Doctor wondered.

'You are wondering how much I know, aren't you, Doctor?' the Professor observed. 'I can assure you that I know enough.' Scabellax clicked his fingers. The four tribes-men pulled a poisoned dart from their loincloths and placed the deadly darts inside their blowpipes. 'I thought I'd save time by making it very clear what will happen to you if you don't cooperate.'

'If you are as informed about me as you claim, then you know that I am a responsible scientist. I will research things further and then publish my findings. The information you want will be available in less than a year,' said the Doctor.

'But not just available to me,' said Scabellax. 'Available to all. I'd rather have more . . . *exclusive* ownership of the knowledge.'

'What do you want to do with it?' the Doctor demanded.

'You appear to have forgotten who is asking the ques-tions again,' said the Professor, clapping his hands and squashing a blue dragonfly which had flown too close to his face.

'If I tell you, how can I be sure that you will let me go?'

The Professor smiled.

'That question I will allow you. You are aware of my power and also of the lengths I will go to to get what I want. I assure you that if you so much as hint at this information when you return to civilisation, I will take immediate action to have you silenced. I know, therefore, that there is no need to worry.'

The Professor looked the Doctor straight in the face.

'So I can promise you that I will not kill you now.'

7

Upon the words 'not kill' the Doctor knew his fate was sealed. For one brief moment the Professor's eyes could not meet the Doctor's. The Doctor had studied language all his life, including body language, and he knew very well that when a person looked away suddenly it meant they were lying.

'Now we've got that little unpleasantness out of the way,' the Professor went on, 'I await your explanation.'

He leant on his cane and prepared to listen.

'Where to start?' the Doctor began. He could feel adrenalin pouring into his veins. His body demanded action but he knew he had to time his escape attempt perfectly.

'Doctor?' the Professor sounded impatient.

Will Forest opened his mouth as if to speak. Instead, he turned and ran full speed across the clearing. His heart was pumping as he dashed towards the safety of the trees. Cover was almost in reach . . .

However, the tribesmen had reacted instantly. They were sure and swift and, despite the Doctor's best efforts, they were faster than him.

Leaning on his cane in the centre of the clearing, Professor Scabellax watched with an air of amusement. For the Doctor was no longer fleeing; he was being hunted down. Years of chasing wild boar had made the tribesmen experts at cutting off routes of escape. Trapped like a wild animal, the Doctor charged desperately one way and then another.

'I do hate to see energy wasted so pointlessly,' the Professor observed, spying an ant on his suit and smacking it dead immediately.

Having cornered him against an enormous tree, the tribesmen approached the Doctor, their blowpipes held to their lips. He slumped back against the trunk, resigning himself to capture. The tribesmen sensed his surrender and allowed themselves to relax also – taking their blowpipes from their mouths and looking at him with broad smiles.

And then something extraordinary happened.

From nowhere a cascade of sticks rained down from the canopy, hitting the tribesmen. Yelping with pain and surprise they cowered down, glancing about them in alarm. In all their years of hunting, this had never happened before. Their ancient superstitions filled them with doubt. Was the forest displeased with them? They looked at each other in confusion and fear.

For not a single stick had struck the Doctor.

But Professor Silus Scabellax did not believe in ancient superstitions. He knew that if there were sticks falling from the sky, then someone or something was throwing them and they were doing it for a reason.

The Doctor saw his opportunity, reached for the lowest branch and began to climb.

'Fools!' shouted Scabellax at the tribesmen. 'He's getting away. You're being outwitted by monkeys.'

The rage of Professor Scabellax was so terrible that for a

moment it outweighed the tribesmen's fear of the wrath of the forest. They looked up to see the Doctor scrabbling up into the canopy.

'Remember I want him alive,' the Professor shouted.

But it was too late. Dishonoured by seeing their prey on the verge of escape, the tribesmen lifted their blowpipes and took aim.

Above him the Doctor saw a thick branch. If he could reach that he would be safe. Below him the tribesmen, their blowpipes raised to their mouths, were trying to make out his body between the thick leaves.

He jumped for the branch and tried to haul himself up. He willed himself to cling on but already the strength was fading from his muscles. He clawed wildly at the slippery resin but he couldn't get a grip . . . His arms were in agony . . . digging his nails in didn't work . . .

There was a cry of excitement from the ground. The tribesmen had spotted him.

And then, suddenly, there she was on the branch, undoubtedly the same monkey that he had spent an hour with in the clearing. She had come back. He looked into her eyes and found more understanding than he could ever hope for in the murderous members of his own species down below. In that moment, deep in the Amazon, the Doctor rediscovered a communication that had been lost ages ago when mankind had first climbed out of the trees and gone to walk on the open plains. The monkey extended her hand and the Doctor was tugged to safety, as the underside of the branch was peppered with darts.

'Don't think you've got away with this, Doctor,' the raised, though still calm, voice of Professor Scabellax rang mockingly through the trees. 'There are more ways in heaven and earth to make a man bend to my will than you could ever dream of. All you've done is to ensure that the next time will be far, far worse.'

The Doctor turned back to the monkey, who sat calmly on the branch beside him.

'Thank you,' he said.

Three days later, the Doctor rushed up the stairs of his hotel in Rio de Janeiro two at a time. He fumbled for the key and burst into the tiny living room.

'Lily!' he shouted to his wife. 'Lily, are you still here? Are you all right?' He heard the cry of his young son, Adam, from the bedroom and his face relaxed. They were here.

'Lily,' he said, striding to the bedroom door, 'I think I've done it. I've broken the code. It's going to be difficult but I'm going to be able to communicate with every single animal in the world!'

Triumphant, he flung open the door to the bedroom. He was met by the hungry screams of his three-year-old son. His wife was nowhere to be seen.

He picked up Adam to comfort him and saw a note pinned to his clothes.

Dear Doctor,

One day you will beg me to learn your secret. Until that day comes, you will not see your wife again.

Regards,

Professor Silus Scabellax

All his success forgotten, the Doctor let the note drop from his hand – it fluttered slowly to the floor. Meanwhile, the familiar scent of his father had begun to calm Adam and his hungry screams were dampened to sad whimpers and then suddenly choked off altogether . . . The toddler had seen something he had never seen before and it had surprised him so much he had forgotten his empty stomach and the disappearance of his mother.

The Doctor turned to the monkey standing in the doorway.

'Do you still want to travel with me, Simia?' he asked, and there was a hard, cold edge to his voice which had never been there before. 'I hope so, because now we have something very important to find.'

Ten years later

CHAPTER 1

'Land ho!' cried Adam.

The *Ark of the Parabola*, the fastest yacht in the sea, skimmed over the waves in the fresh wind.

Doctor Forest looked quizzically up from his book. This was the third time Adam had claimed that he could see land. Both previous sightings had turned out to be big waves in the distance.

But this time there was no mistaking it. The Doctor stood up and Adam, one hand still on the helm, passed him the telescope. Scanning the coastline, he saw a harbour and, behind the wharf, rising steeply, the white houses that lined the streets of Buenos Sueños, the most isolated city in the world. And in the far distance lay the reason for its isolation: Los Puntos Afilados, lower than the Himalayas, less extensive than the Alps but filled with more treacherous avalanches and crevasses than any other mountain range in the world. No climber had ever returned from one of its icy peaks. And so a self-governing city had grown up, cut off from the rest of the world.

'How did Mum get here?' Adam wondered.

The Doctor was asking himself the same question. But he was not prepared to admit it to his son. He had searched for his wife for ten long years, diligently following up any reported sighting, exhausting every lead. Along the way, he and Adam had visited cities and towns on every continent and during the time spent at sea, sailing from one place to the next, he had perfected his research. Now he and his thirteen-year-old son could communicate with almost every kind of animal, and some of the animals they had met on their journey had joined their boat, determined to see the world for themselves. These animals were the Arkonauts. Thanks to the Doctor's teaching, most of them could even understand the language humans spoke. But important as this work was, it would always take second place to Doctor Forest's primary objective: finding Lily.

'The telegram from the Mayor I received in Istanbul was quite clear,' he told Adam. 'Your mother left him a message.'

'What was it?'

'He refused to say,' the Doctor replied. 'He insisted that if I wanted to know, I must come in person.'

'Do you think it could be a trap?' said Adam.

'We will not judge until we get there,' his father said firmly. 'Groundless speculation is the enemy of science.'

'Why do you think Scabellax has never contacted you?'

asked Adam. 'Do you think he's discovered how to talk to animals by himself?'

'We are not going to think about that,' said the Doctor firmly.

He was angry at Adam for reminding him of his own terrible fear: that Scabellax, too, had cracked the code and therefore no longer needed the Doctor's wife as a hostage. But to think that way was to risk giving into despair.

'But what if –' Adam began.

'I said we are not going to speculate,' repeated the Doctor firmly.

Adam sighed. His father was probably right about speculation. Maybe it didn't help. But Adam couldn't stop himself wondering about things he had no way of knowing . . . wondering about his mother, snatched away from him by Professor Silus Scabellax when he was only three years old.

Adam could not remember her. Now he was thirteen and he felt as though his whole life had been spent trying to find something he had never known. Sometimes when he closed his eyes in his cabin at night, he felt that he was so close to remembering her, but she remained tantalisingly out of reach, just beyond the edge of his memory.

The *Ark of the Parabola* was touching twenty knots. Soon they would begin their approach into the harbour.

'I think you should take us in,' said the Doctor.

'Me?' said Adam, looking at the jam of boats bobbing in and out of the harbour.

17

'You're ready,' his father replied.

Adam was far from sure he was ready. It was one thing navigating the *Ark* on the open sea, when there was an empty blue vastness in front of him and nothing to crash into, quite another to steer it through the chaotic port of Buenos Sueños.

The Doctor seemed to sense what Adam was feeling.

'Don't worry,' he said. 'Much of the chaos will resolve itself into patterns the closer we get to it.'

Adam knew better than to argue with his father. If it can be done, his father always said, then with enough practice and patience we can do it too. He said things like that with great confidence – a confidence that Adam rarely felt. He wondered, yet again, if he took after his mother more than his father. He gripped the helm tightly.

Behind him, out of the hatch which led down into the living quarters, emerged a monkey. It looked at Adam controlling the wheel, shook its head, then loped along the deck, chattering anxiously before tugging at the Doctor's sleeve.

'What is it, Simia?'

The monkey pointed at Adam and jabbered in a series of high-pitched shouts and yelps.

At least that's how it could have sounded to anybody else's ears. The Doctor and Adam, both being fluent in the monkey's language, heard, 'I can't believe you're letting him steer. Don't you remember what happened last time?'

The Doctor replied, yelping and chattering back in the monkey's language. Listening, Simia thought that, however hard he tried, the Doctor would never get his accent quite right. He sounded much more like he was speaking baboon. But apart from that, his yelps made sense.

'Adam is ready, Simia, he just needs practice.'

'He nearly crashed. Right into the Governor's yacht in Jamaica. What trouble that would have caused! Lots and lots of trouble.'

'That was ages ago,' yelped Adam indignantly.

Simia had to admit to herself that Adam's accent was perfect. But then, he'd been brought up learning both monkey and human language. Still, she was in no mood to praise his accent.

'Tch!' Simia turned to the Doctor. 'He is a very, very, very stupid boy.'

'Don't call me very, very, very stupid,' Adam said. 'Just stupid would do.'

'Let me steer like always,' the monkey pleaded.

'He needs to learn, Simia,' the Doctor said.

'What kind of coordination do you humans have, tch? Can you swing from branch to branch? No. Yet another thing you lost when you decided to leave the trees and walk on the land. Tch!'

'But –' began the Doctor.

'When I think of how I had to rescue you all those years ago,' continued Simia. 'Perfectly good tree to escape up but you couldn't climb it because of all this clever evolving you'd been doing.'

The Doctor had spent ten years being reminded by Simia that she had saved his life, and all the more often since he'd explained to her Darwin's theory of evolution and the survival of the fittest. Simia had interpreted the whole concept as a gigantic insult to monkey-kind.

'Chill out, girlfriend,' said a long, slow, smooth voice. Malibu, the ship's cat, had woken up.

He had joined them in California, having previously lived the pampered life of a film-star pet, only to be thrown into the streets of Hollywood when his breed stopped being fashionable. He stretched himself out in the early-morning sun.

Simia scratched her head in irritation.

'This is nothing to do with you, cat,' she said. 'Nothing at all.'

'Morning, Doc,' purred Malibu, showing no interest in the monkey's concerns.

'Good morning, Malibu,' said the doctor, bending down to tickle him behind the ears.

Sensing that she was not going to get her way, Simia stomped off to the rail, muttering darkly.

'I don't want to attract attention to us yet,' the Doctor called to the retreating monkey. 'And nothing attracts attention like having your boat steered by a monkey.'

They were now on the final approach to the port of Buenos Sueños. Fishing vessels seemed to be all around them and he could hear the unconcerned shouts of the anglers on either side.

'Hola!'

'Ciao!'

A fishing smack sailed so close that Adam heard the crack of the wind in its sails. Once past the harbour wall Adam knew that there would be calm water and easy sailing. But before that he had to negotiate the bottleneck of boats that had jammed together at the entrance to the harbour. He gripped the wheel tightly.

'Just keep a steady course,' counselled the Doctor.

The shouts of the sailors mixed with those coming from people on the wharf and the cries of the seagulls overhead who followed the boats, hoping for any of the catch that was rejected. There were boats behind the *Ark*, in front of the *Ark* and on both sides of the *Ark*. One veered suddenly towards them, its skipper distracted by a swinging rope. Adam wanted to steer the other way. Moments later he was glad he hadn't, as another boat nearby tacked round unexpectedly when a fisherman discovered he'd forgotten his lunch. Another boat shot right in front of them.

'Don't panic,' said the Doctor calmly. 'A man who panics is lost.'

Adam didn't want to panic. He wanted to shut his eyes and open them again when they were in the calm blue water of the harbour – but this would be to rely on fate, which, according to the Doctor, was even worse than panicking. The

boat in front got closer and closer and closer, and then, with an expert flick of the rudder, the fisherman took it safely past.

'Muy bien, chico,' he shouted across to Adam.

Adam's faith in his ability was growing. He kept his eyes open and his course steady and, following one final gust of wind, the *Ark of the Parabola* surged triumphantly into the harbour.

Simia tutted. 'Beginners' luck.'

'Remember to breathe, Adam,' said the Doctor.

Embarrassed, Adam took a huge gulp of air.

'I didn't think they were ever going to get out of the way,' he said.

'Of course they were going to,' his father remarked. 'The interesting thing to observe from a scientific point of view was how.'

Adam was more interested in the way his heart was beating like it wanted to force its way out of his chest and the way he felt dizzy with the success, but he knew better than to say so. His father would have dismissed this as putting sensation over science, and if there was anything he despised more than giving into fate, it was overemphasising sensation.

'Right,' said the Doctor. 'Let us find a discreet berth where we can keep the Arkonauts as far as possible from the gaze of prying eyes. And Simia, I'm afraid you'll have to retire below for a little while.'

At these words the monkey picked a flea out of her fur,

ate it and then loped across the deck to the hatch and disappeared down below.

'Right,' said the Doctor. 'Let us go and see the Mayor of Buenos Sueños.'

CHAPTER 2

'There's no time to waste,' Doctor Forest urged his son. 'Whistle for Sniffage and then we can leave.'

There was a mewl of disapproval from behind them.

'That dog makes soooo much noise,' moaned Malibu.

Moments later, an orange and white patched head with large floppy ears stuck out of the hatch to the hold. The spaniel never did anything slowly. He bounded down to the front of the ship, barking.

'Yeah! Yeah!' Sniffage yapped. 'Where are we going? We going for a walk? Let's go for a walk!'

'We are going for a walk, Sniffage,' the Doctor assured him.

'Let's go somewhere smelly. Can we? Yeah! Yeah!' Sniffage shook his floppy ears from side to side with enthusiasm.

'Eww,' said Malibu. 'Dogs are so gross.'

Sniffage ignored Malibu. He had spotted a stick. He grabbed it between his teeth, padded over to Adam and dropped it at his feet.

'Throw it for me, yeah! You won't lose it. I'll bring it back! Yeah! Yeah!'

Adam picked the stick up and threw it to the other end of the ship. Sniffage charged after it, scooped it up in his mouth and charged back, his tail wagging with pleasure. He dropped the stick at Adam's feet.

'Do it again! Yeah! Throw it further! I'll get it again!'

Adam picked up the stick.

'I don't know who's stupider,' mewled Malibu. 'You for throwing it or him for getting it.'

'There's no time for this,' said the Doctor, leading the way down the gangplank.

'I'll keep an eye on things here while you're gone,' said Malibu, and promptly fell asleep.

Standing on the quay, it was obvious to the Doctor and to Adam, though perhaps not to Sniffage, that finding anything in this maze of higgledy-piggledy streets lined with tall white houses was not going to be easy. And what is more, there didn't seem to be anybody about to ask. All the people that they had seen on the wharf as they sailed into the harbour had vanished.

'Strange,' remarked the Doctor.

They crossed a wide road and entered the labyrinth of Buenos Sueños.

'Smelly!' Sniffage barked approvingly.

'Sometimes,' remarked the Doctor, 'I almost regret learning to understand what they're saying.'

'A signpost!' said Adam, pointing to a crossroads at the end of the narrow street.

'A very detailed one,' added the Doctor, noticing that the signpost was bristling with directions. 'Surely one of the signs will point to the town hall.'

They hurried over to it. The town hall was signposted to the left.

'Come on,' said the Doctor.

But Adam tugged at his father's sleeve and pointed again. He had noticed that the town hall was also signposted to the right.

'And look,' he said.

The town hall was also signposted on the road that went straight on and even on the road that they'd just walked up. In fact, walking in any direction, according to the signpost, would lead them to the town hall.

'Strange,' repeated the Doctor. 'And not particularly helpful.'

'Over there,' said Adam. A little further down the street was a small kiosk. A sign above it said 'Tourist Information'.

Sitting by the door, with his feet stretched out and a faded brochure perched on his face, was a sleeping man. He was wearing a vest which featured an interesting mixture of sweat patches and holes. A badge attached to the vest informed Adam and the Doctor that his name was Señor Gozo and he was here to help.

The Doctor coughed.

Señor Gozo opened his eyes. They were red-rimmed and hostile.

'What?' he growled.

'We'd like some information, please.'

'Why?'

The Doctor was taken aback.

'Because we're in a strange city and a little confused about the directions.'

'What do you want to go visiting new cities for, eh? You should stay in cities that you know. That way you don't get lost.'

'But you're the local tourist information officer,' said Adam. 'Aren't you supposed to help us?'

'No,' said Señor Gozo.

'What are you supposed to do, then?'

Señor Gozo growled, 'I am here to give information *about* tourists, like they wear shorts even when it is cold and are taking photos of everything in a place, even the really boring things. And are always getting their wallets stolen. We have so few visitors to Buenos Sueños, people need advice on how to deal with them.'

The Doctor and Adam exchanged puzzled glances. Buenos Sueños was obviously a city unlike any other.

'Errr . . . we're looking for the town hall,' persisted the Doctor.

'There's a signpost over there.'

'We know,' Adam said, 'but it says that the town hall is in

27

four different directions. We were wondering if you could tell us which is the best.'

'Depends,' said Señor Gozo, 'on whether you want the direct route, the scenic route, the route avoiding low bridges or the route including low bridges.'

'The route including low bridges?' said Adam. 'Why do you have that signposted?'

Señor Gozo scratched his hairy stomach.

'The Buenos Sueños Society for the Appreciation of Low Bridges is a thriving local organisation. They crouch every Tuesday underneath the Puente Pequeñita near the swimming baths.'

'We'd like the direct route, please.'

'Well, good luck,' said Señor Gozo. 'You've got a one in four chance of being right.'

Sniffage, having become bored during this conversation, had gone off to investigate. Now he reappeared.

'Your dog appears to have a dead thing in his mouth,' observed Señor Gozo.

Sniffage dropped the unidentified dead thing at Adam's feet and began to bark enthusiastically.

Señor Gozo closed his eyes and leant back. It seemed that he had given them as much help as he was prepared to.

'Thank you,' said the Doctor. 'I suppose if we get lost we can always ask a policeman.'

'Ask a policeman?' said Señor Gozo, opening one eye, and his face broke into a broad smile. He disappeared into the dark recess of his kiosk, laughing uproariously.

The Doctor and Adam looked at each other in confusion. Above them the sun burnt down, reflecting off the white houses, steadily raising the early-afternoon temperature.

'Yeah! Yeah!' barked Sniffage, bounding around their legs. 'Is anybody thirsty? Bet you are. I am. Yeah! Found this puddle. Couple of dead things floating in it. Come and have a drink! Yeah!'

'No, thanks.' Adam shook his head.

'Sniffage,' cautioned the Doctor, 'how many times have I told you not to drink from pools with dead things in? They could make you seriously ill.'

'Dead things?' Sniffage cocked his head to one side as though he was hearing this for the first time. 'Dead things aren't good for you?'

'Not in drinking water,' insisted the Doctor.

'Yeah! But all the rest of the time. Yeah!'

'Pick a direction. Any direction,' he said, turning to Adam.

'That one,' said Adam, pointing straight on.

CHAPTER 3

At every crossroads there were directions, always pointing in four different ways. The sun beat down mercilessly and the streets of Buenos Sueños shimmered in the intense heat. Sniffage's tongue lolled out of his mouth and his breathing was heavy.

'Look,' said Adam suddenly.

Standing at the next crossroads, dressed in a smart, perfectly pressed white uniform, with a whistle in his mouth and pistol in his holster, was a policeman.

'We will ask him.' The Doctor strode directly up to him. 'Good day, my good man. I am looking for –'

PHEEEEEEP! PHEEEEEP! The policeman blew loudly on his whistle.

'Thank you,' said the Doctor drily. 'My ears were in need of a cleansing blast of high-pitched sound. Now, I was wondering if –'

'Do not distract me. I am directing traffic,' the policeman snapped.

The Doctor and Adam looked left and right. There wasn't a vehicle in sight.

'As there doesn't appear to be any traffic perhaps –'

'You give me no option,' said the policeman. 'It is a crime in Buenos Sueños to distract an officer in the course of his duty. I am imposing an on-the-spot fine. Diego, come here.'

A small man with a ponytail, who had been hidden in a shady corner, rushed over. He was carrying a can of paint and a brush.

'Paint a spot, Diego,' the policeman instructed.

'Immediately, Officer Grivas,' said Diego.

He dipped his brush into the pot of red paint and, with a practised hand, painted two perfectly circular red spots on the ground.

'Stand on the spots,' Officer Grivas ordered Adam and the Doctor. 'You have been found guilty of endangering the life of the innocent citizens of Buenos Sueños by attempting to sabotage the smooth running of the Buenos Sueños transport system in contravention of Section 81 of the Buenos Sueños Crime and Punishment Code. You are officially classed as dangerous terrorists. Fine: two pesos,' he announced.

'This is an outrage,' said the Doctor.

Officer Grivas shrugged.

His face reddening, Doctor Forest reluctantly handed over two pesos.

'You may go on your way,' said Officer Grivas, waving

them off. 'But no more of this terrorism, you understand.'

A moment later: *PHEEEEP! PHEEEEEP!*

They turned round.

'Back on the spot, please.'

'I don't understand, Officer,' said the Doctor testily. 'You said we could go.'

'I didn't say you could vandalise the streets of Buenos Sueños. That is a crime under Law 22.'

'Vandalise the streets?'

Officer Grivas indicated the ground with his pistol. Coming from the newly painted spots they had just been standing on were two sets of red footprints.

'But this is madness,' protested the Doctor. 'If we get back on the spot now, we'll get our shoes covered with wet paint again, and as soon as we get off we'll commit the crime once more.'

'You are stuck in a cycle of crime,' observed Diego, contemplating his paint brush philosophically. 'You offend. You are punished. You offend again. You are punished again. And so it goes on. Tragic in its inevitability.'

'Wait a minute,' said Adam. He bent down and removed one shoe, stepping out of his spot with his bare foot as he did so. He then removed the other and placed his two bare feet outside the spot. His feet appeared to be crime free.

'Ingenious, Adam,' his father complimented him, removing his shoes in exactly the same way and stepping from his spot.

Barefoot, and carrying their shoes in their hands, they set off to look for the town hall, noticing a large number of red spots painted on the ground in every street they turned into. Buenos Sueños, it seemed, had a very serious crime problem.

CHAPTER 4

As they walked rapidly through the streets, their feet burning on the sizzling cobbles, Adam asked the question which had been niggling at him since the moment they had moored in Buenos Sueños harbour. 'How did Mum end up in such a weird place? There are so many cities in the world – why here? And why is everyone so obsessed with rules and laws?'

'I'm afraid I can't enlighten you,' Doctor Forest admitted. 'Since the first travellers stumbled upon it, Buenos Sueños has developed a reputation for eccentricity, fostered by its remoteness. Perhaps it's that no one wants to be the odd one out in such a close-knit community. I've often observed this kind of behaviour in other animal groups.'

Before they could discuss things further, they reached a little square with a fountain where they could surreptitiously bathe their burning feet and wash the red paint from the soles of their shoes. A little alley led to a much grander square beyond. And there, on one side of the church, was the

'Ayuntamiento' – the town hall.

After a brief wait in the cool, whitewashed foyer, the Mayor's secretary, Señorita Ratti, announced that he was ready to see them.

'Doctor Forest,' said the Mayor warmly, standing up as they walked in. 'Welcome to Buenos Sueños.'

'Thank you, Mayor Puig,' said the Doctor. 'Please allow me to introduce Adam, and this is . . . *Sniffage!*' he said in a severe tone. 'Get out of there at once!'

Sniffage pulled his head out of the Mayor's bin – his jaws gripped tightly around a mouldy sandwich. He padded over and dropped it at the Doctor's feet.

'Blue spotty mould – that's my favourite,' woofed Sniffage enthusiastically, pointing out what to him seemed to be the strong advantage of the half-eaten sandwich.

'I thought you preferred yellow mould,' said Adam.

'What?' said the Mayor.

The Doctor gave Adam a warning look. Together they had taught the Arkonauts to understand some of their own language. But the Doctor was very clear that Adam should never speak an animal language in front of anyone else, nor say anything that would hint that he understood one either.

'It's just he brings so many mouldy yellow things back to the *Ark*,' Adam explained a little desperately.

'Thank you, Adam,' said the Doctor. 'I'm sure the Mayor doesn't want to hear about that. Sit down, Sniffage.'

Obediently Sniffage sat.

'Now, Mr Mayor,' said the Doctor, 'I am immensely grateful for your telegram and, as I'm sure you understand, after ten years' silence I am very eager to read the message you have received from my wife.'

The Mayor leant forward conspiratorially.

'First, there is something I need to . . . share with you. I am standing for re-election in a week's time, an election which, until two weeks ago, I was certain to win. I had no opponents because my policies were supported by almost everyone: I hoped to embark on an amazing programme of reform, to change Buenos Sueños for the better, for ever. But then a terrible crisis befell Buenos Sueños, and straight away another candidate entered the mayoral race, promising to solve it. I fear that people's faith in me may be ebbing. Buenos Sueños's one chance to change, to rejoin the world it has been separated from for so long, might be about to slip away. And I thought that, while you're here, you, a man rumoured to be the greatest scientist in the world, might be able to help me tackle this crisis.'

The Doctor had been reading angrily between the lines of the Mayor's speech. He could contain himself no longer.

'You are saying there is no message? We travelled all this way under false pretences?'

'No! No! You don't understand,' said the Mayor anxiously, leaning even further forward. 'Of course I have the message. But I was hoping that you might . . . give something in return. Bad forces are at work. A terrible thing is happening to our citizens.'

'What do you mean?' said the Doctor. 'What terrible thing?'

'Let me tell you . . .' began the Mayor, but then he glanced at his watch. 'Better than that, let me show you. Come with me.'

He beckoned Adam and the Doctor to follow him. His office led directly on to a balcony which overlooked the main square – all white except for the large number of red spots painted on the ground.

'Look at the clock on the police headquarters.'

The Doctor and Adam looked at the building directly opposite. Standing on the balcony, smoking a cigar, was a man in the bright white uniform of the police, but even at this distance they could see the gleam of medals on his chest. Above him was a clock showing the time at precisely 3.29.

'Three . . . two . . .' counted down the Mayor, 'one.'

The minute hand of the clock clunked to half past the hour and at exactly that moment they heard a sound.

BRRRRIIIIIIIIIIINNNNNNNNGGGGGGGG!

It was the loudest sound they had ever heard.

CHAPTER 5

Even with their ears covered it was deafening. It rang out across the whole city, over each narrow street and white house, through the main square and onwards and upwards into the hills and the mountains, echoing and intensifying as it bounced off sheer rock faces. It drove Adam and the Doctor and the Mayor off the balcony and back into the Mayor's office, where they cringed under its assault, their fingers jammed in their ears. It rang until Adam and the Doctor were convinced their ears could bear it no more and then, as suddenly as it had started, it stopped, its echoes drifting over the harbour and out to sea. All was quiet for a moment apart from the distant hum which seems to linger after a great noise.

'Wow!' said Adam. 'That was really loud.'

'Two weeks ago this started,' said the Mayor sadly, 'and now, every day it happens. And every day it is getting louder and longer.'

'It's certainly very annoying,' agreed the Doctor. 'But things could be worse.'

'Worse?' said the Mayor. 'Forgive me, Doctor, but how could things be worse?'

'Imagine if it was three thirty in the morning. Everyone would be asleep.'

The Mayor's brow furrowed and his dark brown eyes flashed with anger. He poked a stubby finger at the Doctor.

'Are you joking?' he demanded, his moustache quivering in anger. 'Have you not heard of the siesta?'

'Ah, yes,' said the Doctor awkwardly. 'How could I have forgotten?'

'What's a siesta?' asked Adam.

The Mayor turned to him in disbelief.

'The siesta is the most important part of the day in Buenos Sueños. In the morning you work. But in the after-noon it is too hot to work so you return to your home, eat a big lunch and then have a siesta.'

'Is it like a pudding?'

'A pudding?' said the Mayor in horror.

'I thought you said it came after lunch,' explained Adam. 'I'm a big fan of custard.'

'Boy, a siesta is a sleep.'

'A sleep?' Adam repeated.

'Of course.' The Mayor nodded. 'Here in Buenos Sueños we pride ourselves on being the best sleepers in the whole world. We have a saying: "Any man can get up, but it takes a clever man to stay in bed."'

'Most inspiring,' said the Doctor drily.

'In his later years,' continued the Mayor proudly, 'my own father slept almost constantly.'

'Really?'

'May the saints forgive me,' the Mayor added sadly, 'but I am almost glad that he did not live to see these terrible days. The Dreadful Alarm has destroyed the siesta.'

'But why can't you stop it?' asked the Doctor.

'We would if we could,' said the Mayor, 'but you must remember that Buenos Sueños is an isolated city without many modern resources. Still, of course I have done everything I could. I asked the police to investigate but they had almost no success.' The Mayor shook his head. 'In fact they seemed more concerned with minor offences than with the appalling sound that was plaguing the city. So instead I asked Fidel Guavera, my chief political adviser, to try to discover what was happening. He was convinced he was close to finding the source of this Dreadful Alarm, but then, without warning, the police arrested him.'

'What for?' said the Doctor.

'He apparently acted in contravention of Law 478, which bans "brandishing a pole in the street".'

'I suppose that could be dangerous.'

'It was an opinion poll! I have protested, but he is still in jail. So with the police failing and my own best man failing, I have been forced to beg for outside assistance. Without your help, I fear the city will be lost.'

'Lost?'

'Lost,' repeated the Mayor. 'The election is coming and if my opponent, a man whose name I will not speak within these walls, is victorious, then the city will return to the dark ages.'

'I don't understand,' said the Doctor. 'Surely the people would not vote for such a candidate. Surely they would not vote against their own interests.'

'That was true once,' the Mayor replied solemnly. 'But then the Dreadful Alarm came. The citizens have not had a proper siesta for weeks. In their sleep-deprived state anything could happen . . .' His speech trailed off. He seemed almost on the point of tears.

The Doctor coughed awkwardly.

'Mr Mayor, if you can produce the letter from my wife, then . . . I give you my word to do what I can to help you.'

'Thank you,' said the Mayor, suddenly pulling himself together. He rushed round the desk, grabbed the Doctor's hand and pumped it enthusiastically to demonstrate his gratitude.

'But,' the Doctor added, withdrawing his hand as quickly as he could without seeming rude, 'I can offer no guarantees.'

'Of course not, of course not,' said the Mayor. 'But now that you, a wise and worldly man of science, are here, I feel there is hope for us.'

'And now,' said the Doctor more sternly, 'if I might have the message that my wife left with you.'

'Of course,' said the Mayor. 'Whatever must you think of me?'

He hurried to a picture behind his desk. He pulled it back to reveal a dull metal safe. Instinctively, the Doctor and Adam leant forward in their chairs.

'Now what was that combination?' the Mayor muttered, scratching his head.

However, he was distracted by a knock on the door. Señorita Ratti poked her head round.

'We have found your daughter, Señor Mayor. She is waiting outside.'

At the mention of his daughter, the Mayor's face darkened.

'Send her in!' he said.

CHAPTER 6

The door to the Mayor's office swung open and through it came a pretty girl with dark hair and a mischievous look in her eyes. She was about the same age as Adam.

'This is my daughter, Anna,' said the Mayor.

Anna winked at Adam.

'She is the only person in the whole of Buenos Sueños who has not been affected by the Dreadful Alarm,' he continued.

'Why's that?' Adam asked.

'Because she's deaf,' said the Mayor.

'Oh,' said Adam. 'I was going to say hello.'

'Please do. She can lipread every word you say and speaks with her hands.'

'Hello!'

Anna winked once more.

'Unfortunately,' continued the Mayor, 'my daughter has been up to her tricks again. I have just had to listen to yet another complaint from the Chief of Police about her behaviour. Anna, can you explain to me why it was necessary to put itching powder in his underpants?'

Adam couldn't help himself. He'd lived a sheltered life with the Doctor and he'd never heard of a trick as audacious as that. He burst out laughing.

'Adam!' the Doctor snapped.

Anna signed an answer to the Mayor.

'An accident?' shouted the Mayor. 'You deliberately sneaked into the laundrette and found his underpants.'

Anna signed something else.

'It was an accident because you meant to put the itching powder into his pyjamas?' cried the Mayor in disbelief.

Anna nodded.

'You are a very bad girl!'

Anna signed once more, her hands and fingers moving rapidly.

'Don't try and shift the blame on to me. I may not like the man, but that doesn't justify this sort of behaviour,' interrupted the Mayor. 'You must not do this again.'

Anna nodded.

The Mayor turned to the Doctor with a sigh.

'What can you do with these unruly children?'

The Doctor made a sympathetic noise.

'I do what I can, but still she seems to get into trouble.'

As soon as the Mayor had turned away, Anna's solemn nod of regret became a defiant shake of the head and a bright grin. The moment the Mayor turned back to look at her, the nod of regret returned. The timing was so perfect that Adam couldn't help bursting into laughter again.

'Adam,' the Doctor warned sternly.

With the Doctor and the Mayor's attention fixed on Adam, Anna took the opportunity to pull an extraordinarily strange face behind their backs. It made Adam laugh even more.

But the Mayor, who knew his daughter well, suspected she could be at the root of Adam's laughter and swung round, to find his daughter not only looking remorseful but also seeming to wipe away the beginnings of a sorrowful tear. The Mayor was not wholly convinced.

'Perhaps an afternoon in your room will be enough if you promise not to misbehave again. Do you promise?'

Anna nodded solemnly.

'Good,' said the Mayor. 'Off you to go to your room to think about what you've done.'

Anna turned to go, but as she did so Adam was sure he caught the very slightest hint of a wink in his direction.

'I apologise for the delay,' said the Mayor. 'Now, where were we?'

'You were about to give me the –' began the Doctor, but yet another knock at the door interrupted him. Señorita Ratti came into the room.

'You told me to pass on any news relating to Felipe Felipez and the election straight away,' she said, holding out a piece of paper for the Mayor to read.

Mention of the election drove everything else from his mind. The Mayor grabbed the paper, then slumped into his chair with a low groan.

'I cannot tell you how bad things are now – even my troubles have troubles.' He sighed. 'The other candidate – Felipez – do you know what he has promised the voters now?'

The Doctor and Adam shook their heads.

'Ear mufflers! For every citizen in Buenos Sueños. To block out the sound of the Dreadful Alarm!'

'Is that such a terrible idea?' asked Adam.

The Mayor stared hard at him. 'It is his idea. The people will praise Felipe Felipez.'

'That doesn't mean you can't be the one to make it happen. Surely the job of a mayor is to do the best thing for the people of his city. That should be all that matters to him,' Adam said passionately.

'This is why I don't do school visits,' grumbled the Mayor to himself. 'Children are such idealists.'

But it was obvious that Adam's words had affected Mayor Puig, for a few moments later he reluctantly pressed the intercom on his grand desk.

'Señorita Ratti,' he said to his secretary. 'Get me Los Mufflers de Ears.'

'Putting you through now.' Señorita Ratti spoke through the intercom.

'Hola?' came a voice after a few seconds.

'Ciao,' said the Mayor. 'This is Mayor Puig. The city of Buenos Sueños wants to –'

'This is Jordi Iniesta, head of research and development at Los Mufflers. Please state your business.'

'If you will let me finish,' said the Mayor. 'The city will buy your –'

'Hola? Whoever you are, stop it with these silent phone calls. You have been doing them all day. I warn you, I will report you to the police.'

'What do you mean silent phone calls?' said the Mayor. 'I'm talking perfectly –'

'They can trace your call, you know.'

Suddenly Adam realised what the problem was. He leapt out of chair and ran round to the Mayor's side of the desk.

'TAKE YOUR MUFFLERS OFF!' he shouted as loudly as he could into the microphone.

'What is that you're whispering?' said Jordi. 'Take my – oh, I see. Well, that explains why we haven't been getting any business.'

'You have all the business you need now,' said the Mayor. 'The city of Buenos Sueños will buy your entire stock of ear mufflers immediately. Deliver them to every house in the city.'

This time there was silence on the other end of the line. Eventually Jordi spoke.

'We may have a small problem.'

'What is it?' asked the Mayor.

'Our entire stock is two pairs of ear mufflers.'

'What?' he roared.

'You see,' said Jordi, 'only one week ago a man called Elipe Elipez came to our factory and bought the entire stock.'

The Mayor took his finger off the intercom and crashed his fist against the table.

'Curse Felipe Felipez,' he shouted. 'You see what kind of devious man we are dealing with?' The Mayor looked up at the Doctor. 'Now can you tell me what I am to do?'

The Doctor's usually well-controlled temper was beginning to shorten.

'Give me the message from my wife that you have been promising me ever since Adam and myself arrived.'

The Mayor slapped himself on the forehead, clearly harder than he had intended.

'Ouch,' he said.

He went to his safe and twiddled the knob left and then right, before the door swung slowly open. Reaching inside, he pulled out a letter, which he handed to the Doctor. The Doctor looked at the envelope.

'It is her handwriting,' he said excitedly. 'I would know it anywhere, even after all this time.'

'I am sorry that it has taken so long –' began the Mayor, but he was interrupted by a buzzer on his intercom.

'Chief of Police Grivas is here to see you.'

'Send him in!'

'Come on, Adam,' said the Doctor. 'We will –'

'No,' said the Mayor, holding up his hands. 'If you are to understand Buenos Sueños at all, you must meet the Chief of Police. Just this one last thing. And then I will leave you to your letter.'

The Doctor nodded frostily just as the door opened and the uniformed figure of Chief Grivas marched into the room. He had a huge moustache and was smoking the biggest cigar Adam had ever seen.

'Chief Grivas,' said the Mayor, 'may I present Doctor Forest and Adam.'

The Doctor rose and held out his hand. The Chief of Police did not extend his. Instead, he removed his cigar and exhaled a large puff of acrid smoke in the Doctor's face.

'I do not shake hands with criminals,' he said.

Sitting at Adam's feet, Sniffage growled. Adam had never known the spaniel to growl on meeting a stranger before. Normally he was the friendliest dog in the world.

'Criminals?' said the Mayor. 'What are you talking about? These are distinguished guests of Buenos Sueños who arrived only this morning.'

'You can call them all the fancy names you like,' said Chief Grivas with a sneer. 'But within minutes of setting foot in our proud city, a very promising young officer found them guilty of trying to destroy the transport system of Buenos Sueños and vandalising the streets.'

The Chief of Police blew more black smoke into the Doctor's face.

The Doctor stared impassively back.

'Is this true?' asked the Mayor.

'All we did was ask for help,' said Adam.

'I see.' The Mayor sighed as he turned back to Chief Grivas. 'Some more of your ludicrous laws.'

'They are not my laws,' answered Grivas. 'They are the laws of the city.'

The Mayor shook his head with frustration.

'The sooner these laws are changed the better.'

'That is a matter for you.' Chief Grivas shrugged.

'How can I change them if I do not have access to the Buenos Sueños Crime and Punishment Code?'

'I don't understand,' said the Doctor. 'You are the Mayor but you don't know what the laws are in your own city?'

'There is only one copy of the Crime and Punishment Code of Buenos Sueños,' the Mayor explained. 'And it is in the possession of Chief of Police Grivas.'

'But can't he make a copy?'

'Apparently the law states that it can't be copied,' said the Mayor.

Chief Grivas nodded.

'Can't he let you see it, then?'

'Of course,' said Grivas. 'The Mayor is the Mayor – he is welcome to see the Crime and Punishment Code at any time.'

The Mayor's face began to go red.

'I have been asking to see the Crime and Punishment Code for four years.'

The Chief of Police nodded.

'And I am hoping that any day now it will become available,' answered Grivas, taking a puff on his giant cigar. 'In order to be a successful policeman it is necessary to learn the code by heart. And because of the number of laws we have in Buenos Sueños this takes some time, particularly as there is only one copy. My nephew, Trainee Constable Grivas, has been studying for a year now.'

'I think he must be the officer who fined us,' Adam mused.

'No, it is not the same man,' said Chief Grivas. 'I am referring to Trainee Constable Paolo Grivas not Constable Jordi Grivas, who apprehended you.'

'The entire police force of Buenos Sueños appears to be related to you, Chief Grivas,' remarked the Mayor pointedly.

'A coincidence,' said Grivas.

'It is also a coincidence, I suppose,' said the Mayor, 'that the Grivas family are the only ones who have not committed a crime in the last four years.'

'You criticise my family for abiding by the law!' shouted the Chief of Police. 'Why not save some of your politician's breath to criticise those who break it? Without the Buenos Sueños Police Force this city would be a criminal's paradise.'

'I didn't notice any crime,' said Adam, who was beginning to seriously dislike Chief Grivas.

'Of course you didn't,' answered Grivas, taking a puff on his giant cigar and breathing out more choking black smoke.

'Three years ago I introduced a policy of zero tolerance. The tiniest infringement would be clamped down upon. Thanks to that my force has these people under control. But let me tell you, underneath they are animals.'

'You're an animal too,' remarked the Doctor mildly.

Grivas choked in indignation. He marched up to the Doctor and poked a stubby finger into his chest.

'What did you call me?'

'I called you an animal,' answered the Doctor. 'Because that is what you are. Kingdom: *Animalia*. Class: *Mammalia*. Order: Primates.'

The Chief of Police spluttered with rage.

'Are you calling me a monkey?'

'Stop this!' the Mayor intervened. 'I wanted to ask you about progress in the search for the source of the Dreadful Alarm.'

'There has been no progress,' said Grivas. 'Perhaps if my officers were not constantly interrupted in their work by the crimes of strangers, there would be more.' And with that, Grivas flicked ash contemptuously on to the carpet and stomped out.

The Mayor thumped his desk in frustration.

'Our citizens have always had a reputation for being law-abiding. But over recent years, so many laws have been implemented that even the laws have laws. Due to the zero-tolerance policy of Chief Grivas, most of the people in the city have been fined so often they are weighed down with debt, for the fine doubles with each new offence. This is why I based my entire campaign on one policy only: to introduce a new Crime and Punishment Code for Buenos Sueños. If all the people voted for it, then even Grivas would be forced to concede and the citizens of Buenos Sueños would be happy again. But that was before the Dreadful Alarm started. Since then, Felipe Felipez has begun to campaign with his policy of ignoring new laws and promising instead simply to deal with the Dreadful Alarm, and my support has fallen away. Do you see how vital it is that I stop the alarm before the election? Only then will I be able to win and change the laws to save the city.'

'We have said that we will help,' said the Doctor. 'But now I must *insist* that you finally permit me to open this letter from my wife.'

The Mayor looked momentarily confused as though he didn't know what the Doctor was talking about, before his eyes lit up with understanding. He raised his hand to slap himself for being so forgetful, but then remembered, too, how much that had hurt last time.

'Of course, of course. Please, go ahead,' he said, lowering his hand.

The Doctor needed no further encouragement. He deftly opened the envelope and slipped out a single folded sheet of paper. Next to him, Adam craned his neck. The Doctor unfolded the paper and looked at its contents.

'What is the meaning of this?' he asked.

'Is something the matter?' said the Mayor.

'What is it?' said Adam.

The Doctor's face was dark with anger. Adam had never seen him like this before. He held the paper out towards Adam.

It was blank.

Adam couldn't believe it.

Neither could the Doctor. He always maintained that one should keep one's emotions in check and respond to any situation, however difficult, with logic and restraint, but this was too much. Such was the strength of his anger that the Mayor backed away behind his desk.

'I have sailed halfway round the world for a blank piece of paper.'

'A message was left for you and I passed it on,' the Mayor protested. 'What else was I to do?'

'After ten years!' the Doctor shouted. 'Ten years of searching.'

For a moment, Adam actually thought that his father would hit the Mayor. But instead the Doctor, with what appeared to be a tremendous effort of self-control, thrust the message into his pocket and turned away.

'Come on, Adam,' he said, striding to the door. 'Come on, Sniffage.'

'I hope this doesn't affect your agreement to help me solve the mystery of the Dreadful Alarm,' the Mayor ventured.

The Doctor spun round to give the Mayor a withering glare.

'I assure you that any agreement we had is now terminated.'

'But the people of Buenos Sueños, the election, Felipe Felipez . . .' pleaded the Mayor.

'Are none of my concern,' said the Doctor.

He turned and led Adam and Sniffage from the room, slamming the door behind him.

CHAPTER 7

'Where have you been?' chattered Simia as Adam emerged from the hatch on to the deck. 'The Doctor said we were to make an early start this morning and yet you've been a lazy slug-a-bed, not helping at all with the preparations.'

Adam looked at the sun. It still sat low in the east and its weak rays sent out none of the heat they would doubtless do later in the day.

'It's only just light,' he protested.

'Only just light,' mocked Simia. 'That's humans for you all over. Centuries of evolution and what do they do with it? Stay in bed!'

'Where's my dad?' asked Adam, trying to avoid yet another tirade.

'The Doctor needs his rest,' said Simia, whose criticism of the entire human race always excluded the Doctor. 'He had a terrible shock yesterday.'

The monkey indicated the letter, which lay discarded on

the table where the Doctor had thrown it on his return to the boat last night. He had locked himself in his cabin and Adam had not heard from him since.

'I had a shock too,' Adam protested.

'You're young. You'll get over it!' said Simia. 'We monkeys have a saying: "An old monkey drops his banana and he is hungry for the rest of the day. A young monkey drops his banana and he eats some berries instead."'

'What does that mean?' asked Adam, puzzled.

'It's a saying,' said Simia severely. 'Who knows what it means? Now hurry up and help me order the sails. We need to be gone on the morning tide.'

'Excuuuusssse me!' yowled Malibu from his perch on a nearby barrel. 'Could you pipe down over there? Some of us are in the middle of our winks.'

'For your information, cat,' said Simia, 'there is no need for any further discussion. The boy here is going to help me with the sails.'

'Tell him to do it quietly,' said Malibu, closing his eyes.

'I don't know why the Doctor keeps you on board,' Simia muttered.

'I do what any ship's cat does,' Malibu replied dreamily. 'I keep down vermin.'

'The Doctor collects vermin,' the monkey pointed out.

'Ah well, whatcha gonna do?' said Malibu. And he fell asleep again.

'Come on, boy,' said Simia.

But the talk of bananas had reminded Adam he hadn't had any breakfast yet. On the wharf there was a stall selling fruit and vegetables. He felt in his pocket. He had five pesos.

'I'm going to get some breakfast first,' he said to Simia.

'Another human excuse,' Simia sighed. 'Survival of the fittest. Survival of the laziest more like.'

And shaking her head in disapproval, the monkey scampered over to the sails. Adam headed down the gangplank on to the wharf, past the fishermen who sat mending nets, towards the stall. Piled high were ripe oranges, mangoes, grapes and pineapples, to name but some of the fruits, and in front of them were glasses filled with their juice, shaded by stirrers with little novelty sombreros. Adam felt hungrier than ever. Above the stall was a sign: Ferdinand and Isabel's Fruit and Vegetable Emporium. It was staffed by a friendly-looking woman aged about fifty, who Adam decided must be Isabel.

'I'd like an orange, an apple, a banana and a grapefruit, please,' he said.

Isabel shook her head.

'Do I look like I was born yesterday, chico?' she said.

'No,' said Adam truthfully. 'You look like you were born yesterday fifty years ago.'

'Exactly,' said Isabel. 'And so, unlike some, I'm old enough to buy fruit.'

'What do you mean, old enough to buy fruit?'

'You have to be eighteen to buy fruit in Buenos Sueños,'

she explained. 'So show me some identification or move along. I don't want to attract the attention of the police.'

'But fruit is healthy,' protested Adam. 'It's got vitamins and minerals and things,' he added, vaguely remembering a rather tedious lecture the Doctor had given him one day on the benefits of eating fruit on long sea voyages. The only bit Adam had been really interested in was the symptoms of scurvy.

'Exactly,' said Isabel. 'Vitamins and minerals keep everyone healthy.'

'So why is there an age limit on buying them?'

Isabel looked around. Seeing there was no one in earshot she leant forward and whispered confidentially, 'Because people who eat lots of fruit live longer.'

'But why is that a problem?'

'It means that the undertakers don't have as many bodies to bury. Therefore they can't make as much money. Grivas the undertaker calls it "restraint of trade". And, under the Buenos Sueños Crime and Punishment Code, restraining the trade of a legitimate business is punishable by a large fine.'

Adam noticed a fading painted red spot next to the stall. Obviously in the past Isabel had been in receipt of a fine for restraining the trade of the undertaker by prolonging life by selling fruit and vegetables to an the under-eighteens.

'What did you say the name of the undertaker was?' asked Adam.

'Grivas,' Isabel repeated.

'It's odd how many of the laws in Buenos Sueños seems to benefit the Grivas family,' Adam mused.

'I know. I was going to vote for the Mayor and his plans for change, until this blasted alarm started. My husband, Ferdinand, hasn't had a siesta in weeks. His temper is terrible.'

'But that's not the Mayor's fault.'

'All I know is that Felipe Felipez has promised to end the alarm if he's elected,' said Isabel. 'And that is good enough for me. Now please be on your way, chico. Just by standing near a fruit stall a young boy can attract the attention of the police.'

Adam looked at the ripe fruit and felt his mouth water. Soon they would be out at sea again and he wouldn't see fresh fruit for days. His forlorn face touched Isabel's heart.

'Quick!,' she hissed, reaching over to pass him a couple of bananas and a glass of orange juice. 'Have these to show there's no hard feelings. Now, adios, chico, before the police come.'

'Thank you!' he said, but Isabel was already serving another customer.

Not wishing to get caught, Adam rushed straight back to the boat. Although still early, the sun's rays now flooded the deck of the *Ark*. Adam sat down by the table, pushing the useless letter that the Mayor had given to the Doctor to one side.

'Where have you been?' demanded Simia. 'I could have

gone to the Amazon rainforest and back to get fruit in the time it's taken you to buy it.'

But Adam was not going to allow the monkey to spoil his breakfast. He placed the bananas and the juice on the table.

'Hey, what's with all the noise?' Malibu yowled. 'What is it with you primates and your nonstop yakking?'

'Don't you compare me to him,' said Simia. 'We're totally different.'

'Different!' said Malibu, fully awake now and not at all happy about it. 'The only difference between the two of you, girlfriend, is that *he's* got a decent haircut.'

Simia was outraged. She was very proud of her fur.

'I'll tell you what,' the cat went on. 'I know a place on Sunset that does a mean fur trim. Next time we're on the west coast I'll get the Doc to take you there.'

'I don't want to hear about your pet barber,' snapped Simia.

'We ain't talking about no pet barber here, monkey. We're talking high-class animal coiffure.'

'You're a disgrace, cat,' whooped Simia angrily. 'You've betrayed your species.'

'Just the sort of response I'd expect from a lower-class species,' Malibu hissed.

'Come over here and say that!'

'You come here, it's just as far.'

Monkey and cat glared at each other. Adam decided it was time to step in.

'I think we should all calm –'

But it was too late. In the same instant the animals sprang, crashing into one another on top of the table and becoming a rolling, snarling, fighting ball of fur. Adam's juice was sent flying.

'What on earth is going on up here?'

The Doctor climbed up on deck, looking angry.

At the sound of his voice, Simia and Malibu stopped immediately. They looked at one another and a flash of wordless understanding passed between them. Both knew the Doctor's views on animal-on-animal violence and they risked a long, tedious lecture.

'Nothing, Doctor,' said Simia.

'Just playing, Doc,' Malibu added.

'It sounded like a very loud nothing,' said the Doctor. 'Especially when we should be preparing to sail today.'

'Catch you later, cat,' Simia muttered.

'Not if I see you first, girlfriend,' hissed Malibu.

'Look!' shouted Adam suddenly.

'What is it?' asked the Doctor.

Adam pointed to the table. 'The letter!'

'The letter,' corrected the Doctor, 'is simply a piece of paper. I can't believe I didn't throw it away yesterday.'

'No, it isn't,' said Adam. 'Come here and see!'

There was an unusual urgency in Adam's tone. The Doctor hurried over and looked where Adam was pointing. Orange juice had spilled across the table and wherever it touched the letter, faint shapes were appearing, some of them beginning to resemble words.

Already Adam could make out two.

'*Help me.*'

CHAPTER 8

'How could I have been so stupid?' Doctor Forest cried, grasping the letter.

'You're not stupid, Doctor,' said the ever-loyal Simia.

'I am, Simia, I am,' insisted the Doctor.

'The man says he's stupid, monkey,' said Malibu, 'you gotta respect that. He's got a lot of qualifications, so he oughta know.'

'How could I forget?' the Doctor went on.

'Forget what?' Adam asked.

'Before you were born, before we were even married, your mother and I used to send each other letters. But they had to be secret. Her father disapproved of me because of my circumstances. My mother was poor and my father was . . . well, we need not dwell on what my father was, or is, whereas your mother's family were rich and powerful. So I would write her letters – on one side they would be about innocent scientific matters, but on the other side they would be blank. Blank until you added a little acidic juice, that is, which would make the real words in my letter appear.'

The Doctor's eyes seemed to mist over as he lost himself in the memory.

'And they would say how I felt, how I . . .'

Suddenly, he shook himself back to reality.

'What they said doesn't matter.'

Adam looked at his father and tried hard to imagine him many years ago sending secret romantic letters, but he just couldn't see it. The ten years of fruitless searching had hardened him too much.

'Pour some more juice on the rest of it, Adam,' the Doctor ordered.

Slowly more words began to appear. Two minutes later the whole communication was laid out in front of them:

Will and Adam,

I have very little time. I am in Buenos Sueños. Scabellax and his henchmen watch my every move. But I am sure that you are still looking for me and if anyone can find me I know you can. I pray this message reaches you. Help me!

Your loving wife and mother,
Lily

Adam glanced at the Doctor, who appeared to be wiping a tear from his eye.

'Bit of grit,' said the Doctor, noticing his son's look.

'Uma used onions in scenes when she needed to turn on

65

the waterworks,' Malibu observed, remembering the actress who used to own him, 'whereas Brad would pull out a nose hair. Whatever it takes to get the shot in the can, they used to say.'

'The Doctor is not crying,' said Simia firmly. 'I suppose this means we will not be leaving.'

'Of course we won't,' the Doctor replied. 'Hidden somewhere in that city, desperate for us to find her, is my wife and Adam's mother.'

Adam looked out into the city, with its identical white houses and narrow streets. How would they ever find her?

And then he remembered something else.

'If the letter is real,' he said to his father, 'that means we really should help the Mayor find the source of the Dreadful Alarm of Buenos Sueños and get rid of it. Like we promised before.'

The Doctor agreed. 'But that would mean having to tell him the letter was genuine. I would rather as few people as possible knew about that at this time. Buenos Sueños is a strange place where, I suspect, all is not what it seems. Therefore let us try to help the Mayor as we promised but without telling him, until we have more of an idea about what is going on in this city and whom we can trust.'

'That's a very clever idea, Doctor,' said Simia. 'Fancy you saying you were stupid.'

'Thank you, Simia,' said the Doctor.

But Simia wasn't finished.

'Now had you been talking about the rest of your race –
those furless late developers who can't climb trees – then
you'd have had a point.'

The Doctor decided not to engage with Simia's views on
humans and instead changed the topic of conversation.

'What time does Vlad wake up?' he asked Adam.

Realising that she was being ignored, Simia flounced off.

'Vlad?' said Adam. 'He's out all night and sleeps all day.
He's not normally awake until dusk at the earliest.'

'I'm afraid he's going to have to get up a little earlier
today. I have a job for him to do.'

'He won't like it,' said Adam. 'He hates daylight.'

'That's why I need you to prepare him,' said the Doctor.
'He can be so precious, but you seem to have acquired the
skill of talking to him.'

*That's because I don't talk to everyone like they're a scientific
machine*, thought Adam. But he didn't say that. There was
something else he was far more interested in which the
Doctor had mentioned earlier.

'You talked about your father before,' he said to the
Doctor. 'I thought he was dead.'

'I have never said that,' answered the Doctor. 'He left
when I was very young.'

'But you never talk about him,' said Adam. 'He's my
grandfather and I know nothing about him.'

Perhaps it was the recent letter from his wife, for something seemed to have briefly softened the Doctor. He sighed.

'All right, Adam,' he said. 'I will tell you this once and once only.'

Adam leant forward excitedly. His family had always been a mystery to him. His father was the only relative he had ever known. Except for his mother, he thought bitterly, but he wasn't even able to remember her.

'Your grandfather was a student of human behaviour, just as I was,' the Doctor began.

'So you took after him?' said Adam. 'He was a doctor too?'

'No,' his father answered firmly. 'He was not a doctor. His study was outside academic circles.'

'What did he do?'

The Doctor looked uncomfortable.

'I suppose you are old enough to know, Adam. But I must stress one thing before I tell you: that if one makes scientific discoveries, then one should never use them for personal gain. One should share them with humanity for the good of all.'

Adam tried not to look bored, but he'd heard this lecture many times before.

'Your grandfather used his knowledge of human behaviour for the basest of all possible motives,' said the Doctor shortly. 'Financial gain. He left my mother and me when we were very young to become a conman and a gambler – travelling the world searching for the foolish and the ignorant and parting them from their money.'

'He just left you and your mother alone?' said Adam in disbelief.

The Doctor nodded. 'One day we woke up and he was gone.'

'What about money?'

'Some mornings we would wake up to discover a bag of money had been left on our doorstep overnight,' acknowledged the Doctor grudgingly, 'coming from who knows where but doubtless taken from some poor fool. But being a father is not about providing money. Being a father is about supporting your family day in and day out.'

'Did your mum tell you about him?' asked Adam.

'She never spoke about him,' said the Doctor, 'and neither did I. On the day he left it was as though he had never existed.'

'So how do you know what happened to him?'

'Reports in the papers and on the news, policemen coming to the house wanting to know if we knew where he was. And one time, when I was your age, men worse than policemen – gangsters who threatened to kill us if we didn't help them find him. But how were we to help? If I could have forgiven him before, I could never have done so after that.'

For the second time that day, Adam saw tears glinting in the Doctor's eyes as he remembered the day when he'd stood powerless to protect his mother in front of three heavy-set men in dark glasses whose guns bulged under their jackets.

'What happened to him?' asked Adam.

'The last I heard he was in prison,' said the Doctor matter-of-factly.

'Prison! What did he to do to end up there?'

'I don't know and frankly I don't care,' said the Doctor. 'And as far as I'm concerned he can rot there.'

Adam had never heard his father speak with such hatred for anyone, even Professor Silus Scabellax.

'And now,' said the Doctor, 'you know everything you need to know about your grandfather. That is the first and the last time I will speak of it, so I would be grateful if you would never refer to it again. Go down below and prepare Vlad for the daylight.'

Even though this was not going to be easy, as Adam climbed below deck he couldn't concentrate on the task in hand. His mind was still on his grandfather – conman, gambler and convict. Adam could barely permit himself to think of him when he remembered the anger in the Doctor's face, but he couldn't stop himself either. Bad as his grandfather obviously was, his life sounded exciting. Adam wondered what it would be like to actually meet him.

CHAPTER 9

'What time is it?' asked the Doctor

Adam looked up. During a voyage across the Pacific Ocean his father had taught him how to use the sun to calculate the time, and these days he only wore a watch when it was cloudy.

'Around quarter past three.'

'I need to know exactly,' said the Doctor a trifle testily. 'We need to be ready when the alarm goes off.'

'I'm not happy about this,' squeaked a voice. 'Not happy at all.'

The voice came from under the table, which was entirely covered, legs and all, by a thick brown blanket to prevent any light getting in.

'Adam,' said the Doctor, 'the exact time, please.'

Adam went into the navigation cabin to retrieve his watch.

'It's twenty-one minutes past three and forty-six seconds,' he announced.

'Pull the blanket slowly off the table and hopefully Vlad's

eyes will become accustomed to the light.' said the Doctor.

'Make sure it's very slowly,' squeaked the voice from under the blanket.

'Come on,' said the Doctor to Adam, and together they grabbed the blanket and began to pull.

'Ooooohhhh,' squeaked Vlad, as the burning afternoon sun seeped under the table.

'Now, now,' said the Doctor, continuing to pull the blanket away. 'It's not that bad.'

'Ooooooooooohhhhhhhhh.'

Vlad had a reputation on the *Ark* for being overdramatic.

'Ooooooooooooohhhhhhhhhhhhhhhhh.'

With one final tug the blanket was removed to reveal the vampire bat hanging upside down from the bottom of the table. He didn't hang around for long. With a thud he dropped on to the deck.

'I'm blind,' he squeaked. And to prove it he stood up and walked into one of the table legs.

'Don't be silly, Vlad,' said the Doctor.

'Dark, dark, amid the blaze of noon,' cried Vlad, banging into the table leg again and collapsing on his back.

'It's way past noon,' Adam pointed out.

'I know you're doing this on purpose,' said the Doctor. 'Your sonar would have told you about the table legs even if you couldn't see them.'

'I think the sun has sent it all haywire,' piped Vlad.

'Of course it hasn't,' said the Doctor.

Tentatively the vampire bat opened one of his eyes. And shut it again.

'It's so bright!'

'Am I ever going to get any winks?' demanded Malibu, awoken by Vlad's high-pitched squeaks of discomfort.

'Be quiet, Malibu,' the Doctor snapped.

'Quiet is all I want,' grumbled the cat.

Despite Vlad's melodramatic protests the Doctor knew the vampire bat was genuinely finding it difficult to function in the glare of the strong sun.

'If only we had something to cover his head . . .' he mused. 'If his eyes were shaded I'm sure things wouldn't be so bad.'

'The sombrero!' shouted Adam suddenly.

'What are you talking about?' demanded the Doctor.

Adam reached into his pocket and pulled out the novelty stirrer from the glass of orange juice that Isabel had given him earlier in the day. One swift tug was all that was needed to detach the sombrero from the top of the stick.

'Vlad could wear the sombrero to keep off the sun!' cried Adam, waving it at the Doctor.

'Do you think I'm running a circus, boy?' said his father. 'I do not believe . . .' Then his voice trailed off. 'I suppose it just might work.'

But not everybody was convinced. Under the table, Vlad drew himself up to his full height, which unfortunately for him wasn't actually very tall.

'I am a vampire bat,' he squeaked. 'A near-legendary creature who strikes fear into the hearts of all who see my fangs. I have my dignity. I will not be seen wearing a sombrero. My reputation would be – ow, that sun is bright.'

'We haven't time for this,' said the Doctor.

He reached under the table, grasped Vlad and pulled him out.

'I warn you I will bite,' said Vlad, showing his fangs.

'You won't bite me,' said the Doctor calmly, placing the miniature sombrero on the vampire bat's head. It was a perfect fit.

'If either one of you laughs, then I'm not going,' threatened Vlad.

The Doctor rarely laughed, so to him this was no great challenge. It was a different matter for Adam, though. Seeing a vampire bat wearing a sombrero was an extremely comical sight.

'He's laughing,' said Vlad, ever sensitive to mockery.

Adam couldn't trust himself to speak so instead he shook his head.

'His shoulders are shaking,' said Vlad accusingly.

'Perhaps he's cold.'

'Cold?' echoed Vlad. 'Cold? We're in Buenos Sueños in the summer and the sun is burning down, it's not –'

The Doctor interrupted Vlad's protests. 'Just remember when the alarm goes off to use your sonar to try to find its source.'

BRRRRRRIIIIIIINNNNGGGGG!!!

The Doctor threw Vlad into the air and the sombrero-topped bat disappeared towards the city. Adam and the Doctor wasted no time in jamming their fingers in their ears. The alarm was louder and longer than before.

CHAPTER 10

'Do we just wait for Vlad to come back?' asked Adam.

The Doctor shook his head.

'Vlad may be able to pinpoint the location of the Dreadful Alarm but while he is doing that we must look for your mother.'

'But she didn't give us any clues.'

The Doctor picked up the letter his wife had sent them. Discreetly printed in the bottom corner were the words 'Hotel Dormir, Calle Cama'.

'She did give us one,' said the Doctor. 'Let's start walking.'

There was a sudden flurry of activity and out of the hatch, his ears flopping like crazy, bounded Sniffage. He skidded up to the Doctor and Adam.

'Did someone just say walk? Yeah! Yeah! I know they did. I heard them! Let Sniffage come! Can we go down smelly streets with dead things? Yeah! Yeah!'

'You can come, Sniffage,' said the Doctor, 'but try not to

do anything to attract the attention of the police.'

'The police!' said Sniffage. 'Don't you worry about the police! I'll chase 'em off! I'm a very scary dog! Look at my teeth! Yeah! Yeah! Oops! I mean, Grrr! Grrr!'

Adam started laughing. He couldn't help it. With his floppy ears and brown button eyes, Sniffage was the least frightening dog in the whole world.

'Come on, then,' said the Doctor impatiently. 'We must find the Hotel Dormir and see if anyone recognises your mother. I still have the last picture taken of her two days before she went missing.'

'But it's ten years later,' said Adam. 'Will she look the same?'

'We will have to hope that ten years in the clutches of Scabellax will not have changed her too much.'

With the sun burning hot above them, the Doctor, Adam and Sniffage headed down the gangplank and into the narrow, quiet streets of Buenos Sueños.

'Look!' said Adam as they arrived at a crossroads. 'There's a sign for the Hotel Dormir.'

But of course there wasn't just one sign for the Hotel Dormir, there were four. Like the town hall, every road seemed to lead to the Hotel Dormir with no indication as to which route was the quickest.

'Pick a direction,' said the Doctor.

'Yeah! Yeah! Left smells nastiest!' yapped Sniffage.

So they went left.

The route led them through darker and narrower streets than any they had seen before. When Adam looked up it seemed as though the tall buildings above him were leaning in towards each other. While he knew it must be an optical illusion, a part of him still felt that the houses were about to collapse in on them.

'Look out!' the Doctor cried out.

Adam looked in front of him and managed to duck just in time to avoid crashing his head into a low bridge which spanned the narrow road.

Two men and two women stood on the other side of the bridge, gazing admiringly at it. They all had large angry red bumps on their heads.

'Greetings!' said one of the women as Adam and the Doctor straightened up. 'My name is Carla. Are you Bajapuentalists too?'

'Bajapuentalists?' said Adam, looking at the Doctor.

'Si,' said Carla. 'Bajapuentalists. Members of the Society for the Appreciation of Low Bridges. Doubtless you can see that this is one of the city's greatest examples. It arches perfectly across the street with a pleasing symmetry, combining flamboyant wrought-iron effects with a genuine lack of altitude.'

Not wanting to offend the Bajapuentalists, the Doctor and Adam looked back admiringly at the low bridge.

'It is one of architectural jewels in the crown of Buenos Sueños,' Carla went on. 'Would you mind taking a picture of us in front of it?'

Adam smiled and nodded. She handed him an ancient camera and the four Bajapuentalists stooped in front of the bridge.

'Try and get our bumps to stand out,' said Carla.

'Why do you all have bumps?' asked Adam.

'It is an occupational hazard of the Bajapuentalist,' Carla explained. 'Even one as experienced as me can stand up too early or crouch too late. But they show that we have suffered in our quest for lower bridges.'

Adam pointed the camera at the Bajapuentalists.

'Say ouch!' Carla called.

'Ouch!' cried the other Bajapuentalists, and the camera flashed in the dark street.

'Thank you,' said Carla. 'Would you like a picture of yourselves in front of it?'

'That won't be necessary,' said the Doctor. 'But you could help us by looking at a picture.'

'Is it of a low bridge?' asked Carla optimistically.

'No,' said the Doctor. 'It is of my wife.'

'Is she standing in front of a low bridge?'

The Doctor shook his head. He reached into his pocket and carefully pulled out a small black and white snap of a woman holding a toddler. The toddler was Adam.

'She will be older now,' said the Doctor.

Carla and the other Bajapuentalists scrutinised the picture. All shook their heads.

'It was a long shot,' said the Doctor.

'More of a close-up, I'd say,' said Carla.

'I meant . . . Oh, it doesn't matter,' the Doctor sighed.

'We must be going,' said Carla. 'But if you want to join our society we meet every night on the Puente Pequeñita near the Plaza de los Valiente Hombres.'

'You're very kind,' said the Doctor.

'And a bit crazy,' added Adam.

But luckily the Bajapuentalists were already on the way to their next low bridge.

'Come on,' said the Doctor. 'It's obvious we're on the route to the Hotel Dormir that does not avoid low bridges. Let us hope it gets us there soon.'

Adam thought his father should have known better. This was Buenos Sueños, after all. Two streets later the road opened into a wide square jammed with people. The signpost unhelpfully pointed straight across the square, through the most tightly crowded part.

'We must make our way through as best we can. Stay close,' said the Doctor. And he turned to a man on the edge of the crowd. 'Excuse me.'

Two hundred and thirty-eight 'Excuse me's later and they had reached the middle of the square, when suddenly there was a surge in the crowd and a voice boomed out of a loud-speaker, 'Señors and señoras, please welcome the next Mayor of Buenos Sueños, Felipe Felipez!'

There was a loud roar of approval. The Doctor and Adam (with some difficulty because he was smaller) looked towards the platform set up on one side of the square to try to get their first glimpse of the mysterious man who was taking Buenos Sueños by storm. They were only able to catch the glint of his unnaturally white teeth shining in the sun.

Felipe Felipez grabbed the microphone.

'Señors and señoras, thank you for your coming out to this rally today. I know how much effort it has taken you, how weary you must be, thanks to the hopeless inability of the Mayor to stop the Dreadful Alarm.'

Felipe Felipez looked at the crowd.

'Tell me, señors and señoras, are you tired?'

'Si,' shouted the crowd.

'Are you yawning?'

'Si,' they shouted once more.

'Are you irritable and prone to lose your temper too easily?'

'Si.'

'Are you beginning to forget things?'

There was a silence and then a bit of muttering. Felipe Felipez asked again.

'Are you beginning to forget things?'

'Possibly,' shouted back the crowd.

'I feel your pain,' Felipe Felipez told the crowd, holding his hands out towards them. 'I too have wax on my fingers after jamming them deep in my ears to keep out the terrible ringing of the Dreadful Alarm. But still it rings – while the

Mayor snores in his soundproofed office, oblivious to our pain.'

'The Mayor's office isn't soundproofed,' said Adam, but nobody was listening. Felipe Felipez was building up to the grand finale of his speech.

'We have had enough. We're not going to take it any more!'

'Si,' shouted the crowd.

'We do not need to be distracted by worrying about changing the laws of this fine city.'

For the first time there was a rumbling of disagreement in the crowd. Felipe Felipez heard the rumblings and quickly changed tack.

'What I mean is that we need to focus our attention on the most urgent problem. Other things can wait until the alarm is silenced. Unlike the Mayor, we aren't all lucky enough to have a soundproofed office and a pair of luxury ear mufflers.'

'Why would you need ear mufflers if your office was soundproofed?' wondered Adam.

'I promise you,' said Felipe Felipez, 'that on the first day of my office, the Dreadful Alarm will be found and silenced and you, the people of Buenos Sueños, will sleep soundly once more.'

'How will you do it?' a voice in the crowd demanded.

'Yes,' cried another voice. And then another, and another. Doubt was beginning to sweep through the crowd.

Felipe Felipez raised his hands for silence.

'Citizens! I can tell you that I have found the only man on the planet capable of switching off the alarm. He is already in Buenos Sueños. He is ready to save us.'

'Why doesn't he do it now?' a voice demanded.

'Yes,' shouted the crowd.

'A good question,' said Felipe Felipez, 'and one deserving an answer. It is because he believes so passionately in the rule of law and order that he refuses to act to save a city that may vote to throw away its Crime and Punishment Code.'

The crowd began to hiss at the mention of the Code. For a moment it looked as though Felipez was in trouble.

'I am not saying the Code must stay in its current form for ever,' he said to mollify them, 'but what I am saying is that we must have priorities. And instead of this crazy personal vendetta the Mayor has against the Code, we must first think of you, the citizens of Buenos Sueños. And unlike the Mayor, who promises you nothing but noise and sleep disturbance, I promise you pyjamas, I promise you pillows, I promise you snoring! So vote for Felipez! Vote for sweet dreams!'

All around the Doctor and Adam the crowd roared their approval. It appeared that Sniffage had also been convinced by Felipez's powerful words, because he began to bark enthusiastically.

'Sniffage,' said Adam, 'we're supposed to be supporting the other guy.'

CHAPTER 11

The Hotel Dormir, when they eventually arrived, was an impressive white building with two ornate golden lamp-posts on either side of the staircase which led up to its grand entrance. A man in a ridiculously elaborate uniform stood by the door. When the Doctor, Adam and Sniffage reached the top of the steps he saluted.

'Can I help you with your luggage, señor?'

'I don't have any luggage,' explained the Doctor.

'Would you like me to lend you some? Then I could help you with it.'

'There's no need,' the Doctor assured him.

The concierge looked momentarily disappointed. Then he noticed Adam and seemed to brighten again.

'Perhaps I can carry him?'

'I don't need carrying,' said Adam.

'You look tired,' the concierge insisted. 'And you have very weedy legs.'

'Leave my legs alone,' said Adam.

'They could give out on these steep steps. It happens all the time.'

'No, thank you,' said the Doctor.

'Are you sure there isn't anything I can carry?'

The Doctor shook his head. 'I'm afraid not.'

The concierge held out his hand expectantly.

'I said there's nothing for you to carry,' said the Doctor, raising his voice.

The concierge continued to hold out his hand.

'What do you want?' said the Doctor, both puzzled and irritated.

'My tip,' said the concierge.

'Why do we have to give you a tip?' asked Adam. 'You haven't carried anything.'

'I am carrying the burden of my disappointment that there is nothing to carry,' said the concierge firmly. 'It is a very heavy burden and I expect a large tip.'

With a sigh, the Doctor reached into his pocket and handed over a peso.

'Have a nice day,' said the concierge, holding the door open for them.

The lobby of the Hotel Dormir was air-conditioned and cool after the boiling heat of the street. There were luxurious leather chairs and tall green plants in pots. A well-dressed white-bearded old man was taking a cup of coffee and reading a newspaper in one corner. It was a haven of tranquility after the heat of the square and the sweltering crowd.

A tall young woman with long dark hair was sitting behind the reception desk. She stood up when she saw them come in.

'Welcome to the Hotel Dormir,' she said. 'The only four-and-a-half star hotel in Buenos Sueños.'

'Four-and-a-half stars?' said Adam.

'We lost half a star for bad punctuation and spelling,' explained the receptionist ruefully. 'The inspectors are ruthless.'

Sniffage sat down at Adam's feet. The hotel seemed disappointingly clean and lacking in dead things.

'My name is Arantcha,' said the receptionist. 'I am here to help you. Would you like a room?'

'No, thank you,' said the Doctor, fishing into his pocket and pulling out the picture of his wife. 'Would you mind looking at this photograph and telling me if you've seen this lady before?'

'Of course,' said Arantcha. 'Please pass it to me.'

The receptionist glanced at the photo.

'She would be a little older now,' said the Doctor, an edge of pain in his voice as he thought of all the years they had been apart – years that, even if he found her, they could never replace.

'I'm afraid I don't recognise her,' said Arantcha, quickly handing back the photo.

'You didn't look very hard,' said Adam.

'Adam!'

'She didn't. I watched her. It was like she'd decided she hadn't seen Mum before she even looked at the photo.'

'This is your mother?' asked Arantcha sharply.

'Would it be possible to look at the hotel register?' said the Doctor quickly, casting Adam an angry look. Adam couldn't believe his own stupidity. He told himself for the millionth time to think before he opened his mouth.

'I'm afraid the register is confidential,' said Arantcha. 'And now, if there is nothing further I can assist you gentlemen with, then I would be grateful if you would allow me to attend to the interests of our paying guests.'

She turned away from them dismissively, but Adam could see that his father was reluctant to go. He remained rooted in front of the reception desk.

'I must tell you that permitting me a look at your hotel register may be a matter of the utmost importance,' Doctor Forest urged her.

The receptionist looked up. This time her eyes were hard.

'Would you like me to call the concierge to escort you out into the street?' she said coldly.

'That will not be necessary,' said the Doctor, a hint of defeat in his tone. 'Come on, Adam.'

They turned to go.

Adam was thinking. There had to be a way. The Doctor would always use the most straightforward, the most logical and scientific method when he wanted something. But perhaps there was a different way to solve the problem.

Sniffage was the only one of them who was eager to be out of the hotel, with its disappointing aroma of cleanliness. It gave Adam an idea. He bent down and pulled the dog back.

'Yeah! No! Whatcha doing?' barked Sniffage.

Arantcha looked up from her desk. Adam crouched as close as he could to Sniffage's ear and whispered something to him.

'Really!' yelped Sniffage.

Adam nodded.

'Yeah! Yeah! Yeah!'

Suddenly the dog leapt out of Adam's hands and charged madly across the lobby.

'Sniffage!' shouted Adam.

But the dog ignored him.

'Control your dog!' shouted the receptionist.

'Sniffage!' ordered the Doctor. 'Come here!'

But Sniffage was not listening to anybody. He bounded over to the armchairs and jumped up on the one next to the old man and licked his face.

'I say!' said the surprised old man.

'Sniffage!' shouted the Doctor.

Having licked his face, Sniffage seemed to take a fancy to the old man's newspaper. But not reading it. Eating it. He took a large bite out of a corner.

'I was reading that article,' said the old man. 'This really is too much!'

But if it was too much, then it turned out that Sniffage only had more in mind. He leapt on to the table, upending the cup of coffee which sat there. Its contents landed in the old man's lap.

'Miguel!' cried Arantcha, rushing out from behind her desk. The burly, uniformed concierge rushed into the lobby. 'Get rid of that dog!'

Miguel, hampered only slightly by his extra-large tasselled lapels, which flapped into his face as he ran, dashed towards Sniffage. But Sniffage was not going to be caught so easily. He leapt into the pot plants, sending them toppling one way and then another, soil spilling in all directions.

Meanwhile, Arantcha hurried over to the old man. 'Señor Le Blacas,' she simpered, 'the hotel cannot apologise enough for this appalling incident. Allow me to immediately sponge your trousers.'

The Doctor watched the scene in utter horror. He had always believed that animals, like humans, would behave reasonably if they were treated well, yet here was Sniffage, with no provocation, causing complete pandemonium. It was throwing his scientific theories into chaos.

It was also throwing the lobby into chaos. Miguel's pursuit of Sniffage was far from nimble, and any plant that Sniffage had neglected to topple over the concierge did instead as he desperately tried to get a hold on the crazy dog. Sniffage charged back and forth across the lobby, barking joyfully. This was even more fun than finding a dead smelly thing and Sniffage hadn't thought there was anything more fun than that.

Finally, however, the concierge, red-faced and with one torn tasselled lapel hanging awkwardly from his uniform, cornered Sniffage.

'Hah!' he said triumphantly to the trapped dog. 'Now I will kick you into the street like a —'

But Sniffage took Miguel by surprise and sprang forward, straight at the concierge.

'Oh!' Miguel shouted as Sniffage slipped through his legs.

On the other side of the room, Arantcha was still tending to Señor Le Blacas.

Adam followed Sniffage, slipping past the concierge while he was still cursing the dog for escaping. They fled down the front steps and waited round the corner for the Doctor to emerge from the hotel.

Worse was to come.

PHEEEEEEP!

Officer Grivas, whistle in mouth, dashed down the street and up the staircase into the lobby. Inside, the concierge had a grip of iron on the Doctor's right arm.

'Look, my good man,' the Doctor was saying. 'I'm very sorry, but it was all a complete accident and . . .'

He spotted Officer Grivas staring at him and stopped talking.

'This man has disturbed the peace of a hotel lobby,' Arantcha informed the policeman.

'Which piece?' said Officer Grivas.

'All of it.' She indicated the general chaos.

The Doctor sighed. 'I suppose I have earned another on-the-spot fine.'

'If the hotel had less than four stars you would be right,' said Officer Grivas, advancing with an evil grin on his face. 'But for a four-and-a-half star hotel the punishment is a night in the cells.'

CHAPTER 12

'I have never been so embarrassed in all my life. A night in prison. A poor old man traumatised, his trousers stained. Innocent pot plants upended. The apology and the money I immediately handed over will be scant compensation for the stress you have caused.'

It was the next morning. The Doctor had just returned to the *Ark of the Parabola* and Adam and Sniffage were being told off.

'Have I not always told you that in order to get others to treat animals with respect it is important to avoid the kind of stereotypical behaviour which permits people to think that animals are lower forms of life?'

'But –' Adam began.

'No, Adam,' said the Doctor. 'There is no excuse for it. When Sniffage starts charging round a hotel, it feeds into the prejudices of those who regard dogs as dangerous. And don't say that you had nothing to do with it, because I know you connived with Sniffage in this appalling display. You should both be ashamed of yourselves.'

'But –' Adam tried again.

'I agree with the Doctor,' said Simia, who had been watching the telling-off and was eager to offer her views. 'Creatures like you two let the rest of us down.'

'Creatures like the four of you are keeping me awake,' yowled Malibu from his barrel. 'I am running a big winks deficit over here.'

'But –' began Adam.

'I don't want to hear another word,' said the Doctor. 'I couldn't be more disappointed in you both.'

Adam reached under his jumper and pulled out a sheet of paper, which he dropped on the table in front of the Doctor. 'It's the top page of the hotel register. I slipped behind the desk and ripped it out while Sniffage was distracting everybody.'

The Doctor was speechless.

'You mean,' he said after a shocked silence, 'that not only have you vandalised the property of others, but you have also used deception in order to do so? This is your grandfather's influence.'

'I've never met him,' Adam pointed out. 'So how could he influence me?'

'I meant his genetic influence,' said the Doctor, 'wired deep in your DNA. Believe me, it is not a good sign.'

But as he spoke, the Doctor eyed the torn page keenly.

'Leave it with me,' he said gruffly. 'I don't trust you to be responsible for anything!'

There was a sudden fluttering above them and, with a clunk, Vlad landed on the deck. The Doctor rushed over to the bat.

'Are you all right, Vlad?'

'Blood!' gasped Vlad. 'I need blood.'

'Adam,' said the Doctor, 'Vlad needs some blood.'

'I haven't got any.'

'You have approximately four litres circulating your body as I speak.'

'I'd like it to stay there.'

'Don't be so sentimental. You know any blood you spill will soon be replaced. Get a knife, cut your finger and dribble the blood into a cup.'

Reluctantly, Adam did as he was told.

Meanwhile Vlad decided that he was dying.

'I . . . would like . . . to make . . . a will,' he informed the Doctor between squeaks of pain.

'You don't have anything to leave,' Doctor Forest pointed out.

'I have my sombrero,' the bat insisted indignantly, temporarily forgetting his squeaks of pain.

'Hurry up with that blood, Adam,' said the Doctor.

'I would like to leave my sombrero to my sister,' continued Vlad. 'You will find her hanging upside down in a deserted mine shaft somewhere near La Paz.'

'Thanks for the precise directions,' said the Doctor.

'And now,' said Vlad, preparing himself bravely, 'I must go to the great bat cave in the sky.' And he closed his eyes.

Adam arrived with the cup.

Vlad opened one eye.

'Is that fresh blood I smell?'

Adam nodded.

'I am too far gone now to recover but perhaps if you were to tip it towards my fangs, then I would have one last drink to soothe me on my way.'

Adam tipped the cup towards the bat's mouth. He couldn't help shuddering when Vlad's fangs shot out greedily to suck up the blood. Whatever the Doctor said, there was something altogether unpleasant about it.

'Mmm,' said Vlad, licking the last dribble from his fangs. 'Remind me what year you were born.'

Adam told him.

'An excellent year,' Vlad remarked, evidently having made a complete recovery. 'Full-bodied and rich with fruity overtones.'

'As you seem to have revived,' interrupted the Doctor, 'perhaps you could tell us what you found out about the location of the Dreadful Alarm.'

'My life dangles yet on a thin thread,' cautioned Vlad. 'But I suppose we may hope that I'll pull through.'

'Tell me' There was steel in the Doctor's tone. Vlad decided to answer with uncharacteristic speed.

'I honed in on the sonar waves from the alarm and

followed them inland as fast as I could. They led me over the city and into the hills beyond, and just as I felt I was about to locate the source of the alarm it ceased. By now, the sun had weakened me so much I could barely go on. Nonetheless, I perservered.'

'So you know where the alarm is coming from!' cried Adam excitedly.

'Not exactly,' admitted Vlad. 'Once the alarm had ceased, the echoes could only give me an approximate location. But if you find the fairground in the hills – it will not be far.'

'Thank you, Vlad,' said the Doctor.

Vlad saw he had the attention of the others and decided to bleed it for all it was worth.

'I hope,' the bat said dramatically, 'that I can find a way to recover from this traumatic near-death experience.'

'I can recommend a therapist in LA,' Malibu drawled. 'He helped me through some issues.'

'What issues?' said Adam.

'I wasn't sleeping well,' Malibu explained. 'Sometimes only sixteen hours a day. It all went back to my relationship with my mom apparently. You see –'

'Shouldn't we go there right away?' Adam cut in, turning to the Doctor.

'Not so fast,' his father said. 'We need to gather more intelligence on the precise location. This would be far easier from the air.'

'But we can't fly,' pointed out Adam.

'And I'm not going,' announced Vlad. 'I'm exhausted. I'm going to hang upside down until I feel better.'

'I wasn't thinking of you,' said the Doctor.

Adam guessed who he was thinking about. There were only two other Arkonauts who could fly.

'Gogo,' he called. 'Pozzo!'

Two green parrots fluttered down from the crow's nest, where they had been perched.

'Nice to see you,' squawked Gogo, who had a slightly bigger beak.

'To see you nice,' added Pozzo, who was a slightly lighter green. Unlike the other animal Arkonauts, the parrots could speak human language.

'Hello,' said the Doctor. 'We need you –'

'I say, I say, I say!' Gogo continued. 'What's the difference between a bag of millet and a drunken magpie?'

'That's –'

'I don't know,' said Pozzo. 'What's the difference between a bag of millet and a drunken magpie?'

'One's bird seed and the other's a seedy bird.'

Both parrots looked expectantly at the others. None of them smiled.

'That one might need some more work,' conceded Gogo.

Gogo and Pozzo had joined the ship in Jamaica. They had escaped from a birdcage which hung in the bar of a small comedy club. Despite being parrots, they were convinced they could make it big in show business and so spent most of their days high in the rigging of the *Ark of the Parabola*, honing their double act.

'No more jokes,' commanded the Doctor. 'I need you to do something. This is very important.'

Gogo and Pozzo decided to shut up and listen.

'First, I need you to find the Buenos Sueños fairground. There is a large feral population of parrots in Buenos Sueños. Talk to them. Find out whether they have seen anything unusual recently. Somewhere near there is the location of the alarm that has been disturbing the city. It is vital that we find the alarm's source!'

Gogo looked at Pozzo. 'I've heard of tomato sauce.'

Pozzo looked at Gogo. 'I've heard of chilli sauce.'

They both looked at the Doctor. 'But we've never heard of alarm sauce.'

Each joke added a new wrinkle to the Doctor's already furrowed brow. Deciding that they were pushing their luck, Gogo and Pozzo both bobbed their heads to Adam and the Doctor and rose into the sky, fast becoming little green blurs which darted across the city in search of the fairground.

'What do we do now?' said Adam. 'Just wait for them to get back?'

'Of course not,' said the Doctor. 'We must go through the hotel register.'

'But I thought you were too annoyed with the way I got

it to use it,' said Adam mischievously.

The Doctor gave his son a hard look.

'I do not approve of what you have done,' he said, picking up the page, 'but, in the circumstances, I am prepared to overlook it.'

'Fine,' snapped Adam. 'I'm going out.'

CHAPTER 13

Adam stomped off the boat, feeling that life was very unfair. It was one thing for the Doctor to tell him off for the chaos he'd caused in the hotel, another thing entirely to tell him off for doing it to get the hotel register, and then to go and use it without saying thank you.

Something touched his leg.

Sniffage.

'Yeah! Yeah!' barked the dog. 'Going for a walk without me! You'd hate it! There'd be no dead things!'

Despite his bad mood, Adam smiled. Sniffage would never let him down.

In the streets, people scuttled past him, yawning and grumpy. They had bags and dark shadows under their eyes. The Dreadful Alarm was certainly having an ever-increasing effect on the citizens of Buenos Sueños, and it wasn't a good one. There were clunks, bangs and curses echoing up and down the street as people bumped into one another, dropped items of shopping or walked into doors by mistake.

'Watch it, can't you?'

'Get out of my way.'

'I've dropped a mango in the gutter.'

'Your dog's eating my mango.'

'Sniffage! Regurgitate that lady's fruit.'

Phrases like these, spoken in tired, angry voices, followed Adam as he picked his way through the city. The people were exhausted and it was showing in their mood. Adam told Sniffage to stay as close as possible to him.

It was funny, he reflected, but Buenos Sueños was much easier to walk through when you weren't actually intending to go anywhere. You could ignore the signs pointing in all directions and just pick a road at random, which is how Adam turned one way, then another, to find himself in a tiny deserted square that the sun just managed to squeeze into.

It was surprising it was empty, because it was the most beautiful square Adam had come across in all of Buenos Sueños. In the centre an elegant fountain trickled water, and cooling shade was provided by three tall palm trees. In one corner there was a café with tables outside, but they were all deserted.

Sniffage was not so impressed.

'Yeah! Yeah! No bad smells,' he barked. 'Let's go somewhere else.'

But Adam was happy to stay a little longer. Above him he heard shrill bird calls. He looked up. Flying at the level of the highest houses in the square were dozens of swifts, their neat, dark bodies swooping and veering in all directions. It was a fantastic sight. The birds were catching insects on the wing, which they then fed to their chicks, nestled in the eaves of the tall buildings surrounding the square. Adam knew swifts love to fly and hate to land – even sleeping in the air. The only thing that will make them land, and even then just for a moment, is feeding their chicks. So within a second they were back in the air.

Adam wanted to say hello. He knew the Doctor's rules about only using the ability to talk to animals when it was absolutely necessary and never when anybody might see. All right, it wasn't strictly necessary now, but there was nobody around and, anyway, what was the point of being able to talk to animals if the only place you got to do it was on board the *Ark of the Parabola*?

Adam took one more look about him to check that Sniffage was the only creature, apart from the swifts, within earshot. Then he took a deep breath and in bird language cried, 'Hello!'

The surprised swifts froze mid-flight and looked down.

'Hello!' repeated Adam.

The swifts realised they were all about to plummet to the ground and promptly flapped their wings again. And they started talking.

'Hello!'

'Hello!'

'Hello!'

'How are you?'

'Where did you learn our language?'

'Is that your dog with its head in a bin?'

They were bombarding him with questions now. This was one of the hazards of talking to creatures who travelled in flocks: they had developed sophisticated methods of having multiple conversations at once, a skill that creatures who only moved alone or in small groups, like humans, lacked.

'Hello! Well! On a boat! What bin?' cried Adam, answering the questions as fast as he could.

'Can you fly?'

'Why don't you have a beak?'

'Where's your feathers?'

This was undoubtedly the first time a human had ever spoken to them and it was not surprising that they were so interested. Now they swooped and dived around Adam, shrieking more and more questions.

'Have you got any flies?'

'Do you go south for the winter?'

'Why are humans always sitting down?'

'I think your dog has got his head stuck.'

'Hang on,' said Adam, as a swift fluttered past his face, while another perched briefly on his head. 'One at a time.'

His mind was whirling as he tried to order his answers. Maybe talking to the swifts wasn't such a good idea after all. Suddenly, all the swirling dust and feathers gave Adam a violent urge to sneeze.

'Achoo!'

PHEEEEEEEEP! PHEEEEEEEEEEEEP!

The blasts from the whistle sent the swifts flying back up, high above the square. Adam turned round. Coming towards him was Officer Grivas. Behind him was Diego, with his paint pot.

'Halt! Police!' cried Officer Grivas. 'You are under arrest.'

'What for?' Adam said. 'I wasn't doing anything.'

'Not doing anything?' shouted back Officer Grivas. 'You were breaking the oldest law in the Buenos Sueños Crime and Punishment Code. Law 1, Section 1, Subsection 1, Paragraph 1. You were spreading plague.'

'Plague?' cried Adam. 'I don't have plague.'

'A likely story,' said Officer Grivas. 'You were sneezing in a public place without using a handkerchief. Under the Buenos Sueños Crime and Punishment Code that constitutes an attempt to spread plague.'

'But something flew up my nose,' Adam protested.

'Your nose is your own responsibility,' said Officer Grivas. 'Consider yourself under arrest. Diego, paint a juvenile spot for the little señor to stand on.'

Diego did as he was told.

'Little señor, stand on the spot, please. You owe 224 pesos.'

'Hey, there's the blackguard who stained my trousers!'

Both Adam and Officer Grivas turned to see Señor Le Blacas emerging from the café.

'Officer,' demanded Señor Le Blacas, marching angrily across the square, 'that boy is responsible for the staining of my trousers. Arrest him immediately.'

'I've already arrested him,' said Officer Grivas.

'Arrest him again!'

'I'm not sure I can arrest someone who is already arrested,' said Officer Grivas, looking confused.

'Can't arrest him again? Pah!' fumed Señor Le Blacas. 'Liberal nonsense. Why, when I was young you could be arrested twenty or thirty times in a day. The whole of society is going to the dogs.'

It was unfortunate that at this moment Sniffage finally managed to liberate his head from the bin he had stuck it in. He heard Señor Le Blacas's words and barked approvingly – society going to the dogs seemed a very good idea to him.

However, Sniffage's enthusiastic bark had a decidedly unenthusiastic effect on Señor le Blacas. He looked at the dog and shook with rage.

'That's the beast that spilled coffee on my trousers. Arrest the boy again and shoot the dog!'

Adam gasped in horror. 'Run, Sniffage, Run!' he cried.

Sniffage didn't have a clue what was going on, but the terror in Adam's voice made it very clear that it was something extremely serious. Before Officer Grivas could unholster his weapon, Sniffage was running away at top speed.

'He's getting away,' cried Señor Le Blacas.

Officer Grivas raised his revolver, aimed and fired. The bullet flew over Sniffage's head.

'Lower, you fool, lower,' cried Señor Le Blacas.

'Faster, Sniffage! Faster,' shouted Adam.

Sniffage disappeared round the corner. Plaster was blasted off the wall where, a moment earlier, his head had been.

With Sniffage gone, Officer Grivas turned towards Adam again.

Adam looked frantically around for some means of escape, but found himself cornered. Then he looked up. Above him, the swifts still circled the small square. It would mean breaking his father's golden rule, but surely even the Doctor would see that this was a special case where he was left with little option.

Adam opened his mouth and shrieked.

'What are you doing?' demanded Officer Grivas.

The swifts shrieked back and Adam called to them again.

'Is he talking to them?' said Señor Le Blacas.

'Nobody can talk to – eurgh!'

A large white bird dropping landed on Officer Grivas's collar.

'Eurgh!'

Another landed on his shoe.

'Eurgh!'

A further one landed on his head.

The swifts circled above.

'Stop that!' Officer Grivas ordered the birds.

While Señor Le Blacas and Diego retreated beneath the parasol of a table in the nearby café, more droppings rained down upon Officer Grivas. But the policeman stood resolutely next to Adam.

'Why aren't they pooing on you?' he demanded angrily. 'You're the criminal.'

But the swifts diving and swooping over Officer Grivas showed no desire to change their target. Desperately, he raised his hands to ward off the plummeting poo, but to no avail. Swifts, it appeared, could poo with great accuracy.

'Aaarggh!' shouted Officer Grivas. 'It's stinging my eyes.'

'Shelter over here, Officer,' shouted Señor Le Blacas from under the parasol.

'I'm blind,' the policeman cried, staggering left and then lurching right. 'I can't see where I'm going.'

'Follow my voice,' Señor Le Blacas called.

Officer Grivas doubtless would have managed to reach the safety of the parasol had not the gurgling fountain lain in his path. He tumbled into it with a large splash.

'Officer down! Officer down!' he shouted, waving his hands wildly. 'Call for backup! Officer down!'

Adam saw his chance to escape. He stepped off the spot and ran.

Though Officer Grivas couldn't appreciate it at first, falling in the fountain was a very lucky turn of events for him. Until then he had been unable to depoo himself fast enough, but his sudden immersion in the waters of the fountain cleaned him up in an instant. He raised his head just in time to see Adam dash out of the square and down a street.

'Officer backup!' he shouted again. 'Prisoner escaping!'

He clambered out of the fountain, reaching for his whistle as he did so. A loud blast would bring other officers of the Buenos Sueños Police Force to his aid in the pursuit of this dangerous felon. He put it to his lips.

Phep!

'Your whistle is soggy,' observed Diego.

Officer Grivas was crestfallen. But not for long.

'Come with me, Diego,' he shouted. 'That boy will stand on the biggest spot in the world by the time I'm finished with him.'

Señor Le Blacas didn't follow them out of the square. Instead he looked thoughtfully up at the swifts and stroked his beard.

CHAPTER 14

Pheeeep!

Adam ran. He turned left, then right, then left again. Surely he could lose Officer Grivas.

There were whistles from all sides now. Other policemen had heard the call and were determined to join the chase. Adam needed a miracle. He charged round the corner and ran straight into a bike.

'Owww!'

The cyclist didn't say anything. Adam realised why. It was the Mayor's daughter – dark, pretty, mischievous Anna. She seemed to think riding her bike into Adam was funny. She rocked with silent laughter.

'I'm glad you find it funny,' said Adam, remembering that, although Anna was unable to hear or speak, she could lipread every word he said.

PHEEP! PHEEP! PHEEP!

'The police are after me,' he told her. 'I've been running as fast as I can down all the narrowest, darkest roads, but they seem to be able to follow me wherever I go.'

Anna pointed behind him. Adam turned to see a line of red footprints. *How could I have been so stupid?* he thought.

He turned back to the dark girl.

'This is really important, Anna. I've got to get away.'

PHEEP! PHEEP! PHEEP!

The police were very close now. Adam had no idea which way to run. With a dangerous smile, Anna stood up on her pedals, leaving the seat of her bike free. She nodded to Adam to climb on. He wasn't sure he liked her smile, but he didn't have any other option.

As Officer Grivas sprinted round the corner, Anna swung her bike away from him and pedalled for all she was worth. Two more policemen were running up the road towards them. As Anna swerved to avoid the first one, the second officer jumped to block their path. She swerved back the other way and sped past.

But there was worse ahead. Another two policemen had formed a human cordon. Only by riding into them could Anna hope to get by. She pulled hard on both brakes and her bike juddered to a halt. Officer Grivas was behind them. They were trapped.

Or maybe not. Spotting the door of a house slightly ajar, Anna whirled her bike round and cycled straight at it.

The Marquez family were sitting down to lunch. Señor Marquez was pouring the wine, while Señora Marquez was spooning out portions of fish stew to the children. In the corner, Grandma Marquez was knitting a scarf. It was a scene of domestic tranquillity . . . which was abruptly shattered when the door flew open and a young girl riding a bike, with a boy sitting behind her, shot through their living-room-cum-dining-area, accelerated into their kitchen and sped out through the open back door.

The Marquez family's mouths dropped open.

Moments later four large policeman burst into the house.

'I am Officer Grivas. These are other Officer Grivases. Hand over the criminals or face the consequences.'

'Never!' screeched Grandma Marquez, waving her knitting aggressively at the police officers.

The rest of the Marquez family, their mouths getting wider every moment, turned to her.

Officer Grivas was taken aback but swiftly regained his air of authority.

'I insist you hand over the criminals hiding in this house.'

'You'll never take me alive!' shouted Grandma Marquez. 'I've got a thimble and I'm prepared to use it.'

'What are you talking about, Mother?' said Señor Marquez.

'I said we should have put her in a home,' said Señora Marquez.

'I thought I'd got away with it,' Grandma Marquez muttered.

'Got away with what?'

'Sixty-seven years I've been on the run,' the old lady went on.

'You haven't run much in the last few years,' said Señora Marquez drily.

'On the hobble, then,' she conceded.

'But what have you done?' said Señor Marquez.

'I can't remember,' admitted Grandma Marquez. 'I think it was something to do with peas.'

'Peas?' cried Officer Grivas. 'I know of nobody in Buenos Sueños wanted for a pea-related offence.'

Grandma Marquez wasn't listening.

'Take one step nearer,' she warned the policemen, 'and I kill my hostage.'

'You haven't got a hostage, señora,' Officer Grivas pointed out.

'What do you call this?' shouted Grandma Marquez, holding her scarf up in the air. 'Try to arrest me and I'll unravel it. I'm not bluffing.'

'Now, now,' said Officer Grivas, 'let's all stay calm. Just put the scarf down and . . . What am I saying? Destroy your scarf if you like. I don't care. I want to know where the two criminals are who just cycled into your house.'

'They went out the back,' said Señor Marquez.

'It's a dead end out the back. They've got nowhere to go,' Señora Marquez added.

The four policemen charged out of the back door. The yard behind the house was enclosed on all sides, and there were Adam and Anna astride the bike.

'Arrest them!' cried Officer Grivas joyfully.

Adam slumped in his seat. They were caught.

But Anna wasn't giving in so easily. She stood high on the pedals for a moment and then cycled furiously towards the far wall.

'You can't escape,' Officer Grivas crowed triumphantly.

'What are you . . .' began Adam. But he didn't finish the sentence because he saw what she had in mind. An old plank was propped against a box at the far end of the yard. If Anna hit it right, and if she pedalled dead straight, and if it didn't break under their weight, then it just might provide enough of a ramp to launch them over the wall.

These were way too many ifs for Adam's liking, but there was no stopping Anna. He gripped the saddle tightly.

Would she hit the plank right?

Yes!

Would she cycle dead straight?

Yes!

Would it hold their weight?

Yes!

Would they have enough elevation to get over the wall?

No!

At least it didn't look like it.

The bike rose but not fast enough. The wall seemed to be growing in front of them. If they hit it, it was really going to hurt. Adam closed his eyes and waited for the crushing pain of impact.

When it didn't come, he opened his eyes again.

Anna had jerked the bike back at the last second and then jolted it forward. Like a horse jumping a fence, the bike flew over the wall.

'Yessss . . . nooooo!' shouted Adam.

The 'yes' was for getting over. The 'no' was for what was on the other side. They bike was heading straight down into a swimming pool.

An empty swimming pool!

There was nothing to stop the bike smashing into the tiles at the bottom of the pool . . . except, possibly, the diving board!

Could they land on it? Anna tightened her grip on the handlebars. The bike was plunging almost vertically down now, and with great speed. She crouched, ready for the impact and . . .

BAM!

She hit the board perfectly and pulled with all her might on the brakes.

They screeched along the diving board and stopped right on the edge, teetering over the empty pool.

Adam exhaled.

Anna turned round to him. And winked.

CHAPTER 15

'Doctor! Doctor!'

Adam rushed up the gangplank of the *Ark of the Parabola*. When he reached the top he turned to give Anna a wave but was only in time to see the dark-haired girl on the bike disappear into the narrow cobbled streets of Buenos Sueños.

'Where have you been, Adam?' said the Doctor. 'And why isn't Sniffage with you.'

'He hasn't come back?'

'No.'

'But the shots missed him.'

'Shots?' snapped the Doctor.

'Officer Grivas shot at him for being wild after Señor Le Blacas complained about the coffee on his trousers.'

The Doctor gave Adam a hard stare.

'I warned you such behaviour would have serious consequences.'

It didn't stop you wanting to see the hotel register though, thought

Adam. But he didn't say anything because he had more important things to ask, like . . . 'Can I have an advance on my pocket money?'

'What on earth for?'

'Err . . . I got fined.'

'Fined. Who by?'

Adam took a deep breath and told the story of what had just happened to him. Before the Doctor could launch into one of his lectures, Adam swiftly, and a little deviously, moved the subject on to the hotel register. 'So did you find out anything about Mum?' he asked.

'I'm afraid not,' the Doctor said sadly. 'It turns out your escapade yesterday was all for nothing.'

Adam felt utterly deflated. He was saved from having to think of a reply by a sudden flurry of green feathers from above, as Gogo and Pozzo landed on the deck. The Doctor lost interest in Adam immediately and turned to the parrots.

'Have you located the source?' he demanded impatiently.

'Do we get to tell a joke if you're pleased?'

The Doctor sighed. 'I suppose so.'

'OK,' said Gogo. 'We flew all the way up to the fair.'

'There were lots of parrots there,' said Pozzo.

'None of them with a very good sense of humour,' added Gogo. 'My joke about millet went down like a lead macaw.'

'Concentrate on telling me what you found out.'

'We found out that the tastiest leftovers are from the

takeaway kiosk near the log flume.'

'And that you have to keep an eye out for the local sparrow hawk or your most recent squawk could be your last.'

Adam saw the Doctor bristle with impatience.

'And that further up the mountain in a place called Tibidabo beyond the amusement park, where people never go, is a murky wood.'

'Suddenly, a month ago, just as it was getting dark, this wood became a nest of activity, with people dressed in black going in and out carrying machines – they made sure that they moved about only during the siesta when the rest of Buenos Sueños was sleeping. But the parrots saw them, even though they didn't have much to do with them because they didn't leave any leftovers.'

'The people were working in the forest every night for two weeks, and after that the alarm started.'

'Eureka!' cried the Doctor.

'So would you if you'd been flying all morning in the sun,' snapped Gogo indignantly.

'That wood must be the location of the alarm,' continued the Doctor. 'Whoever built it would have done so far from the view of prying human eyes, but he would not have thought it necessary to conceal it from parrots. Yet again, the Arkonauts have discovered something humans could not. We will head up there immediately.'

'We haven't finished yet,' squawked Gogo.

'The parrots told us the edge of the wood is patrolled by guards. And they all have guns.'

'Guns?' gulped Adam.

Both parrots nodded.

'Hmm,' said the Doctor.

'And now,' said Gogo, 'time for a joke.'

'Did you say it's time for a joke?' said Pozzo.

'I say, I say, I say! What's the difference between a large bird of prey and a dog with mange?'

'One's a golden eagle and the other's a mouldy beagle!'

Neither the Doctor nor Adam laughed.

'I told you nobody was going to find mouldy dogs funny,' Gogo remarked.

'We've got to be more edgy or we'll get stale,' Pozzo insisted.

The parrots flew up to the crow's nest, squabbling about new directions for their act.

'We must go to Tibidabo,' announced the Doctor, 'armed guards or not. If we're to switch off the alarm, that is where we must go.'

'But how will that help Mum?' said Adam, unable to hide his frustration.

'I have a theory about that. I'll explain on the way,' the Doctor replied mysteriously.

'And how will we get past the guards with guns?'

But his father had already disappeared below deck. Adam was left alone. He thought sadly about his mother, possibly so close, but whom he might now never see if things went wrong in the woods. He felt exhausted – so much had already happened today. He slumped down on a chair and covered his face, only to be interrupted by a wet tongue licking his hands.

'Sniffage! You're back!'

Sniffage was indeed back and as cheerful as ever, with a large stick in his mouth.

'What took you so long?'

'Yeah! Got distracted by some dead things. Whatcha doing?'

The spaniel stood in front of him, wagging his tail for all it was worth.

'I was feeling sad,' admitted Adam.

'Sad?' said Sniffage. 'Don't do that! Not when there's sticks to throw!' And he helpfully dropped his stick at Adam's feet. 'Yeah! Yeah! Throw it!'

Reluctantly, Adam picked up the stick and threw it for Sniffage. The dog was right – he did feel better.

But not for long.

Adam turned towards the harbour and saw what looked like the entire Buenos Sueños Police Force, headed by Chief Grivas, descending on to the dock. The Chief of Police stomped up to the gangplank, flanked by all his officers.

Adam gulped.

The noise of their arrival brought the Doctor swiftly back up on deck.

'This young hooligan is going to pay us 1,920 pesos or he is going to prison for a long time,' Chief Grivas informed him. 'Two more offences have been committed: "Escaping without permission" and "Riding a bike through a house during mealtimes." Both are criminal acts according to the Buenos Sueños Crime and Punishment Code.'

The Doctor rushed across to Adam and stuffed some notes in his hand.

'That's almost all our money,' he said furiously. 'Whatever you do, don't commit any more crimes.'

So, beneath the burning sun and under the harsh, watchful eyes of the Buenos Sueños Police Force, Adam walked down the gangplank, stood on the large red spot and handed over the money. Chief Grivas did not seem particularly happy to receive it. It was obvious that he would have preferred to put the boy in jail. As Adam was about to move off the spot, Grivas grabbed his elbow.

'Not so fast. We are going to require you to hand over your wild dog.'

'Sniffage!' said Adam. 'But Sniffage isn't wild.'

'My officer says he's wild, and if my officer says something is true, then it is,' said Chief Grivas. 'Now hand him over to us or we will board your ship and shoot him on sight.'

'What will happen to him?'

'He will be taken to the Buenos Sueños Dog Pound.'

'Can I visit him?'

'Of course not.'

'Will someone throw sticks for him?'

'They will not,' said Chief Grivas. 'My officers have more important things to do than throw sticks for dogs.'

'But he'll be miserable.'

'You have ten seconds to hand over your dog,' Chief Grivas growled menacingly. 'Or he dies.'

Adam looked up at the Doctor. His eyes were blazing, but he said nothing. Sniffage was standing next to him on the gangplank, wagging his tail. Adam had no option. He had to do it.

He whistled and Sniffage trotted down towards him trustingly.

'Yeah! Yeah! Let's hope these policemen go soon. There's still time for some stick throwing. Yeah!'

Sniffage licked Adam's hand. At a signal from the Chief an Officer Grivas stepped forward and grabbed the dog roughly and looped a lead over his head.

'Hey! Hey! Whatcha doing? I don't need a lead! I need to be able to investigate dead things! Take it off! Yeah!'

But to Officer Grivas, Sniffage was just another dog barking. He jolted the lead hard.

'Ow! That hurt!'

'You're being too rough,' protested Adam.

But with every bark, the policeman tugged the lead harder until, eventually, Sniffage was subdued and silent. Officer Grivas led him away. Adam could hardly bear to watch. The dog's head hung low and his tail was lifeless and limp.

'The sooner you leave Buenos Sueños the better,' observed Chief Grivas, tossing his cigar carelessly on to the dock. 'Before you lose any more of your friends.'

'That's litter,' said Adam, pointing at the cigar stub. 'Why isn't anyone arresting you?'

'Arresting me?' repeated Grivas. 'You have a very funny sense of humour, chico. Arresting me! Ha ha ha!'

And with his ugly, jeering laughter echoing round the port, Chief of Police Grivas led his men away.

CHAPTER 16

'I don't know why we're here.'

It was the next morning and the Doctor and Adam were standing by a bus stop on the edge of Buenos Sueños. The Doctor was carrying a white box, the contents of which he had not divulged to Adam.

'I gave my word to the Mayor,' said the Doctor sternly. 'We must investigate the alarm.'

'I don't care about the Mayor and your word,' Adam complained. 'We should be rescuing Sniffage and finding Mum.'

'A man is only as good as his word, Adam.'

'I'm not a man yet,' Adam replied sulkily. 'I'm a boy. And I don't care about words and promises. They're not real. Not like a dog.'

'Words and promises *are* real,' insisted the Doctor. 'And you are beginning to sound worryingly like your grandfather.'

'I'd rather sound like him than you,' Adam grumbled.

'Don't forget that it's thanks to you that we lost Sniffage,' the Doctor snapped, for a moment losing his temper.

'And it's thanks to you that we lost Mum!'

They both lapsed into silence.

The night before had been terrible. Sniffage's absence had taken all the life from the boat. Even Malibu, who had been moaning for years about the amount of winks he had lost due to Sniffage's unnecessary barking, had been sad. But Adam felt Sniffage's loss worst of all because he had got him into trouble in the first place. And what for? The hotel register had told them nothing about his mother's whereabouts. They were back where they started, still in search of Adam's mum *and* now they'd lost Sniffage as well. Even Gogo and Pozzo had stopped telling jokes.

'Listen, Adam,' said the Doctor suddenly, in a softer voice, 'I don't want you thinking it's better to be like your grandfather. He was a bad man, who left his family and used his abilities in wicked ways. I'm going to tell you something. My word is not the only reason that we're still investigating the source of the alarm.'

'What's the other reason?'

'Did I ever tell you about how they discovered the structure of DNA?'

'Only about a hundred times.'

'Then you'll remember,' said the Doctor, 'that the scientists knew that the structure of DNA had to be simple. That, even though human beings are complex creatures, the thing that forms the core of their make-up actually had to be very simple. But they couldn't work out exactly how all the complex things they were discovering could be resolved in a simple pattern.'

Adam couldn't believe it. After everything that had gone wrong, his father was still thinking about science.

'Then they struck upon the idea of the double helix,' said the Doctor, 'one of the greatest discoveries in the history of science. All the things needed to make a complex human being in one simple structure.'

'What has any of this got to do with Mum or Sniffage or the alarm?'

'Everything,' the Doctor replied. 'Ever since we've landed here things have got more and more confusing: the alarm, the letter, the election, the Mayor, the police, notes from your mother, Sniffage and the spilled coffee. It seems as if the whole place is crazy. But science would tell us there is something simple underneath all this madness, something that explains it all and links it together. And if we can only explain one thing, then perhaps everything else will fall into place. Just like –'

'The double helix,' said Adam.

The Doctor nodded. As he did so, a rickety old bus wheezed its way out of a narrow street and lurched towards the bus stop.

'But what if it's not simple?' said Adam. 'What if it's not a double helix? What if it's a great big ugly mess instead?'

The doors of the bus opened and the Doctor climbed

on, without answering the question. Adam sighed and followed him.

'Welcome aboard,' said the bus driver. 'My name is Captain – sorry . . . Señor Torres, and I will be driving you today.'

'Hello,' said Adam.

'Please choose your seat and settle down in preparation for the safety demonstration.'

'Safety demonstration?'

'In case of emergencies.'

'But this is a bus, not a plane.'

'I know that,' said Torres touchily. 'There's no need to remind me I failed my pilot's exam. Please take your seat.'

Adam went and sat by the Doctor. There were no other passengers on the bus.

Bus Pilot Torres got out of his seat and stood in the middle of the aisle.

'Welcome to Aerobus!' he announced. 'The bus which is like a plane in every way. Except it doesn't fly.'

'That's quite a big difference,' muttered Adam.

'Please pay attention to the following safety announcement, even if you are frequent flyers . . . I mean, passengers. The emergency exit is located at the bus door.' Torres pointed to it. 'In fact, it *is* the bus door. If there is an emergency, just go out of it – like you got in, except the other direction. We don't have any low-level lighting to show you the way but I will shine a torch on it – if the batteries haven't run out. In the event of a sudden loss of pressure in the cabin, please put your fingers in your ears until they pop. In the event of the bus landing on water, it is probably because it has been raining and there are puddles on the road. There is no need to adopt the emergency position or shout, 'Brace, Brace!' but you can if you want to. I wish you a pleasant journey on Aerobus.'

Torres returned to the driver's seat, turned on the engine and the Aerobus began its slow crawl up the hill towards Tibidabo.

CHAPTER 17

'Welcome to Tibidabo,' said the driver as Adam and the Doctor got off the bus. 'The hill above the city. I hope you enjoy your stay.'

'Thank you,' replied the Doctor.

They stepped out next to the amusement park that Vlad had described. Today it was closed. It was a forlorn sight: the rides that should have been filled with shrieking children were instead silent and stationary, emitting only the odd creak when a gust of wind blew through them. The Doctor noticed Adam looking longingly at some of them.

'Come on,' he said brusquely. 'We'll have to go the rest of the way on foot.'

Adam tore his gaze away from the rides and followed the Doctor. They soon left the amusement park behind them and were hiking into the dry hills. The harsh yellow sun beat down, making every step an effort. Sweating profusely, they walked for another hour until suddenly the Doctor came to an abrupt halt. He motioned to Adam to keep silent. Remembering the parrots' warning about the guards, Adam did as he was told.

A hundred metres in front of them the mountain plateaued. Adam could see the outskirts of a small wood. And at the edge of the wood stood two guards with powerful machine guns.

The Doctor indicated they should retreat. They crept quietly back for about fifty metres until they found a large rock. The Doctor ducked behind it.

'What are we stopping for?' asked Adam.

'To prepare our attack,' the Doctor answered.

'Attack? Didn't you see the guns?'

'I did,' his father replied calmly. 'But guns have a big drawback.'

'They tend to make holes in everything?' suggested Adam.

'Guns can make holes in *some* things.'

'Like us,' Adam reminded him.

'Like us,' agreed the Doctor. 'But they have problems with other things. Especially little things.'

The Doctor placed his white box on the floor and opened it. Out of it, in strict military formation, trooped a platoon of ants: red army ants. They were led by General Lepti, their commanding officer.

'Attention!' he signalled. Like other insects, they communicated by movement. And mimicking these movements with their own fingers was how Adam and the Doctor communicated with them.

The ants formed into serried ranks. General Lepti saluted them and then approached the Doctor, who put his hand on the ground so the General could march on to it.

'General Lepti and the Special Ant Service reporting for duty, sir.'

'Thank you,' signalled the Doctor. 'There are two guards 150 metres away on the edge of the wood. They are in our way. I would appreciate it if the SAS could remove them.'

'Yes, sir.'

General Lepti was an ant of few signals. He immediately marched off the Doctor's hand and returned to his platoon.

'Listen up, troops,' he signalled. 'The Doctor has ordered us to take out two guards that are blocking his entrance to the wood. Do you understand?'

'Yes, sir,' signalled the platoon.

'We will divide into four groups. A, B, C and D. Groups A and C will perform a frontal assault on the guards while groups B and D will skirt round the back, cutting off their escape. Any questions?'

One army ant raised his feeler.

'Permission to speak,' indicated the General.

'Do they have insecticide, sir?'

'There have been no reports of chemical weapons,' confirmed the General. The tapping of abdomens showed this was good news. 'Any more questions? No. Then on my . . .'

The General stopped. One ant had moved out of formation and was approaching him.

'What do you think you're doing, soldier?'

The army ant signalled something.

'Nobody told you to fall out,' signed the General. 'Get yourself back in formation at the double.'

But the army ant did not get back into formation. Instead he signalled once more to the General, who did an abrupt about turn and marched back towards the Doctor.

'Permission to march up leg, Doctor?'

Intrigued, the Doctor nodded, and General Lepti climbed up the Doctor's leg and into his hand. Adam was not an expert at observing the moods of insects (they were much more difficult to read than mammals), but he could have sworn that the General, normally so confident, seemed ill at ease.

'It is with great regret, Doctor,' he signalled, 'that I am forced to report my platoon has been shamed.'

'What do you mean?'

'Can't say I've never heard of it before, but I never expected to find it in my swarm.'

'What is it?'

'Private Mandible over there,' Lepti indicated the army ant who was out of formation, 'has informed me that he's . . .' The General made a sign with his legs that neither the Doctor nor Adam had seen before.

'Could you repeat that more slowly?'

General Lepti complied.

'Oh,' said the Doctor. 'I can see how that could be quite awkward.'

'What is it?' demanded Adam, who had still not been able to decipher General Lepti's communication.

'I believe,' the Doctor said, 'that Private Mandible has announced he is a conscientious objector.'

'What's one of those?'

'It's someone who doesn't believe in using violence,' his father explained. 'I've never heard of it happening to an army ant before, because . . . er . . . well, they use violence to get pretty much everything. How interesting.'

'Permission to convene a court martial, sir, find Private Mandible guilty of cowardice in the face of the enemy and sentence him to death?' General Lepti requested bluntly.

The Doctor shook his head.

'I'm sorry, General, but when I allowed the SAS to come aboard the *Ark of the Parabola* I made it clear I believed in freedom of signal. The *Ark* was to be a place where animals could express themselves as they choose and there was only one rule.'

'Don't eat each other!' said Adam.

'Can't have him amongst the troops,' insisted General Lepti. 'Bad for morale.'

'Yes, I see that,' said the Doctor. 'Perhaps . . .'

'He can stay with me,' Adam suggested. Something about Private Mandible standing apart from the identical ranks attracted his sympathy.

'That would be helpful, Adam,' said the Doctor.

'Yes, sir,' said General Lepti.

The Doctor lowered him to the ground and he marched over to the solitary army ant.

'Private Mandible, you are a coward and a disgrace,' the General informed him curtly. 'You have dishonoured your species. Report to the Doctor's son and count yourself lucky that you're not subject to the extremes of military discipline.'

Private Mandible sheepishly saluted the General and marched as quickly as he could towards Adam, fearing that at any moment the General would change his mind.

Adam crouched down and held his hand out so Private Mandible could march on to it.

'All I'm saying,' he signalled to Adam, 'is give peace a chance.'

Peace, however, was not to be given a chance. The last thing General Lepti wanted was for other troops to ponder this anti-war message. No sooner had Private Mandible departed, than he ordered his troops to divide into the four assault groups and advance. The army ants marched out from behind the rock and headed towards the wood.

Adam put Private Mandible carefully in his pocket and, along with Doctor, waited to see what would happen. At first nothing did. The two guards patrolled the perimeter of wood, their machine guns slung menacingly in front of them.

'Aiiee!' Suddenly, one guard grabbed at his leg.

'What is it?' The other gripped his weapon tightly and scanned the area nervously. 'Ouch!'

133

Now he knew. Army ants were swarming all over the guards.

'They're on my leg!'

'My arm!'

'In my pants!'

'In my eyes!'

Frantically the guards tried to brush the ants off their hands, legs and faces. But the army ants were used to creatures trying to repel them, and for every ant that was brushed off, another two attacked.

'Retreat to base!' shouted one of the guards.

They turned and fled – right into General Lepti's trap. For waiting behind them were the two other attack groups. They swarmed up the legs of the disoriented guards, who had no chance. Everywhere they turned there seemed to be more ants.

'Aiiee!'

'Ouch!'

'They're everywhere!'

'I can't see!'

'Water! Find some water!'

And desperate to escape the biting attentions of the army ants, the guards stumbled down the mountain.

'Come on,' said the Doctor.

'Aren't we going to wait for General Lepti's platoon?'

'They'll reform and return to base when their job is done,' said the Doctor. 'One of the creatures you need to worry about least is the army ant. We should be more worried about ourselves – we're far more vulnerable. Remember that and keep your eyes peeled for more guards.'

The Doctor led the way into the wood. Adam scampered after him. The sudden disappearance of the sun forced him to blink a few times to allow his eyes to become accustomed to the murkiness. His ears, however, were immediately sensitive to eerie noises. Branches creaked and twigs snapped underfoot. The very air he breathed was heavy and menacing. And looking round, all Adam could see were dark green bushes perfect for an ambusher or a guard to hide behind.

'Are you sure about this?' he whispered.

'I have seen or heard nothing threatening,' the Doctor replied.

'But it feels wrong,' Adam said, looking left and right and back and forth, trying to keep all the potential points of attack under surveillance.

'I hope you're not giving into fear,' said the Doctor dis-approvingly. 'Fear is a most unhelpful emotion that prevents human beings from acting logically and effectively by allowing the imagination to run riot. You will never see an animal imagining things.'

'But what if the imagination is right and there is some-thing to be scared of?' said Adam.

'That is different,' the Doctor answered. 'For example, if we were to come across something in these woods that menaced our lives – let us say, for the sake of argument, ten men armed to the teeth with orders to kill us on sight –'

'Couldn't we say two?' asked Adam nervously.

'If you insist,' said the Doctor. 'In that case, then of course we would give way to terror. Now, I strongly approve of terror. The body shoots itself full of adrenalin and acts at peak performance in an attempt to escape. A real triumph of evolution.'

Adam wasn't so sure that he would give terror the same ringing endorsement. He might instead speak in favour of sitting on the deck of the *Ark of the Parabola* with nothing much to worry about. But that didn't appear to be an option. The Doctor forged ahead. 'If there are ten men armed to the teeth with orders to kill us on sight,' muttered Adam to himself, 'then he's bound to find them.'

Deeper and deeper into the wood they went. Adam's eyes grew more accustomed to the dark and his ears were less spooked by the strange sounds. Suddenly the Doctor stopped. There was sunlight in front of them, seeming extra bright after the murk of the wood. They were on the edge of a clearing. Adam craned his neck round the Doctor and saw that in the very centre of that clearing there was a hatch. He tugged the Doctor's arm.

'I think we've found it,' he whispered.

'It's possible,' conceded the Doctor.

'Let's go back to the city and tell Mayor Puig.'

'We need some evidence,' said the Doctor. 'I'm going to examine it more closely. Wait here!'

Firmly motioning Adam to remain behind, the Doctor cautiously poked his head out of the cover of the trees and into the bright light of the clearing. The noises in the wood seemed to have all quietened. To Adam this felt wrong. But he knew how the Doctor would scoff if he told him that it was too quiet. He watched as his father strode confidently over to the hatch and bent down to examine it. He told himself what the Doctor had told him before, that being frightened when there is nothing to be frightened of is silly and irrational and that he should try to –

What was that?

A black figure on a rope swung out of the trees to his left, another one to his right. Another two emerged from directly opposite. And all four had one thing in common: they were carrying guns.

Each gun was pointed directly at Doctor Forest. He stood up. Though he must have been terrified, he appeared perfectly calm. Adam marvelled at his father's ability to control his emotions.

'Good afternoon, gentleman,' Adam heard him say. 'I left my family at the amusement park and went for a walk. I do apologise if I've wandered into some kind of restricted area.'

The guards kept their guns trained on the Doctor and said nothing.

'Is that the time?' he went on, glancing at his watch. 'I really should be . . .'

The Doctor's voice trailed off. The hatch door was

opening. Out of the ground emerged an old man wearing an immaculately pressed brown suit, sporting a monocle and carrying an ivory cane. He paused for a moment to impale a slug on the end of his cane.

Adam had never seen this man before, but from the Doctor's descriptions he knew exactly who he was: Professor Silus Scabellax.

He fitted the Doctor's description in every detail except one. He was wearing earmuffs. And moments later it became clear why.

The Dreadful Alarm of Buenos Sueños rang out. Adam jammed his fingers in his ears. Down in the city it was so loud it was painful. But up here it was agony. Adam tried everything to shut it out, but he was powerless. The Doctor was even closer and the force of the sound brought him to his knees. Like Adam, he buried his head in his chest, but there was no hiding from the deafening noise, which seemed to go on and on and on. All they could do was wait for it to stop.

The guards did not so much as flinch. In spite of the alarm, they continued to level their guns at the Doctor.

Just when Adam thought his head was about to explode, the noise finally abated. In the clearing, Professor Scabellax removed his earmuffs and approached the Doctor.

'Hello again,' he said.

'I beg your pardon,' said the Doctor, and for the first time Adam could see apprehension on his face. 'Did you say again? I don't believe we've ever met.'

Wow, thought Adam. *He's going to pretend he doesn't know him and hope that after ten years Scabellax has forgotten what he looks like.*

'As I was explaining to these men . . .' the Doctor went on.

Scabellax smirked.

'What is the matter?'

'Forgive my amusement,' said Scabellax, 'but I doubt you got very far. For reasons that have just been demonstrated, all these guards have had their hearing surgically destroyed. They would not have heard a word you said.'

'You destroyed their hearing?' said the Doctor sharply. For a moment his natural repugnance for such cruelty overcame his pretence of being simply a lost tourist. The Doctor was not a very good liar.

'Only *these* guards,' said Scabellax, crushing a spider slowly and deliberately beneath one of his feet. 'It is the simplest way to keep them alert while I conduct my sonic experiment. But the inside of my base is soundproofed, so the guards there still have their hearing intact. Only a cruel man would destroy the hearing of people when it wasn't necessary. And I'm sure nobody would say I was cruel.'

Adam watched the Doctor force himself not to argue with this glaringly false statement.

'Ah,' said the Doctor, trying to look as stupid as he could possibly manage. 'Well, obviously I don't know what you're talking about. As I was telling your guards, I left my family at the amusement –'

'You've aged.'

139

'I'm sorry,' said the Doctor, taken aback. 'I don't understand what – You must be confusing me with someone else. I don't believe we've ever met.'

'We met briefly,' said Scabellax, smiling. 'But I am certainly very well known to at least one member of your family.'

'I –'

'Your wife, Doctor Forest. She has been my close companion for over ten years now. We are firm friends.'

Watching from the edge of the clearing, Adam gasped in shock. Any hope of the Doctor talking his way out of the terrible situation had disappeared.

'How did you know I was here?' demanded the Doctor.

'Oh, I make it my business to know things,' said Scabellax. 'Since my sources informed me that a boat known as the *Ark of the Parabola* had docked, I've been looking forward to this meeting. If you expect to keep a low profile, Doctor, you really shouldn't sail a boat with such a well-known name. I thought of coming to see you, but then I thought, why bother? It wouldn't be long before you came to say hello.'

'How very clever,' said the Doctor sarcastically. 'Well, now that I'm here, you can hand over my wife and switch off the alarm.'

Professor Scabellax threw back his head and roared with laughter.

'That, my dear Doctor, is precisely the *opposite* of what is going to happen. What is going to happen is that my guards are going to escort you down below to my base and then you are going to reveal to me the secret of animal communication that has eluded me for more than a decade.'

The Doctor was reminded of the question that had plagued him the past ten years, the question he had forbidden Adam from asking him.

'Why did you never contact me?' he demanded. 'Why did you never offer to exchange my wife for the secret?'

The Professor shook his head.

'Like so many small men, you overestimate your importance, Doctor. Your discovery, clever though it was, is merely a small part in my grand plan – the scale of which will soon be revealed to you and indeed the world. I had many other things to occupy my considerable talents in the past years. And I knew that eventually you would find me. So why did I need to go to all the trouble of finding you? Besides, I've grown rather fond of your wife.'

The Doctor was silent, his face a picture of fury.

'And of course,' added Scabellax, 'knowing you were suffering all that time made me feel better. But now the time is ripe for you to share your little secret.'

'I'll never reveal it to you,' said the Doctor, through clenched teeth.

'Of course you will,' said Scabellax. 'You do want to see your wife again, after all, don't you?'

The Doctor said nothing.

'Unfortunately,' continued Scabellax, 'I have to travel

down to the city just now on business. But please be assured, Doctor, that I will be back soon and then I will be ready to learn.'

Still the Doctor said nothing.

'Take him down.' Scabellax signalled to the guards and they leapt to obey him.

I should do something, thought Adam. *Now. Before they disappear. I have to stop them.*

But there was nothing he could do except watch as the guards grabbed the Doctor roughly and forced him down the hatch and into captivity. Scabellax looked on, idly killing a butterfly as he did so, and glanced at his watch. Then he, too, departed. Adam was left looking into an empty clearing. Suddenly he felt very alone.

The Doctor was gone. For the first time in his life, Adam had to decide by himself what to do next.

And he didn't have a clue.

CHAPTER 18

'I want to see the Mayor.'

'I want to play centre forward for FC Buenos Sueños,' answered the fat security guard outside the town hall. 'Do you know what our dreams have in common, chico? Neither of them is going to happen. Now be off with you.'

'Don't you remember me? I came here with Doctor Forest. It's very important –'

'Important, chico. Let me tell you what is important to the Mayor: getting as many votes as possible in the election. And do you know who votes, chico?'

'People.'

'People over eighteen years of age. Not little chicos like you.'

'I'm not little,' insisted Adam. 'I'm thirteen.'

'So in five years' time the Mayor will want to talk to you. But, until then, you can go to school or play videogames or do whatever you kids do, but make sure you get out of my face.'

Adam backed away.

He'd sneaked away from the clearing, crept out of the wood, dashed down the mountain, leapt on to a bus and rushed all the way to the town hall, certain that if he told the Mayor about the hatch, the alarm and Professor Scabellax, then he would send the police to rescue the Doctor. It had never crossed his mind that he wouldn't be able to get to see the Mayor. He was discovering that, as far as adults were concerned, children were almost invisible.

Now he was all alone in a strange city, with both his parents in the hands of an evil professor. Adam didn't know what to do next. He felt tears well up in his eyes and then roll down his cheeks. One landed with a plop in the pocket of his T-shirt and Private Mandible crawled out.

'Make nests not war,' he signalled to Adam.

Adam didn't answer.

'All you need is leaves,' he indicated.

Still Adam was silent. Private Mandible scrutinised Adam's face.

'I didn't know humans could rain,' he signalled.

'I'm not raining,' protested Adam.

'There's water falling out of you,' the ant observed.

Normally Adam would have found this funny. But right now things were too serious for him to find anything funny. He could think of nothing to do but to head back to the *Ark of the Parabola*. He had no idea how to rescue the Doctor – or his mother. Scabellax had said that they were friends. But that couldn't be true, could it? He climbed up the gangplank of the *Ark*, telling himself that it had to be a lie.

'Psst!'

Adam stopped and looked about him.

'Psst!'

Adam couldn't think of an animal on board the *Ark* that had a word like 'Psst' in its vocabulary.

'Psst! Over here!'

A human!

'Over here!'

The voice was coming from under the tarpaulin which covered the small lifeboat that sat on the deck.

'Are you alone?' demanded a gruff voice.

Adam backed away towards the gangplank. 'Depends.'

'Does this boat still belong to Doctor Forest?'

Adam gulped. 'Might do.'

'Depends? Might do? Am I ever going to get a straight answer out of you, boy?'

'Don't know.' Adam was poised to run.

The tarpaulin was flung back.

'Excellent. A bit of deception never did anybody any harm,' said an old man, popping up from the lifeboat. 'Adam Forest, you might just be worthy to be my grandson.'

'Grandad!'

Adam had never seen his grandfather before, but he knew straight away it was him. He didn't know how. He just knew.

'Not so loud! And don't call me Grandad. It makes me feel old.'

'But you are my grandad, aren't you?'

'Grandad be damned,' said Adam's grandad. 'My name is Calico Jack. But you can call me Jack.'

'Don't you mean Calico Jack Forest?' persisted Adam.

Calico Jack looked mystified.

'Forest must be your surname,' Adam pointed out. 'It's my surname and it's my father's surname so it must be yours.'

'Surname?' hissed Calico Jack. 'I haven't had one of those in years. Surnames help with records and I've never been a fan of records. Records help the police.'

'What are you doing here?' Adam asked. 'The Doctor said you were in jail.'

'I'll be back there if you don't stop yapping so loud,' said Calico Jack, looking around anxiously. 'Keep your voice down.'

'Back there?'

'I had a bit of a disagreement with the authorities about the length of my sentence.'

'What do you mean?'

'They sentenced me to five years but I felt I only deserved one. So I took matters into my own hands.'

'You broke out?'

'Let's say I decided to serve the rest of my sentence in the community.'

Adam's mouth gaped. His grandad was also an escaped convict.

'What were you in prison for?' he asked.

'You've got more questions than the police,' said Calico Jack gruffly. 'I've never been a fan of questions. Soon as someone starts asking you questions, the next thing you know they're drawing conclusions. And some of us have spent more time than we care to remember in prisons because of juries drawing conclusions.'

'The wrong conclusions?' said Adam hopefully.

'Well, not always,' Calico Jack conceded. 'But it's hard to see them as the right conclusions when you're being led down to the cells.'

The old man shook his head.

Adam hesitated.

'Don't worry, young 'un,' said Calico Jack, sensing his doubt. 'I won't keep you harbouring a prisoner longer than necessary. I know your dad wouldn't want me hanging around, inviting trouble.' Calico Jack experienced a sudden change of mood and paused to rub a tear from his eye. 'Even though I've finally decided to go straight, and it might be then that an old man needs the help of his family.'

'But you can't be going straight,' Adam said. 'You've just broken out of jail.'

'Breaking out of jail was my final crime. But now I'm definitely retired and determined to spend the rest of my life devoting myself to good works. But before I get down to that, there's some information I picked up in prison about a fellow called Scabellax which I think your father will want to know.'

'You're too late!' said Adam angrily. 'Scabellax captured him earlier today.'

'What?' roared Calico Jack, jumping out of the lifeboat with a remarkably sprightly leap for someone of his age. 'Why didn't you tell me before?'

'Before what?' Adam protested.

'When did he catch him? Where? How? Where's he taken him?' demanded his grandfather.

'I thought you didn't like questions.'

'Don't get smart with me, young whippersnapper. We need to get your father back.'

'Shhh,' said Adam. 'Nobody is supposed to know he's my father. He makes me call him "Doctor" when we're not out at sea. He says it's for my own safety.'

'Can't be too careful,' agreed Calico Jack. 'Now, I only just got here so you'll have to tell me what's been going on. But before you do – if the Doctor doesn't think it's wise to reveal your relationship, then perhaps we'd better keep ours a secret too. And don't be surprised if we run into people and I give them a different name to Calico Jack.'

'You mean lie to them?'

'Lie is a very strong term, Adam,' said Calico Jack. 'There's the truth and then there's a lie and there's a large space in between.'

'What's in the space in between?' asked Adam.

'Creativity,' Calico Jack explained. 'Some people need only one name and some people need more. I'm one of the ones who need more. I've got lots of names. In Asia, I am Gregor Ivan Petrovich. In Australia, I'm Brad Outback. In Antarctica, I'm Thor Normquisterson.'

'Antarctica?'

'Got on the wrong boat by mistake when I was leaving Buenos Aires in a hurry. Was stranded for six months with only penguins for company. They are dull creatures – spend the whole day sitting there with eggs on their feet.'

'That's because if they let them touch the ground for even a minute the egg would freeze and the chick would die,' said Adam.

'I'm sure they'd have told me that if I could speak penguin.'

'I'm sure they would,' said Adam. 'They're very chatty.'

Calico Jack gave Adam a hard stare. 'What are you talking about?'

'They were concerned about herring stocks,' explained Adam. 'I told them about global warming.'

'Just my luck,' groaned Calico Jack. 'Finally get to meet my grandson and he turns out to be a gibbering idiot.'

'I'm not a gibbering idiot,' said Adam. 'Well, at least I don't think I am. What does "gibbering" mean?'

'I'm too old for this,' said Jack, ignoring the question, as was his habit. 'I remember your father was interested in some kind of nonsense about talking to animals. But I thought better of him than to expect he'd make his son believe the same crackpot ideas.'

'It's not –' Adam began. But he was interrupted by a chattering from behind. Simia had just discovered that the Doctor had not returned with Adam and wanted to know why. She stormed up to him and tugged hard at his arm.

'Where is he?' she demanded. 'What have you done with him?'

Adam was immediately on the defensive.

'It wasn't my fault! He walked into a trap!'

'A trap. What were you doing leading him into a trap?'

'I didn't. We were in the wood and –'

'A wood?' This made Simia angrier. 'You went into a wood without me? Me, Simia, who can climb a tree faster than you can run down the street. I could have warned you.'

'We didn't know –'

'Woah! What's going on here?' interjected his grandad, who had been watching, though obviously not understanding, the exchange with open-mouthed amazement.

Simia looked at him and then at Adam. Adam realised he'd broken the Doctor's golden rule and revealed his ability to communicate with animals. He didn't know what to do: should he trust his grandfather? For the first time the Doctor wasn't there to tell him what to do. He was going to have to make up his own mind.

'Are you really talking to him?' said his grandfather.

'Simia's a her,' Adam explained.

'Let's not split hairs, Adam,' said Calico Jack. 'You were

talking to a monkey. What was he – I mean, she – saying? Did she want a banana?'

'Not exactly,' said Adam.

'Well, what exactly, then?'

'Actually,' said Adam awkwardly, 'she was giving me a telling-off.'

'Nothing at all about bananas?'

Adam shook his head. Calico Jack was lost in thought for a moment. Then he started chuckling.

'You know, Adam, this opens up an awful lot of possibilities.'

'Does it?'

'A good criminal could make a lot of money if he could talk to animals.'

'But you said you were retired.'

'Did I? I thought I said I was taking a vacation.'

'You said you were going straight,' said Adam firmly. 'I remember.'

'Overrated thing, memory,' muttered Calico Jack, 'as I remember pointing out to the last witness to pick me out of an identity parade. I . . . ugh!'

'Ugh?' said Adam.

'Damned ants everywhere,' said Adam's grandfather, raising his boot.

'Stop!' Adam shouted.

'What for?'

'You're about to step on the Special Ant Service.'

Calico Jack was incredulous. 'Ants! You can talk to ants too!'

'Communicate,' Adam corrected him, and he bent down. General Lepti marched on to his hand.

'General Lepti and the Special Ant Service returning to base!' signalled the ant.

'Any casualties?' asked Adam anxiously.

'A couple of minor thorax injuries and a punctured abdomen. The two enemies were last seen jumping into a pond.'

'Thank you, General,' said Adam.

'Permission to go below deck and eat some leaves,' requested General Lepti.

'Permission granted!'

At a command from their chief, the platoon of army ants disappeared below deck. Having witnessed the exchange with the ant, Adam's grandfather's mouth dropped even wider than before.

'Lucky thing I didn't stamp on your friends,' he said finally.

'Very lucky,' agreed Adam. 'For you.'

'Me?'

'Yes. You'd be no match for General Lepti's platoon,' Adam explained. 'They'd have overpowered you in less than a minute. Army ants can disable any creature that gets in their path. They'd swarm up your legs, biting and stinging. You'd be helpless within a couple of minutes.'

'Could they do that to anyone – say, just for the sake of argument, a security guard in a bank?'

'You said you were retired.'

'So I did, so I did,' the old man agreed. 'But you can't stop your brain from wondering, can you? It's only natural.'

'I suppose,' said Adam. 'But the Doctor would be very angry if he thought that his scientific work was being used for criminal purposes.'

'The Doctor,' said Calico Jack, remembering. 'What are we doing sitting about chatting? We need to –'

PHEEP! PHEEP! PHEEP!

Adam looked round. Rushing across the wharf towards the *Ark of the Parabola* was what appeared to be the entire Buenos Sueños Police Force – again.

Adam turned back.

'Calico Jack? Grandad?'

There was no reply. Calico Jack wasn't answering to any name now. He'd vanished, leaving Adam to face the police all alone.

CHAPTER 19

While the rest of the police force stayed at the side of the wharf, Chief of Police Grivas, accompanied by Officer Grivas, strode up the gangplank towards Adam.

'Hand him over,' he growled, pausing to light one of his fat cigars. Even in the open air, Adam could taste its foul black smoke.

'Hand who over?' he said nervously.

'Harbouring an escaped convict is a very serious crime according to the Buenos Sueños Crime and Punishment Code.'

Adam gulped. They knew about his grandfather already.

'Did you see that?' said Chief Grivas, who had interrogated many suspects in his time. 'That was a gulp of guilt.'

'It wasn't,' Adam protested. 'I don't know where Calico Jack is, I promise you.'

A broad smile broke out on the face of Chief Grivas. 'Who said anything about Calico Jack, chico?'

Adam was horrified.

'I was going to show you this –' the Chief of Police pulled a photo of Adam's grandfather from the top pocket of his uniform '– but now I see that I don't have to. Tell us where Calico Jack is and perhaps things will not be so bad for you.'

Adam opened his mouth to speak. Then closed it. Then opened it again.

As Chief Grivas took a long puff on his cigar and stared hard at Adam, two green shapes swooped down and landed on the barrel next to him.

'I said, I said, I said, are you a policeman?' squawked Gogo.

'Shouldn't it be "I say, I say, I say"?' Pozzo cawed.

'I'm speaking in the past tense,' explained Gogo.

'I was in the past tense,' said Pozzo. 'But then I stopped worrying and learned to relax.'

The parrots paused for some applause. Instead, after a nod from the Chief of Police, who was obviously above dealing with birds himself, Officer Grivas took a wary step towards them.

'Shoo!' he said.

'Shoe to you,' Gogo chirped back.

'And socks too,' added Pozzo.

'Go away!' ordered Officer Grivas, waving his hands.

'Which way?' asked Gogo, stroking his crest with his wing.

'I warn you, parrots,' said Officer Grivas, 'if you don't fly away, you'll soon be under arrest.'

'I'm exhausted,' cheeped Pozzo. 'A rest is just what I could do with.'

Chief Grivas, furious at seeing one of his officers being outwitted by two cheeky parrots, could resist no longer. Forgetting his dignity for a moment, he pulled his cigar from his mouth and prodded it at Gogo and Pozzo, who wisely fluttered just out of reach.

'Listen, parrots,' he said threateningly. 'This is Buenos Sueños. And in Buenos Sueños all parrots should say, "Who's a pretty boy, then?"'

Gogo and Pozzo looked at each other and shook their beaks.

'Why would we say that?' said Gogo.

'When you're so old and ugly,' explained Pozzo.

Chief Grivas secretly spent many hours preening in front of a mirror he kept in his desk back at police headquarters, and he was not prepared to tolerate being insulted by parrots. He reached for his gun.

Gogo and Pozzo decided that it was time to bring their act to an end. Before the Chief of Police could take aim, they flew high up into the rigging.

Adam watched, wishing that he could do the same, as Chief Grivas turned grimly towards him.

'Back to where we were before we were so rudely interrupted, chico. Tell me where Calico Jack is and tell me now.'

Adam didn't know what to say.

'Er . . . um . . . ah . . .'

Chief Grivas continued to stare.

'Ah . . . er . . . um . . .'

Changing the order of his meaningless noises didn't seem to help, but Adam was willing to give it a go anyway.

'Last chance, chico,' said Chief Grivas. 'Or it's prison –'

'Holy moly, jeepers creepers, Mason Dixon and pretzels!'

Standing on deck was a fat man wearing sunglasses, a T-shirt and a pair of bright Bermuda shorts, with a camera dangling from his neck. Adam had no idea where he had come from.

He took one look at the police officers.

'Stars and stripes, ticker tape and the great plains, am I glad to see you!' he said, proffering a paw-like hand in the direction of Chief Grivas.

'We are in the middle of an interrogation,' said Grivas icily. 'Please go –'

'Clackburger. Wyoming T. Clackburger III,' said Wyoming T. Clackburger, grasping the Chief of Police's hand and shaking it hard. 'Mighty pleased to make your acquaintance.'

'I am –' Chief Grivas began.

'The answer to my prayers,' finished Wyoming T. Clackburger III. 'I tell you, I've been wandering round this here town for three days trying to find somewhere to buy a chilli dog, burger and fries. What is it about you foreigners? Don't you like grease and fat?'

'We like vegetables,' said Officer Grivas.

'Vegetables.' Clackburger scratched his head in confusion. 'You can eat them?'

Officer Grivas nodded.

'Goodness gracious, great balls of fire! But they've been in the ground with insects and grubs. That can't be healthy. You need to get munching on an all-American chilli dog and burger and supersize fries with extra mayo. Then maybe y'all would look like people instead of sticks.'

Chief Grivas scrutinised Wyoming T. Clackburger suspiciously.

'What are you doing here?'

'I told ya,' answered Clackburger, 'I was looking for a hot dog . . .'

'On a boat?' Chief Grivas's eyes narrowed.

'I've looked everywhere else,' Clackburger explained, waving his hands impatiently in the air. 'I gotta tell you, a-wop-bop-a-loo-lop-a-lop-bamboo, you gotta improve your provision when it comes to fast-food catering. I'm an American with an appetite. I can't be waiting for vegetables to grow. I need meat now!'

'You expect me to believe this preposterous story,' said Chief Grivas.

'Listen, buddy,' said Wyoming T. Clackburger III, prodding a finger firmly in Chief Grivas's chest. 'If it's a matter of money, I can give you money. Just get me a chilli dog. Here.' He reached into his back pocket. 'Hey! What's going on here?' he shouted angrily. 'Someone's stolen my wallet. I'm an American tourist who's been the victim of a robbery.'

'Are you really a tourist?' said Chief Grivas sceptically. 'They don't normally come to Buenos Sueños.'

'He does look like a tourist,' Officer Grivas observed. 'Señor Gozo at the tourist information kiosk told me they wear horrible shorts and take photographs of everything and they are always losing their wallets.'

'That's what he told me too,' added Adam.

'Silence!' Officer Grivas shouted at him.

Chief Grivas looked at Wyoming T. Clackburger and weighed up the evidence.

'Say full fat cheese!' said Clackburger, and the flash of a camera blinded the two policemen.

The photograph finally convinced the Chief of Police.

'I'll show this picture to my daughter Mary-Beth Jo Honey-Pie when I get back to the States,' said Wyoming T. Clackburger. 'A picture of the two guys who rushed off to find the wallet of a helpless American tourist in a strange fat-free land.'

'Report your loss to the police station tomorrow morning, señor. I am now going to search this ship for an escaped convict,' the Chief of Police thundered.

Adam gulped. If Chief Grivas searched the *Ark of the Parabola*, not only would he find his grandfather, he would also find the Arkonauts. And Adam was pretty sure that he'd find some reason for impounding them all, as he had Sniffage.

159

Wyoming T. Clackburger III seemed to notice Adam for the first time.

'I suppose they've shown you their search warrant, have they, kid?'

'Their search warrant?' Adam repeated. 'No.'

'Well, I ain't no high-paid Manhattan lawyer, but, if I was, then I might say that without a search warrant they can't search the ship.'

'What are you talking about?' interrupted Chief Grivas. 'No such provision is required by the Buenos Sueños Crime and Punishment Code.'

Clackburger shook his head.

'Maybe not, Chief.' And he walked to the rail and looked over the side.

'However, from what I can tell, we're in the water about a metre outside of Buenos Sueños. Here it's the law of the sea.'

Chief Grivas's mouth dropped open. For a moment it looked as though he was going to collapse. Without the Buenos Sueños Crime and Punishment Code, he was nothing.

'But I don't know the law of the sea,' he admitted weakly.

'Well, I guess you'd better go and do some swotting,' said Clackburger. 'And while you're about it, I'd be mighty grateful if you'd keep an eye out for my wallet. Have a nice day.'

Speechless, Chief of Police Grivas, followed by Officer

Grivas, departed the *Ark of the Parabola*. Adam watched as they led the rest of the police force back into the narrow streets of Buenos Sueños.

'Wow!' said Adam. 'Thanks, Mr Clackburger.'

'Mr who?'

Adam turned sharply round. Wyoming T. Clackburger had suddenly lost his American accent. His voice sounded very much like . . .

'Grandad!'

'What did I tell you about that name?'

'Sorry. Calico Jack! But how did you . . . ? You're tanned. Your hair is a different colour. Your clothes.'

'Don't tell anybody else this,' said his grandfather, 'but I never go anywhere without a dressing-up case and my make-up box. Then all you need is a new accent and you can be someone different whenever you want.'

Adam was amazed at the change in his grandfather's appearance. But there was one thing that make-up and dressing up didn't explain.

'But you're so much fatter,' he said.

'Bit of inspiration there,' said his grandfather, shooting a quick glance towards the city to make sure the policemen were out of sight. He pulled up his T-shirt. Hanging from his shoulders, her face buried in his chest, was Simia.

'You can get down now,' he said.

'Not a moment too soon,' said the monkey, dropping straight on to the deck.

'But how . . . ?' began Adam.

'I wagered that if they could understand you, then they could understand me,' explained Calico Jack. 'I told them that if they didn't provide me with some extra bulk, the police would be searching the *Ark* and taking them off to the pound.'

'Them?'

'Oh, I almost forgot.' Jack swung round. Hanging down his back, fast asleep, was Malibu.

'Wow!' said Adam.

'What is it?'

'You've done something nobody else has ever managed,' said Adam. 'You've made Malibu help. He's been on this boat five years and he's never done anything useful before.'

'I resent that,' yowled Malibu, opening one eye. And to demonstrate his readiness for action, the cat promptly nuzzled his head back into the gap between Calico Jack's shoulder blades and fell asleep.

Adam picked him up and placed him on the barrel where he normally slept.

'I hope you noticed,' chattered Simia, 'that no human could have clung on as long as I did without moving. Upper-arm strength. Another thing you lost when you came out of the trees and started all that unnecessary upright walking. Didn't think about your arms, did you? Hanging down by your sides for generation after generation, doing nothing. They've got so weak they're practically useless.'

'Hardly useless,' Adam protested.

'And don't even get me started on the way you let your tail waste away.' she went on, jabbing her finger critically at him.

'Don't blame me!' cried Adam defensively. 'I never had a tail in the first place.'

'That's what you say.' The monkey sounded dubious.

'Hey! Calm down!'

Adam's grandfather couldn't understand anything that was being said, but he could tell from the agitated tone of the discussion and Simia's aggressive body language that they were having some kind of disagreement.

Adam and Simia eyed each other angrily.

'She's always going on at me for not having a tail,' moaned Adam. 'Or laughing because I've got no fur.'

'We can't be thinking about that now,' said his grandfather. 'We may have seen off the police for now, but I know from experience that they have a nasty habit of coming back – usually with evidence and witnesses. And handcuffs. So we must rescue the Doctor as quickly as we can.'

'And my mother,' Adam reminded him.

'Your mother as well.'

'And Sniffage.'

'Who?'

'Sniffage,' repeated Adam. 'He was taken away to the dog pound by the police.'

Adam's grandfather looked at Adam sternly.

'Is there anyone we don't have to rescue?'

'That's about it,' said Adam.

'You're sure?'

Adam nodded. 'Oh, and we've got to stop the Dreadful Alarm,' he added.

Adam's grandfather allowed himself a sigh. 'What on earth is that?' he asked.

Adam opened his mouth to explain. But he didn't need to.

BRIIIIIIINNNNNNNGGGGGGG!

Almost on cue, the alarm began to ring, echoing across the city as it had before. But there were two things that were different about it.

First, it was ringing at night.

And second, it didn't stop.

CHAPTER 20

The alarm kept going all through the night. Adam, Calico Jack, Simia and Malibu were driven below deck in a vain attempt to escape the sound. But it followed them down into the cabins of the *Ark of the Parabola* and boomed through doors and portholes, refusing to be repelled by blankets thrown over heads and fingers drilled into ears.

Morning came and still the alarm rang. There was no sign of life on the deck of the *Ark of the Parabola* or in the streets of Buenos Sueños. Adam lay in his cabin with his face buried in a pillow, hands clamped over his ears, thinking it had to stop soon . . . then thinking it would never stop . . . then thinking if he counted to a hundred, a thousand, a million, it would surely stop. But the Dreadful Alarm was impervious to Adam and his thoughts. It rang and rang as the sun rose and as the sun set.

And the next night brought no respite. If anything, the air grew stiller and the sound grew louder – wave after wave bouncing off the mountain sides, swelling and growing and then descending with all its force on the city and on the port. By now Adam was finding it hard to remember what the normal world sounded like and was having to remind himself that once it had been free of the incessant ring.

On and on it rang. Sometimes Adam thought it was getting louder, sometimes quieter. But the truth was that it was never any different – except that now the sound didn't feel like it was just outside his head. Now it was inside too. And the echoes were no longer against the walls of the mountains; they were against the sides of his own skull. The sound was like a swelling ball inside his head, which grew as it ricocheted back and forth and up and down until Adam couldn't think any more. Was he losing his mind? Was he going mad? Was he . . . ?

It stopped.

Just as the first beam of sun streaked over the mountains and touched the top of the mast of the *Ark of the Parabola*, the alarm stopped.

Two nights and a day hiding from the dreadful sound in his cabin had driven Adam stir-crazy. He rushed up on deck.

Gentle rays of sunshine warmed his face. The taste of the sea was fresh and salty. All that remained of the Dreaful Alarm that had battered the city of Buenos Sueños for thirty-six long hours was a faint hum. The world felt new and bright. He smiled. And then he remembered the Doctor and Sniffage and his smile faded.

'Cheer up, young 'un – it's stopped, hasn't it?'

Calico Jack emerged from the hatch. He went and stood by the rail, looking at the city and swallowing big lungfuls of air.

'I was thinking about the Doctor and Sniffage,' Adam explained.

'That's no reason not to enjoy a beautiful morning,' said Calico Jack. 'When you've been cooped up as much as I have, you learn to appreciate such things.'

Adam felt uncomfortable as he remembered that his grandfather had spent time in prison. Should he really be trusting this man who lied as easily as he told the truth and whom the Doctor had spoken of with almost as much hatred as he had of Professor Scabellax?

'You didn't tell me what you were in prison for,' said Adam.

'Nope,' agreed Calico Jack, looking up at the mountains that enclosed the isolated city. 'I didn't.'

'Perhaps you should,' Adam ventured.

'And perhaps I shouldn't,' said Calico Jack. 'Thing is, young 'un, you'll find out what I've been in jail for, then you'll probably start worrying about things and saying, "Well, I'm not sure I want a murderer on board my –'

'Murderer!' cried Adam.

'There, I've gone and said it,' said Calico Jack, shaking his head. 'Me and my big mouth.'

'Murderer!' repeated Adam. 'But who . . . how . . . when . . . why?'

Calico Jack opened his mouth and roared with laughter.

'What's so funny?' demanded Adam furiously. 'There's nothing funny about being a murderer.'

'You've spent too long with the Doctor,' said Calico Jack, making no attempt to hide his amusement despite Adam's fury. 'You can't even see when someone's pulling your leg.'

'What are you talking about?' said Adam. 'You said –'

'Didn't you think that perhaps I might have planted that little clue in there so as you would think you had stumbled across the truth by yourself?'

Adam wasn't sure what Calico Jack was saying.

'You mean you aren't a murderer?'

'Whether I'm a murderer or not is neither here nor there,' said Calico Jack. 'The point is, I got you to think I was one.'

'But you could have just told me you were one,' said Adam, even more puzzled.

'I could have,' acknowledged Calico Jack, whose raucous laugh had now been dampened down to a broad smile which Adam found marginally less insufferable. 'But one of the things you've got to learn, Adam, is that people always believe things much more when they think they've found them out by themselves. Especially when they think they've done it by outwitting the other person.'

Adam felt foolish.

'Don't look so down, young 'un,' said Calico Jack, reaching over and cuffing Adam gently on the head. 'It's not you. It's all of us. Overestimating our own intelligence is a human trait. Remember this: nobody is ever quite as clever as they think they are. Now, it's that gap between how clever people really are and how clever they think they are where people like me can take advantage.'

This was a lesson unlike any Adam had been given before. The Doctor had taught him facts about the world. He had never shown him how to exploit them.

Calico Jack gave him a wink and wandered back down below deck. Adam watched him go, remembering that his grandfather had never actually denied being a murderer. With Calico Jack, that couldn't be an accident.

'I am soooo tired.' Malibu had appeared on deck and was yowling in protest. 'I have had no winks for, like, years.'

'You're being overdramatic, Malibu,' said Adam.

'Overdramatic? Moi?' said Malibu. 'You don't know how totally wrong you are. When I played "Sleeping cat" in one movie I was the only one Ang didn't tell to "do less".'

'Really?'

Malibu nodded. 'All I heard on set was, "Do less, Kate", "Do less, Hugh", but he never said that to me.'

'That's probably because you were doing nothing.'

'Uh-huh. Which was exactly what the role required,' purred Malibu. 'I'm a method cat when it comes to acting. I live the role. There wasn't a cat in Hollywood that could convey idleness like me. Any scripts needing a sleeping cat came through *my* flap.'

'So are you in lots of films, then?'

Malibu shook his head.

'I didn't want to be typecast,' he explained. 'I wanted to do more action roles. So I auditioned for "Cat jumping off lap" in the last Bond movie, but the director decided to go with a Siamese.' He shook his head and hissed. 'Then Steven cast a Siamese in his next movie, and straight away the scripts dried up. Every cat had to be a Siamese. Sleeping, jumping off laps, playing with cotton wool – it didn't matter. The rest of us in the business were finished overnight. It's not about talent any more; it's about looks, and if you aren't skinny enough, you don't stand a chance.'

Adam didn't know what to say. Malibu had never spoken about his film career before or what had brought him to be scavenging the wharf in Los Angeles when the *Ark of the Parabola* docked all those years ago.

'I took it bad,' admitted Malibu. 'I hit the cat food pretty hard. The pounds piled on, and before you knew it Uma was kicking me out on the street. She said she had allergy issues, but two days later I saw her going into the pet store.'

Malibu paused. Perhaps the memory was too painful.

'She came out with a Siamese too,' he said bitterly. 'And I thought we had a bond.'

'Was that when we found you?'

Malibu cleaned his whiskers and shook his head.

'Things got worse before that. I had a lot of anger issues. Too often, late at night, I'd find myself on top of some roof, brawling and yowling. That's where I got this.' He carefully

170

pushed forward his ear to reveal a deep scar behind it, where his fur refused to grow.

'What happened?'

'I lost a fight one night,' Malibu recalled, bristling at the memory. 'This big ol' tom caught me with a sucker scratch and I went down. I fell off the roof. When I came round, I found myself, bruised and bloody, in a trash can in an alley downtown. I knew I'd hit rock bottom. I was outta control. I had to get help.'

'What did you do?' Adam said.

'Only one thing to do. I joined the Twelve Paw Programme.'

'What did that involve?'

'Sleeping,' said Malibu. 'It was the only way to reconnect with my inner cat.'

He stretched and yawned.

'That's why this alarm thing worries me,' he said. 'I haven't had any shut-eye for ages. Much more and I could go back to my old brawling days. So, if you'll forgive me, it's time for me to catch up on some winks.'

As he finished yowling, a ray of light began to warm his favourite sleeping place. He leapt up on the barrel, settled down and closed his eyes. Soon a steady purring indicated that the cat was soundly asleep.

Adam watched, hardly daring to breathe. Until now he had never understood why it was so important for Malibu to sleep all the time.

'What are you doing?' chattered Simia's voice behind him.

'Shhh,' said Adam.

'Don't you shhh me,' said Simia. 'What I want to know –'

'Please talk quieter,' whispered Adam hoarsely. 'Malibu needs to get some sleep.'

'Sleep!' shrieked Simia. 'All that cat does is sleep.'

'Yes,' agreed Adam. 'But, you see, he's got to because of the Twelve Paw Programme – to stop him losing the connection with his inner cat and to help with his anger-management issues.'

Simia began to chatter wildly, jumping back and forth. 'Anger-management issues? The only time that cat is angry is if some creature wakes him up.'

But Adam wasn't going to be bullied by Simia this time.

'I know you don't believe me, but it's true. That's why we've got to try and keep quiet when he's sleeping. He could snap back at any time. He even showed me a scar from his past.'

Simia, who had been capering up and down the deck to demonstrate her disagreement, stopped suddenly.

'That scar behind his ear where the fur won't grow back?'

Adam nodded.

'He got that scar when he rolled off the barrel in his sleep last year. I know. I assisted the Doctor while he stitched the wound.'

Adam looked at Malibu and sighed. Malibu winked.

Adam was beginning to wonder if the Doctor had left out rather a large and important topic when he was educating him. True, Adam knew things that no other child would ever know – how to talk to every species of animal – but what he couldn't tell was when a creature was lying or telling the truth. All his knowledge was wasted because he was too easily taken in.

'I cheep, I cheep, I cheep! You look a bit down in the mouth.'

Adam looked up. Fluttering in front of him were Gogo and Pozzo.

'I had some down in my mouth once,' said Gogo.

'Serves you right for biting ducks,' said Pozzo.

Adam managed a small smile.

'What do you call a bad-tempered seabird?'

'An alba*cross*.'

Adam managed a slightly bigger smile.

'What do you call a seabird that won't stop talking?'

'A cormo*rant*.'

Adam started to laugh.

Gogo and Pozzo allowed themselves a small bow.

'Thank you, thank you, thank you and once again, we thank you.'

And satisfied that they had cheered Adam up, they flew back to their perch at the top of the mast.

Calico Jack appeared at the hatch and hobbled back towards Adam.

'Come on, lad. If we're gonna find the Doctor and your dog and whatever else you've managed to lose in this city, then we need to get going before the police get themselves a warrant.'

Adam nodded.

'What's the matter with your leg?' he asked. 'You're walking really strangely.'

Calico Jack shook his head. 'Ah, my arthritis is playing me up something terrible. I knew I should have waited until the summer before breaking out of Alcatraz that time. The freezing cold water plays havoc with your bones.'

Suddenly Adam stopped.

'What is it, young 'un?' his grandfather asked.

'I don't know,' said Adam. 'I feel like I don't know what is true and what isn't any more. When the Doctor was here, everything seemed simple and black and white, but now it's all confusing. I think I might need to learn more about lying.'

A broad smile cracked across Calico Jack's face.

'Well, if that's what you're looking for, young 'un,' he said, 'you've found just the right guy.'

CHAPTER 21

The narrow streets of Buenos Sueños were deserted. After two nights and a day of the Dreadful Alarm pounding down upon them, the townsfolk were using the quiet to get some sleep. Adam and Calico Jack seemed to be the only two people alive. Everywhere else was silent and shuttered.

'Where are we going?' asked Adam.

'We need to see the Mayor,' answered Calico Jack. 'We're going to need his help to sort this mess out.'

'A guard wouldn't let me see him yesterday.'

'Probably because you told him the truth,' Jack explained. 'Your first mistake.'

'CITIZENS OF BUENOS SUEÑOS . . .'

A harsh voice suddenly boomed across the city, making them both jump.

'Where's it coming from?' said Calico Jack, instinctively shrinking into the shadows at the side of the street.

'CITIZENS OF BUENOS SUEÑOS . . .'

The voice was horrible, low and yet loud, emotionless and yet somehow hypnotic. It echoed through every street, just as the Dreadful Alarm had.

'It must be coming through the same sound system as the alarm,' muttered Calico Jack.

'CITIZENS OF BUENOS SUEÑOS, WAKE UP!'

'They've probably only just got to sleep,' said Adam.

'COME OUT INTO THE STREET!'

After a few moments, a man in a pair of striped pyjamas stepped out into the street. Two doors down from him a woman emerged. Then three doors up, a whole family came out. But these Buenos Sueñosians did not move in the way people normally move. Instead they shuffled silently out, their red-rimmed eyes vacant and dead. They seemed to be in a trance.

'CITIZENS OF BUENOS SUEÑOS, GATHER TOGETHER IN SMALL GROUPS.'

'What's going to happen?' asked Adam nervously.

'I don't know, young 'un,' said Calico Jack. 'Let's keep out of sight until we do.'

They shrank further back into the shadows, watching as the people of Buenos Sueños shuffled obediently into small groups.

'CITIZENS OF BUENOS SUEÑOS, FORM YOUR GROUPS INTO CIRCLES.'

It was weird to watch. Not a single citizen objected to the booming voice. They moved to form themselves into circles.

176

Adam noticed two people collide, then carry on without even acknowledging each other's existence. It was like they were robots.

When the last of the Buenos Sueñosians in the street had found their place in a circle, they stood patiently waiting for new instructions, not even acknowledging with a friendly nod or wave neighbours they had known for many years.

Something must be going to happen? But what? Adam imagined each circle being sucked suddenly into the air, or the ground opening and swallowing each circle up.

Suddenly, as though someone had switched on a giant ancient record player, there was loud hissing and crackling. And then music blasted out across the city. Party music. It was a song.

'YOU PUT YOUR LEFT LEG IN . . .'

Each member of the circle put their left leg in.

'YOUR LEFT LEG OUT . . .'

Then pulled their left leg out.

'IN, OUT, IN, OUT . . .'

The Buenos Sueñosians' feet went robotically back and forth.

'YOU SHAKE IT ALL ABOUT.'

And so the people of Buenos Sueños continued to obey the song's instructions.

'YOU DO THE HOKEY COKEY AND YOU TURN AROUND, THAT'S WHAT IT'S ALL ABOUT.

OH! THE HOKEY COKEY!

OH! THE HOKEY COKEY!'

By now the Buenos Sueñosians were holding hands and moving, like zombies, in and out of the circle in time to the music. But there was no party atmosphere. There were no whoops or cheers as there would be at a genuine fiesta, just mechanical obedience. One old woman seemed about to collapse with the effort of shaking it all about.

'How long did you say the alarm has been going on for?' Calico Jack asked Adam.

'More than two weeks,' Adam replied.

Calico Jack nodded. 'That would be about right.'

'Right for what?'

'The citizens of Buenos Sueños have had their normal sleeping patterns completely disturbed,' explained Calico Jack. 'And for the last thirty-six hours they have been deliberately deprived of any sleep whatsoever. In my experience, that is about the time it takes to lose your free will.'

'In *your* experience?' said Adam.

'There you go with your questions again. Take my word that, thanks to the CIA, I know all about sleep deprivation. After two weeks you'll do anything. This is what has happened to the Buenos Sueñosians. They'll obey any command because they've lost the ability to think for themselves.'

'That's terrible,' said Adam. 'Why hasn't it happened to us?'

'Because we haven't been here as long,' Calico Jack replied, 'so we haven't suffered as much. This is bad news. It means Scabellax is getting closer to successfully bringing the dastardly plan he has in mind to fruition. If we're to stop him and rescue the Doctor, then we need to get to the town hall as quickly as possible. We must hope that the Mayor is truly on our side against Scabellax, as we're going to need all the help he can give us.'

Adam led the way through the city streets. Everywhere they passed reluctant circles of Hokey Cokeyers. If Scabellax was behind this, then he appeared to be determined to exhaust the poor citizens even more. Left leg, right leg, left arm, right arm – all had to be in, out, in, out and shaken all about. The music was relentless, and its relentless cheeriness in contrast to the dopey obedience of the dancers made the whole absurd show all the more sinister.

But Adam was determined not to be distracted by what was going on around him. Now experienced in navigating the city, he led Calico Jack straight to the square with the town hall and the police headquarters. Here, the largest circle in the whole of Buenos Sueños had reached the final verse of the 'Hokey Cokey'.

'YOU PUT YOUR WHOLE SELF IN . . .'

Putting their whole selves in was proving difficult for the sleep-deprived citizens. They accidentally tripped over each other, jumped into each other and headbutted one another.

'YOU PULL YOUR WHOLE SELF OUT . . .'

Desperate to obey, the Buenos Sueñosians yanked their own limbs free from the people with whom they had just become entangled. It was painful to watch. Arms and legs were twisted and pulled in unnatural directions. There were yelps of pain. Blood ran freely down faces after clashes of heads. But hypnotised by lack of sleep, the dancers were unable to stop.

Adam could hardly bear to look as the song urged them, 'IN, OUT, IN, OUT . . .' It was carnage. The music rose to a jaunty climax. In stark contrast, the citizens collapsed on the ground, wheezing and groaning.

There was a short silence and then a voice boomed over the city. 'CITIZENS OF BUENOS SUEÑOS, YOU MAY RETURN TO YOUR HOMES AND AWAIT FURTHER INSTRUCTIONS. WHEN YOU GET THERE YOU WILL FORGET ALL ABOUT THE HOKEY COKEY. YOU WILL THINK YOU HAVE BEEN DOING THE WASHING UP.'

This voice undoubtedly belonged to the master of the citizens of Buenos Sueños. They dragged themselves to their feet and began to shuffle towards their homes, many of them not seeming to notice that they were bloodied and injured.

'I don't know how much more of this they can take,' said Calico Jack grimly.

Adam looked towards the town hall. As all those who could still walk had obediently returned to their houses, the route was now clear. They rushed across the square, up the grand steps, and were almost through the great door when . . .

'Stop!'

Slumped against a pillar, yawning, was the guard who had stopped Adam two days before. He was almost asleep but not quite. With an effort, he dragged himself upright and pointed his gun.

'What's the meaning of this?' he demanded. 'Trying to sneak past while I was washing up and get me into trouble, eh?'

'Er . . . we were . . .'

'We?' demanded the guard. 'What do you mean "we"? There's only one of you.'

Adam looked behind him. The guard was right. Calico Jack had vanished.

'Well, when I say we,' said Adam. 'I mean . . . er . . . I don't know exactly . . . er . . .'

'All I know,' said the guard, 'is you tried to get past me the other day. That time I sent you on your way nicely. This time it's not going to be quite as nice.'

The guard advanced menacingly.

Adam backed away.

'There you are!'

From behind the pillar stepped a man wearing a bearskin hat, with a bushy moustache and snow on his eyebrows.

'Who are you?' demanded the guard.

181

The man with the bearskin hat turned to him.

'Permit me to introduce myself,' he said with a Russian accent. 'I am Ivan Ivanovich Ivanivov and this is my nephew Igor. I am afraid he is very stupid. Please take no notice of him.' Ivan Ivanovich Ivanivov clunked Adam round the head. 'I am the official representative of Grobilov-Plodvov – a small city in Siberia. We must see the Mayor.'

'You're a long way from home,' said the guard.

'I know, comrade,' said Ivan Ivanovich Ivanivov. 'I have been ordered by the Mayor of Grobilov-Plodvov to find a twin.'

'A twin?' The guard was puzzled. 'Like a brother or sister?'

'No, no, no.' Ivan Ivanovich Ivanivov laughed heartily, and for good measure cracked Adam merrily across the skull again.

'Ow!' said Adam.

'When I say "a twin", I mean a twin city. London said no. Paris said *non*. Berlin said *nein*. Buenos Sueños is our last hope. I must ask the Mayor if he will permit Buenos Sueños to be our twin city.'

'I've never heard of a twin city before,' said the guard suspiciously.

'Oh, it is very common, I assure you. Every city has at least one twin.'

'Why?'

'There are cultural exchanges,' Ivan Ivanovich Ivanivov

explained. 'We see what we have in common and celebrate it. For example, what is Buenos Sueños famous for?'

'Sun, strange signposts and sleeping,' said the guard. 'Except we haven't been able to do much sleeping recently. What is Grobilov-Plodvov famous for?'

'Snow, pig iron and nuclear waste,' Ivan replied cheerfully. 'So, as you can see, we are a perfect match.'

'That doesn't sound like a perfect match to me,' said the guard.

'Of course it is,' Ivan Ivanovich Ivanivov assured him. 'Snow and sun are both types of weather. And signposts can be made out of pig iron, so that's almost exactly the same thing.'

'And sleeping and nuclear waste?'

Ivan Ivanovich Ivanivov paused. Could it be that Grobilov-Plodvov might not be a perfect twin for Buenos Sueños, after all? Then the Russian's face suddenly lit up.

'The amount you have can seriously affect your health,' he said triumphantly.

Carried away with enthusiasm, Ivan Ivanovich Ivanivov proceeded to launch into a long list of the cultural benefits that Buenos Sueños might receive if they would only twin with Grobilov-Plodvov.

'You could see bad weather for the first time. Think how exciting this would be. And you would be able to sample our famous beetroot stew, the recipe of which has been handed down from generation to generation across the icy steppes.

183

And you would have the opportunity to meet our great Siberian bears, and some of them might eat you.'

Adam noticed that even though much of what Ivan Ivanovich Ivanivov offered was horrible, his tone made them sound like the most desirable things in the world.

'Yes,' nodded the guard, carried away by Ivan's enthusiasm. 'Twinning would be good for Buenos Sueños. I only have one life. Why should I spend it all in the sun, eating good food? I should be able to be cold and eat beetroot!'

'Don't forget the man-eating bears,' said Ivan.

'How could I forget?' said the guard. 'Go in! Go in! The Mayor told me that he is not to be disturbed, but this opportunity is too good to pass up. Buenos Sueños and Grobilov-Plodvov should be twinned. It will be a great day for international relations.'

'Come, Igor,' said Ivan Ivanovich Ivanivov to Adam. 'We owe it to our friend here to complete the twinning process.'

Ivan Ivanovich Ivanivov marched into the town hall.

'You are Calico Jack, aren't you?' whispered Adam as soon as they were out of earshot of the guard.

'I am young 'un. I am.'

'But how did you change so quickly?'

'Always keep a couple of disguises on me, wherever I go,' said Calico Jack. 'You never know when you might need to be somebody else.'

CHAPTER 22

Señorita Ratti knocked on the door to the Mayor's office and, hearing a distracted 'Si', pushed it open to reveal the Mayor slumped over his desk with his head in his hands.

'What is happening to my city?' he groaned. Then he looked up and saw Adam and Calico Jack standing at the door beside his secretary. 'Who is this?' he demanded.

'They come from Siberia and they would like to be your twins,' said Señorita Ratti.

'My twins!' roared the Mayor. 'Don't they know I am an only child?'

'No, no, comrade . . .' protested Ivan Ivanovich Ivanivov.

Adam decided that the whole twin thing had gone far enough. It had been necessary only to get them into the Mayor's office. Now they had achieved that, they could drop the pretence.

'Don't you remember me?' he asked the Mayor.

The Mayor looked closely at Adam without any sign of recognising him.

'I was with the Doctor,' Adam went on.

'Ah,' said the Mayor, remembering. 'How could I forget? But I don't understand, chico. You were not a Russian when I last saw you.'

'No,' said Adam. 'Neither of us are Russians.'

Calico Jack removed his bearskin hat and rubbed the fake snow from his eyebrows to show this was true.

'But we had to get past the guard,' explained Adam, 'because I have to tell you about the terrible things that have happened to the Doctor and Sniffage.'

'Sniffage?'

'The dog.'

Again the Mayor remembered.

'The spaniel . . .'

'Yes,' said Adam. 'They are both in trouble and –'

The Mayor held up his hand.

'Why should I help them after they refused to help me?' he said. 'I have my own problems. First, I have had to do the washing-up this morning, and second, Felipez has revealed he has an expert who can stop the alarm.'

'You're wrong about the Doctor and Sniffage,' cried Adam passionately, forgetting that mayors are not normally people you shout at. 'They were both trying their best to help you and stop the Dreadful Alarm.'

'How was your dog helping?' said the Mayor.

'Er . . . he was sniffing dead things,' Adam ventured, realising that in his enthusiasm to defend Sniffage, he had

186

strayed a little way from the truth.

'Dead things?' repeated the Mayor. 'How would sniffing dead things help?'

'It doesn't sound like it would help,' Adam admitted. 'But that's because everything on the surface seems confusing. But underneath there's a very simple solution which makes everything make sense. It's like a double helix.'

'What's a double helix?' demanded the Mayor.

'It's the building block of life, the structure of DNA. All we needed to do was figure out what it was and then we'd find out what was causing the Dreadful Alarm and where my mother was and everything would make sense. Do you see?'

Adam looked at the Mayor, Calico Jack and Señorita Ratti. Each of them looked blankly back. *Why*, wondered Adam, *did it make so much more sense when the Doctor said it?*

'But it doesn't matter if you don't understand,' he said desperately. 'All that's important is that the Doctor and Sniffage were trying to help you even if you didn't know it. And now they're in trouble and you're going to have to help me rescue them or we won't stand a chance of stopping the alarm.'

The Mayor opened his mouth to respond.

PHEEP! PHEEP! PHEEP!

Chief of Police Grivas and ten officers from the Buenos Sueños Police Force charged into the room, brandishing pistols and whistles.

The Mayor leapt to his feet furiously.

'What is the meaning of this?'

Chief Grivas, who was sporting a deluxe model of earmuffs with superior padding for all-round protection and extra comfort, motioned to his men to stop blowing their whistles. Then he removed his earmuffs.

'We wanted to attract your attention,' he announced.

'Ten police officers storming into my office is normally enough to attract my attention,' the Mayor informed him drily.

Chief Grivas casually reached for a cigar from his breast pocket.

'This is a non-smoking office,' the Mayor informed him.

Grivas insolently stuck the cigar in his mouth, though he didn't light it.

'My actions are for your own protection,' he told the Mayor. 'We have received credible reports that you are in danger. You have been targeted.'

'Targeted?' said the Mayor. 'Who by?'

'Detergents,' answered Chief Grivas solemnly.

'Detergents?' the Mayor scoffed. 'Surely not.'

'I didn't mean detergents,' the Chief of Police said angrily. 'I meant insurgents. They're a bit like terrorists but –'

'Cleaner?' suggested Señorita Ratti.

Chief Grivas gave her a hard stare. Señorita Ratti glared fiercely back.

'In light of this startling new development,' announced Chief Grivas abruptly. 'I am forced to take over.'

'What?' The Mayor was outraged.

Chief Grivas nodded. 'It is clearly set out in the Crime and Punishment Code of Buenos Sueños that if the Mayor is threatened, then democracy itself is threatened. Therefore we must institute martial law. The police must take over immediately.'

'You mean you're suspending democracy in order to save it?' said the Mayor incredulously.

'Of course,' replied the Chief of Police. 'Now, for your own protection I order you to remain here under the supervision of these officers while I run Buenos Sueños until such time as it is deemed safe enough for you to assume control again.'

'And who will judge that?'

'Me,' said Chief Grivas confidently. And now, flushed with power, he lit his cigar, inhaled deeply and blew black smoke into the Mayor's face.

'I will not allow this,' said the Mayor, coughing. 'Not until I have finally seen the Buenos Sueños Crime and Punishment Code for myself.'

'Unfortunately it is not currently available,' Chief Grivas explained. 'Trainee Officer Anna-Luis Grivas is currently studying it for her final exams tomorrow.'

'I don't believe you,' cried the Mayor, who could feel his power ebbing away. 'You have shown no evidence that there is a threat to me and, until you do, I will not submit to your orders.'

'You have no choice,' snapped the Chief of Police. 'You must obey my orders.

He had tired of the Mayor's protests. He put on his deluxe earmuffs with superior padding for all-round protection, saluted his officers and nodded a perfunctory farewell to Señorita Ratti, Calico Jack and Adam.

Then he looked once more at Calico Jack. And this time he looked hard.

Horrified, Adam realised that his grandfather had forgotten to don his disguise again after showing the Mayor he wasn't a Russian. Too late, now, did Calico Jack jam his bearskin on his head and alter his expression. The Chief of Police tugged off his earmuffs and then whipped a photograph out of his pocket.

'What have we here?' he demanded, holding the photo up next to Calico Jack's face.

'I am Ivan Ivanovich Ivanivov —'

'No, you're not,' said Chief Grivas. 'You are Calico Jack, escaped murderer, robber, thief, fraudster, confidence trickster, swindler, smuggler and litter lout.'

'I was framed for the litter,' said Calico Jack.

'Arrest him!'

Adam expected his grandfather to do something amazing. But for once he seemed lost. Dumbfounded at his stupidity at forgetting to put his disguise back on, Calico Jack allowed himelf to be led away by two officers.

Then Grivas's eye fell on Adam.

'What about this little chico here?' he sneered. 'Whenever there is trouble, I always run into him.'

The Chief of Police stared at Adam so hard that he felt as though Grivas could see inside him – almost as if he could read his thoughts. Adam shrank back against the door that led into the Mayor's private apartments in a vain attempt to escape such harsh scrutiny.

'Perhaps,' mused Chief Grivas, 'he too is a threat.'

Fearing the same fate as Calico Jack, Adam slipped his hands behind his back and tried the door handle. The door was locked.

'Yes,' continued Grivas. 'The more I think about it, the better it would be for everyone if this chico was locked safely away in prison too.'

'But I haven't done anything,' protested Adam.

The Chief of Police allowed himself an evil smile.

'Who can tell me,' he asked, turning to the other police officers in the room, 'what we arrest people for when they haven't done anything?'

'Murder,' suggested Trainee Officer Xavi Grivas.

'Don't be so stupid,' said the Chief, rounding on his officers. 'To arrest someone for murder you have to have a body.'

Behind him, Adam heard a little clunk. Someone had just inserted a key into the lock.

'Arson?' suggested another officer.

Chief of Police Grivas snorted.

'Is my police force full of idiots?' he cried. 'Of course not arson. For arson you need a burning building.'

Adam heard a tiny squeak as the key turned in the lock.

'I'm going to have to tell you, aren't I?' he announced angrily. 'The answer is conspiracy: the crime you can always arrest non-criminals for.'

'But conspiracy to do what?' said Trainee Officer Grivas.

'Anything you like,' replied the Chief of Police. 'That is the beauty of it. You can be guilty of it even if nothing has happened. Police work would be so much harder without it.'

Behind him, Adam sensed the handle turn.

Chief Grivas swung round and pointed his cigar directly at Adam. 'Arrest him for conspiracy.'

Two officers stepped forward to obey the command, but before they could reach Adam, the door behind him clicked open and an arm shot out and pulled him through.

Taken by surprise, Adam lost his footing, stumbled and fell backwards. 'Ow!'

Crash! The door was slammed shut again. *Clunk!* The key was turned in the lock.

Adam looked up to see his rescuer.

Anna, the Mayor's daughter.

She was oblivious to the pounding on the door behind her. 'Open this door immediately!'

'How did you know what was happening?' Adam asked, getting to his feet.

Anna pointed to the keyhole.

'You looked through there?'

Anna nodded.

'And lipread what everyone was saying?'

Anna nodded again.

'It's not true, you know,' said Adam. 'I'm not a conspirator.'

Anna pointed to herself.

'You are?'

Anna nodded and shook her fist in the direction of the door.

'You're a conspirator against the Chief of Police?'

Anna nodded again, nodded so hard her head might have fallen off.

Adam smiled.

'If you are, then I am too.'

Anna offered him her hand. Adam shook it. They really were conspirators now.

'If we're going to stop the Chief of Police taking over Buenos Sueños, then we need to rescue my dog, my dad, my grandad and my mum,' said Adam.

Surprised, Anna held up four fingers to check she had read his lips correctly.

Adam nodded. 'Everyone I know seems to get taken prisoner by someone.'

He realised that the pounding on the door had stopped.

'Is there another way into this room?' he asked Anna.

She nodded.

PHEEP!

'I think they might've found it.'

Calmly, Anna signalled that he should follow her.

The two of them sprinted past the long dining table that spanned the room and out of the far door on to a landing. Adam grabbed Anna as she was about to launch herself down the staircase. She couldn't hear, but the police were on their way up the same flight of steps. They headed up the stairs instead, climbing until they reached the top floor.

'Is there another set of stairs we can go down?' Adam asked Anna.

She shook her head.

'We're trapped?' he said in alarm.

Anna shook her head and pointed up. Directly above them was a skylight.

'We can't reach it,' Adam shouted. 'The police are going to be here any second.'

Apparently unconcerned, Anna motioned to a bookcase against the wall. They hurriedly pulled out all the books and swept the ornaments off the shelves, then dragged the bookcase out so that it stood under the skylight. Using the empty shelves as steps, Anna began to climb up.

'You! Conspiracy chico! Stop!'

The police were on their way up the last flight of stairs.

Adam leapt on to the bookcase and climbed rapidly after her. Above him, Anna pushed open the skylight and heaved herself out on to the flat roof.

'Come down here at once!'

Adam was horrified to see a policeman running towards him. He had no intention of obeying, of course. He scrabbled up on to the top of the bookcase and reached for the skylight.

The bookcase shuddered as the policeman leapt on to it, tipping Adam off balance. He wobbled dangerously for a moment, riding the top of the rocking bookcase like a surfboard. As soon as it felt steady again, he stretched for the skylight and, gripping the edge, began to pull himself up.

The policeman made a swipe for Adam's dangling legs. He missed. He took another step up the shelves. He wouldn't miss a second time. Anna grasped Adam under his arms and helped to heave the rest of his body up and through the skylight. Adam felt the policeman's fingers just clip his shoe as he scrambled safely on to the roof.

From there they could see the whole of Buenos Sueños stretched out around them. But there wasn't time to appreciate the view – the head of the policeman popped out of the skylight.

Anna and Adam sprinted across the rooftop of the town hall.

'Stop!'

Still running, Adam chanced a glance behind. More policemen were pulling themselves up through the skylight and giving chase. He reached out and tapped Anna on the shoulder. She turned and smiled when she saw their pursuers, then pointed ahead – there was another skylight.

Adam understood. Anna had lured the police up there in order to get past them. They'd be able to slip through the second skylight, rush down the stairs and disappear into the narrow streets of Buenos Sueños before the policemen could catch up.

Anna put on a spurt of speed and reached the skylight. She tugged at it. And tugged again. Worry creased her face. It wouldn't open. Adam caught up with her and together they gave the skylight a mighty tug. It didn't move at all. This time it was locked. Anna frantically looked about for an object with which to smash the glass, but there was nothing.

Now that the policemen could see that the children were trapped, they slowed to a walk, determined to savour this capture and to make the waiting children suffer. The open skylight was the only way off the roof and they blocked access to it. Adam and Anna had nowhere to go.

But Anna wasn't beaten yet. She gestured to Adam to follow her. The policemen watched with amusement as she led the way to the edge of the roof, which had a thick terrace wall running round it, and with a defiant toss of her dark hair climbed on to it.

'What are you doing?' shouted Adam.

Anna motioned for Adam to get up alongside her. Adam had other ideas.

'It's too dangerous!'

Like a gymnast, Anna danced a few steps along the

wall to show how dangerous she thought it was.

'Be careful,' cautioned Adam.

Anna did a cartwheel.

This display had galvanised the policemen. They wanted their captives alive.

'Get down!' they shouted, and they started running again.

Anna reached down and grabbed Adam. The last thing he wanted was to be hauled over the terrace.

'All right, I'm coming,' he said. 'Just don't pull me.'

Anna let go and Adam clambered on to the terrace and stood up. Anna pointed to the next building. It was lower than the town hall and a narrow street separated them. She grabbed hold of his hand.

'You want us to jump?' Adam cried. 'You're crazy!'

He looked down – the ground was far below him. It began to sway. He felt sick and dizzy. Anna gripped his hand tightly. Adam shook his head. Anna nodded. Adam sighed. Together they took two steps forward. And jumped.

'Aiieeeeeeee!' cried Anna.

It was the first sound Adam had ever heard Anna make. Would it be the last? They were falling fast. Were they falling too fast? If they didn't reach the roof of the next building, the street below was ready to rush up to them and welcome them with a mighty crunch.

'Aiieeeeeeee!' cried Adam.

Hand in hand, the two of them flew through the air and landed on the roof of the building opposite.

'Aieeeee . . . Eeooow . . . Ow!' cried Adam, crashing down, tumbling over and banging his knee hard.

Next to him, Anna rolled into a graceful and painfree landing. It seemed the dark-haired girl had much more experience when it came to death-defying leaps. This did not surprise Adam.

Behind them, the policemen were furious. Already they were wondering how they were going to explain to Chief Grivas that they had been outwitted by two children. None of them wanted to face his wrath.

The fear gave Officer Jordi Grivas an idea. He unholstered his pistol and pointed it at the children.

'Yikes!' commented Adam.

'Stay exactly where you are,' ordered the officer. 'Or we shoot.'

Adam froze. Anna stuck out her tongue and did a backflip.

'What are you doing?' cried Adam. 'They're pointing a gun at you.'

Anna waved her hand contemptuously. She knew the policemen wouldn't shoot at children.

Bang!

It turned out she was wrong. Things in Buenos Sueños were getting very nasty indeed.

CHAPTER 23

A dam and Anna dashed for the nearest skylight in a hail of gunshot from the policemen's revolvers.

Let this one be unlocked, Adam prayed.

Dust flew up in front of him as a bullet ricocheted off the roof and shattered the glass of the skylight.

'Get down,' urged Adam.

Nothing seemed to flurry Anna. She lowered herself easily through the frame of the skylight and dropped to the floor. Needless to say, Adam was not so graceful in his hurry to escape the cracks and bangs of the gunfire around him.

'Ow!' He had hurt his other knee. He tried to ignore the throbbing pain and looked about him. They had fallen on to a landing. It was empty apart from a huge old wardrobe. Anna waved her hands to indicate he should hurry up.

Adam had just got to his feet when he heard a clunk from inside the wardrobe. The old Adam might have pretended not to hear it. But the new, bolder Adam strode over to the wooden doors and flung them open.

Grandma Marquez was standing inside. She was still knitting a scarf. She blinked angrily at Adam.

'How did you find me?' she demanded.

'You clunked.'

'You try knitting in the dark,' the old lady said defensively.

'I was just explaining,' said Adam.

'Are you the police?' she asked suspiciously. 'Because I warn you, if you are, I have a knitting needle and I'm prepared to use it!'

'No,' Adam replied. 'Actually, we're on the run from the police.'

Anna clenched her fists in frustration. Adam's honesty would surely get them caught.

'I'm on the run from the police too,' confided Grandma Marquez.

'Really?' asked Adam, in surprise. 'Why?'

'I don't remember exactly. It was sixty years ago or so,' said Grandma Marquez, 'but I committed a crime – something to do with peas.'

'Peas? You're sure you can commit a crime with peas?'

The old woman nodded.

'I thought I'd got away with it,' she said. 'But just the other day the police found me and I've been forced to hide in my sister Jordina's wardrobe ever since. It is a terrible way for an old woman to spend her declining years. Have you ever tried to have a conversation with a coat hanger?'

Adam shook his head. Next to him, Anna suddenly came

to life. Her hands flew backwards and forwards.

'What is the matter with your friend?' asked the old lady, looking alarmed.

'She doesn't talk,' explained Adam, without taking his eyes off Anna. He had to concentrate hard to understand her gestures.

'Anna wants to know if anything unusual happened just before the police came into your house?'

Grandma Marquez thought for a moment and then nodded.

'Two children I'd never seen before rode through the dining room on a bicycle.'

'That was us,' said Adam.

'I hope for your sake you don't run into my daughter-in-law,' said the old lady. 'You got oil on her favourite rug.'

'You don't understand,' Adam began.

'What's there to understand?' said Grandma Marquez. 'There is oil on a rug. She will kill you.'

'No,' said Adam. 'Not the rug. The police. They were after us. They didn't know anything about you and the peas.' The old lady looked confused. 'It means that you don't need to worry about staying in this wardrobe for the rest of your life.'

Her face broke into a wide wrinkly smile as she realised this was true. She stepped out on to the landing.

'I am free,' she said. 'Thank you, chicos. You must let me do something for you in return.'

From three floors below there was a tremendous banging on the door.

'I wonder who that could be,' she said.

'I think I can guess,' said Adam.

'Oh good,' said the old lady. 'I like guessing games too. Is it the butcher?'

'No, it's –'

'Don't tell me. The baker?'

'No, it's the police,' said Adam. 'They're after us and we need to get away.'

The sound of more thunderous knocks reached them.

'You're not very good at giving clues,' said the old lady frostily.

'I'm not playing a game,' said Adam.

'I'm an old-age pensioner who has spent the last few days with only coat hangers for company. You'd think that a little guessing game wouldn't be too much to ask. But the youth of today only think of themselves . . .' she muttered.

'I'm not only thinking of myself,' said Adam. 'I'm thinking of my dog and of my dad and of my mum and of my grandfather. They are all locked up and I'm the only person who can help them escape . . .'

Anna was reading Adam's lips and she stamped her foot. Adam looked at her, surprised. Anna pointed firmly to herself.

'I mean, Anna and I are the only people who can help them to escape,' he added.

'Well,' said the old lady grudgingly, 'I suppose you can't be blamed for your bad manners. It's obvious you come from a family of criminals.'

'But I don't,' said Adam. 'Well, not the whole family. I mean, my grandfather is a criminal, and I haven't seen my mum since I was two.'

'I see,' said Grandma Marquez. 'You come from a broken home as well. What can one expect?'

'I don't come from a broken home. My mum was kidnapped by an evil scientist.'

'Is that what your parents told you?'

'Yes,' said Adam.

'Well, it makes a change from "We married too young and your mother's gone to find herself."'

There was more thunderous knocking downstairs.

'Is there any other way out of here?' Adam pleaded.

'There might be,' Grandma Marquez replied cryptically.

'Will you show it to us?' he begged.

'All in good time,' said the old lady. 'First I'd better answer the door.'

'But it's the police at the door!' said Adam desperately. 'You can't let them in.'

'Who said anything about letting them in?' said the old lady with a smile as she set off down the stairs.

CHAPTER 24

Grandma Marquez opened the door a fraction.

'Ciao,' she said.

'Why have you taken so long to answer?' the policeman demanded.

Behind the door, Adam and Anna shrank back. If Grandma Marquez decided to betray them, they would be caught for sure.

'I have bad knees,' said Grandma Marquez. 'And bad ankles. And my elbows are nothing to write home about.'

'Shut up about your elbows,' said the policeman rudely. 'I am Officer Grivas of the Buenos Sueños Police Force. Two wanted criminals were seen entering your premises. I demand you allow the officers of the law to come in and search for them.'

'All right, officer,' said Grandma Marquez.

Adam and Anna couldn't believe it. She was going to let them in. The old lady reached up to undo the chain that was all that was keeping them from the clutches of the police. Adam and Anna held their breath.

Suddenly Grandma Marquez stopped.

'Wait a minute,' she said. 'I haven't got my tights on.'

'That is not important.'

'I don't know what you're talking about, officer,' said Grandma Marquez. 'Let a young man into my house when I'm alone and I haven't got my tights on? Think what people will say. I'll be back in a minute.'

'No,' shouted Officer Grivas. 'Don't shut this door. Don't –'

Grandma Marquez shut the door.

The thunderous knocking resumed.

'It's good being old,' said Grandma Marquez with a cackle. 'Everybody thinks you're crazy. You can get away with anything. Follow me, chicos.'

She led them through the dark house, which was filled with antique furniture, and into the kitchen. There was another old lady peeling potatoes.

'This is my sister, Jordina,' said Grandma Marquez. 'This is Adam and Anna, Jordina. They are on the run from the police too.'

'Have they done something with peas as well?' asked Jordina, who seemed utterly unconcerned about having more fugitives from justice under her roof.

'No,' said Grandma Marquez, shaking her head. 'But he's from a broken home and she waves her arms about. Anyway, the police are searching the streets for them so I am going to show them the secret way out.'

Jordina nodded.

'Would they like a packed lunch?'

Anna shook her head.

'No, thank you,' said Adam. 'It's very kind of you but we've got to get on with rescuing my family.'

'That sounds very hard work to me,' said Jordina. 'You'll need food to keep your strength up.'

'Really,' said Adam, 'we're not hungry. If we could just –'

'It won't take a moment,' said Jordina. 'Sister, you do the bread and I'll do the fillings.'

Neither of the old ladies seemed in the least bothered by the thunderous pounding at the door. They worked together like a well-oiled machine. Minutes later there was a bag full of sandwiches in front of them.

'That's very kind of you,' said Adam.

'Do you like ginger beer?' asked Grandma Marquez.

Anna was standing behind the sisters and she put her finger down her throat and mimed being sick.

'It's Anna's favourite,' Adam replied immediately.

'I'll give her an extra bottle, then.'

Anna shot Adam a hard look. He smiled back. He was getting the hang of this lying business.

'Right,' said Grandma Marquez. 'Follow me!'

She led them out into an enclosed courtyard, where plants and herbs grew in large pots.

'Here it is,' she said, indicating a manhole cover. 'The secret way. Pull it up.'

Adam reached down and pulled. The smell as the cover came up was unbelievably disgusting.

'Ugh!' he said, taking a step backwards. 'That's the sewers! We're not going in there.'

'It's the only way out of here that the police won't be watching,' said Grandma Marquez, adding consolingly, 'and you get used to it after a day or two.'

'A day or two?' said Adam, horrified. 'I don't —'

'Good luck to you both,' said the old lady. 'Do come back and visit one day, but make sure you have a shower first.'

'But which way do we go?'

'Follow the rope,' she replied. 'You'll find it when you jump down. It will lead you to safety. But coil it up as you go so that there is no way the police can follow you.'

'But then we won't be able to get back,' said Adam.

'You won't need to. Just, whatever you do, don't let go of it. The sewers are a maze and without it you will never find your way out.'

And she headed back towards the kitchen.

Adam and Anna sampled the awful odour rising from the manhole. Anna wrinkled her nose in disgust. Adam wrinkled his nose back. Anna opened her hands in a gesture of resignation. They had no other option, so they might as well get on with it. Adam nodded. They smiled at each other. And then they jumped . . .

Into the sewers of Buenos Sueños.

CHAPTER 25

They held the rope and inched their way forward, trying hard to ignore the awful stench that overpowered their noses the moment they dropped into the sewer. Next to them the walls were clammy, damp and dark. Adam and Anna were suddenly cold – the Buenos Sueños sun could not reach them down here. There were strange scurrying noises. The passages were narrow and low – they had to crouch so as not to bang their heads. All they had was the rope, and the further they went into the sewers, the tighter they gripped on to it.

Every passage they moved down seemed to be the same: dripping water, clammy walls, scurrying and scampering. It felt as though the walls were closing in on them. Panicked, Adam had a sudden urge to charge down a passage, any passage, but he fought it off and calmed down. He told himself that if they just stayed calm and followed the rope, they would reach safety.

And then the rope ran out. Someone had cut it.

Adam gulped.

Next to him, Anna gulped too.

They were lost in the maze of the Buenos Sueños sewer system from which there was no escape. It was going to be a very smelly way to die.

Anna tugged urgently on Adam's T-shirt.

He looked in the direction she was pointing. He couldn't see anything. But Anna could. Sometimes, when a person loses one of their senses, the others improve to compensate for the loss. Anna couldn't hear, but she could see better than almost anyone. And glimmering in the distance, at the furthest end of one of the tunnels, she saw a light.

She dragged Adam after her.

'What are you doing?' said Adam. 'We can't just run anywhere. What about the rope? What about the . . . ?'

Adam shut up abruptly. He, too, had just seen the light.

They charged ahead, stumbling and staggering into the clammy walls and banging their heads on the low ceiling. But they didn't care. All that mattered was that they could get to the light before it vanished and left them in this dark under-world for ever.

Adam heard voices.

They were getting closer. Now the first doubts began to surface in his mind. Who were these people? What were they doing down here? Were they friends or enemies? Did they have anything to do with the cutting of the rope?

The last thought struck him hard. But now they were

close enough to hear that the voices were raised in argument. What kind of people would possibly be arguing deep in the sewers of Buenos Sueños except the kind that were up to no good? Adam thought of the Doctor locked underground in Scabellax's base. Could it be that Scabellax and his evil henchmen had access to the sewers from that base? Were he and Anna running directly into a trap?

Adam feared the worst, but there was no stopping Anna. He heard a startled cry from the group of figures as she rushed out of the darkness towards them.

Adam dashed after her and was amazed to discover he recognised the figures. It was the Bajapuentalists of Buenos Sueños – the admirers of low bridges. Carla, their leader, remembered him.

'Welcome, chico!' she said with a warm smile. 'I see that the bug has caught you.'

'What bug do you mean?'

'I can sense when I am in the presence of a fellow admirer,' said Carla. 'And when I met you the other day I thought instantly, there's a chico who admires a low bridge. But even I did not expect you to come so far in the hobby in such a short time.'

Anna could lipread every word but that didn't mean she could understand a thing that was going on. She gave Adam a very puzzled look.

'You must be very advanced,' said Carla, idly fingering a recently acquired bump.

Behind her, the other Bajapuentalists nodded.

'Er, thank you,' said Adam. 'But how exactly am I advanced?'

'You are too modest, chico,' said Carla. 'Normally when one takes up our hobby one admires low bridges above ground for a number of years. It is only when one has been involved in the pastime for a long time that one is prepared to venture into extreme areas, like subterranean bridges. By definition they are even lower than those above ground.'

'I suppose they are,' said Adam doubtfully.

'You have arrived at a most fortunate moment,' continued Carla. 'I believe we may have discovered the lowest bridge in all of Buenos Sueños.'

'Pah!' said a voice from behind them. 'You cannot call that a bridge. It is more of a crossing.'

'This is our difficulty,' Carla explained. 'My fellow Bajapuentalist, Ezzio, is not convinced that it is a true bridge. We would be grateful for your opinion. It would break the deadlock.'

Anna was beginning to fidget.

'I'm afraid we're in a bit of a hurry,' said Adam.

'It will take no time at all,' said Carla.

'But we really have to –'

'There is nothing more important than a low bridge, chico,' said Carla a little sternly.

Adam thought about pointing out that the safety of his father, mother, grandfather and dog, as well as the abolition of democracy in Buenos Sueños, might just be considered more important. But when he looked at Carla he knew none of these arguments would convince her. Her obsession with low bridges wasn't just a hobby. It was a way of life.

'Well, I suppose we could offer an opinion,' said Adam weakly.

Anna stamped her foot in annoyance, which Carla misinterpreted as enthusiasm.

'I see the little chica is eager to see the low bridge. And who could blame her? Well, we will keep her waiting no longer. Look at what the lamp reveals.'

She raised the lamp.

Adam looked up. This was a mistake. Carla tutted in disapproval.

Adam looked down.

Crossing an extremely smelly stream in the sewer was a small bridge. What it was doing there, Adam hadn't got the faintest idea. But there it was.

'So what do you think, chico? Is it a bridge?'

'Of course it's not a bridge,' interrupted Ezzio. 'Where are the arches? Where are the supports? The beams? The cantilevers? The cable stays?'

Not knowing anything about bridges, Adam didn't have a clue.

'You see,' said Ezzio, 'if we cannot identify what type of bridge it is, then we cannot classify it as a bridge. It can only be a crossing.'

The Bajapuentalists sighed with regret. To have come so close to discovering a new low bridge and to have failed. How disappointing.

Suddenly Adam had an idea.

'Perhaps it's a new type of bridge,' he said.

There was a collective intake of breath from the Bajapuentalists.

'Pah!' said Ezzio scornfully. 'A new type of bridge? What are you talking about? Without beams? Without cantilevers? Without cable stays?'

'Yes,' said Adam boldly. 'Exactly that type of bridge.' Before, he might have backed off. But having seen Calico Jack at work, Adam knew that saying things with absolute confidence could work wonders. 'This is clearly a beamless, cantilever-free, zero-cable-stay bridge,' he announced, hoping he'd remembered correctly all the words Ezzio had just said.

Carla released a low whistle of amazement.

'Fellow Bajapuentalists, this is indeed a historic moment in bridge observation. With this discovery we have become pioneers in the world of Bajapuentalogy,' she pronounced.

The group stood in silent admiration for a moment.

'We must celebrate,' Carla continued, 'in the traditional Bajapuentalist way.'

The Bajapuentalists all immediately banged their heads on the ceiling.

'Ouch!'

'The Bajapuentalists are forever in your debt, Adam,' said Carla, rubbing her new bump. 'If ever you need help, just call us.'

Anna gestured to Adam.

'Actually,' said Adam, 'you could help us now.'

'Really?' said Carla.

'Yes. We're lost, you see. We were following a rope, but it's been cut –'

'Because it was an escape route for criminals,' interrupted Ezzio. 'I spend a lot of time in these sewers and I know what goes on.' Adam noticed a sharp knife in his hand. 'So I want to know what you chicos were doing following it?'

Adam couldn't think of an answer. But luckily his recent discovery saved him. Carla rounded angrily on Ezzio.

'I hope you remember, Ezzio, that according to the Bajapuentalist Charter all Bajapuentalists are required to assist each other.'

'One for small and small for one!' cried the rest of the group.

'These chicos are honorary Bajapuentalists because of their discovery of the beamless, cantilever-free, zero-cable-stay bridge. We will help them. Should you choose not to help you may leave our society.'

Ezzio obviously had no wish to help Adam and Anna but he could not bear to leave the Bajapuentalists. He turned away, muttering to himself.

'What can we do for you?' asked Carla.

'If you could just tell us how to get out,' said Adam.

'That is no problem,' she replied, reaching into her pocket and producing a folded sheet of paper. 'In our quest to find the lowest of bridges we have been mapping the sewer system. Where would you like to go?'

'I don't know really,' said Adam.

Anna made some urgent hand gestures.

'But we'd like it to be quite a long way from the police station,' he added, trying to keep his voice casual.

Carla nodded.

'Whatever you like. We can lead you to exits near the hospital – there is quite a low bridge near there – or the theatre, which is also not far from a bridge of only moderate altitude, though to call it low would be a little too generous. Or . . . where are we under at the moment? The dog pound!'

'The dog pound!' cried Adam. 'That's the perfect place.'

'Really?' said Carla, surprised. 'There are no other bridges of note near the dog pound.'

'It doesn't matter,' said Adam.

'It matters to us,' snapped Ezzio suddenly.

'I didn't mean –' Adam began.

'Ask them why don't they want to be seen by the police,' Ezzio added. 'They must be criminals.'

'Be quiet, Ezzio,' said Carla. 'These are fellow Bajapuentalists. Remember our motto.'

'"We all crouch together,"' the other Bajapuentalists quoted dutifully.

But Adam noted that Ezzio did not join in. Instead, he gave Adam and Anna an ugly stare and slunk back into the shadows.

'Follow me,' said Carla, and she took them down a tunnel. Soon they reached a shaft. A ladder led up it. She checked her map once more. 'That should bring you out in the centre of the exercise yard of the dog pound.'

'Thank you,' said Adam.

'It's nothing.'

Adam and Anna shook Carla's hand and climbed up the ladder. For once, Adam went first. When he reached the top, he carefully pushed open the manhole cover, hoping there wasn't a dog warden waiting for them.

But the exercise yard appeared to be empty.

Anna tugged impatiently on Adam's foot. She didn't like being left out and hated the fact that Adam could see something she couldn't. But Adam refused to move immediately. He wanted to be absolutely sure there was nobody around before climbing out of the sewers, because once they were out they were far more vulnerable to capture.

He turned his head left and right, checking to see he hadn't missed anything. There were cages all the way round the perimeter of the exercise yard, each locked with a large padlock. And in each cage there was a dog. There were all types of dogs: big dogs, little dogs, short stubby dogs, long thin dogs, dogs with short tails, dogs with long tails. And then, in the far corner, there was . . .

Sniffage.

Adam forgot about being extra cautious. He pulled himself out of the manhole and ran towards his dog. Anna came straight out after him. There might not have been anyone around to see them, but the other dogs in the pound noticed immediately and exploded into a cacophony of barks and threw themselves against the doors of their cages. Though she couldn't hear the dogs, Anna could sense all this clamour of activity would attract someone . . .

Then Adam opened his mouth and barked.

The dogs calmed down and were silent.

Anna didn't know what to make of it. She could lipread perfectly, but whatever noise Adam had just produced was completely unintelligible to her. She couldn't believe what she had witnessed. Had Adam had just talked to . . . ?

No. It didn't make sense.

Open-mouthed, she pointed to Adam, then to the dogs, then back to Adam. Then to both of them at the same time. Then she shook her head as though whatever she was thinking was impossible.

Adam smiled. For once, *she* was the one who didn't know what was going on.

One dog, however, was too excited to stop barking. He had his nose pressed up against his cage.

'Yeah! Yeah!' barked Sniffage. 'Adam! Yeah! Adam!'

Adam and Anna ran over to the his cage.

'You smell different!' woofed the spaniel delightedly.

'We've been in the sewers,' Adam explained.

'Yeah!' insisted Sniffage. 'You smell really bad. It's fantastic! Yeah!'

Anna had had enough. She tugged hard at Adam, pointed at Sniffage, pointed at him, and with a menacing wag of her finger demanded to know what was going on.

Adam remembered the Doctor's rule that they should never tell anyone, but he was on his own now, making his own decisions, and he knew he could trust Anna better than anyone.

Maybe even better than the Doctor himself.

Adam shook himself. He didn't want to think like that. He looked Anna in the eye. 'I can talk to animals,' he said.

Perhaps it was simply because she trusted Adam in the same way he trusted her, but Anna just nodded and smiled.

Adam turned back to the cage.

'Sniffage,' he said. 'I'd like you to meet Anna. She's our friend.'

Sniffage barked hello.

'Yeah! Yeah! I like her,' he informed Adam. 'She smells as bad as you.'

But there was no more time for them to get to know each other. So far the dog wardens had not been alerted to trespassers, but sooner or later Adam and Anna were bound to be spotted.

'Yeah! Yeah! You got a stick to throw for me?' barked Sniffage enthusiastically.

'No,' Adam told him. 'And even if I did, you couldn't get out to chase it.'

'Grrr!' the spaniel growled. It was very rare to hear him make such an angry sound. 'I hate cages. Stop you going out for walks and don't smell of anything interesting.'

Adam wanted more than anything to be able to throw open the cage door and let Sniffage run out. He hated the idea of animals being locked up. But there was the problem of the large padlock.

He shook it. But it wouldn't budge.

'Yeah! Yeah! Open it!' encouraged Sniffage.

'I want to, Sniffage,' said Adam, 'but I can't.'

He turned to Anna and pointed at the padlock. Could she do anything? The dark girl shrugged hopelessly.

'Yeah! Yeah! Doesn't matter,' barked Sniffage nobly. 'I'll get used to doing nothing. Don't worry about me. Yeah!'

The spaniel turned away. He pretended to wag his tail as he padded across his cage but his heart was not in it and his tail barely moved.

Adam felt tears welling up in his eyes. Of all the animals that he knew, Sniffage would find it hardest being caged. He had to release him. He had to.

'There must be a way to get him out!' he exclaimed

Then Adam felt something crawl on to his hand. He looked down.

It was Private Mandible.

'Ahem,' signalled the army ant. 'Perhaps I can help.'

CHAPTER 26

Adam laughed.

'What are you laughing at?' signalled Private Mandible indignantly.

Once more, Anna's mouth was wide open in astonishment. When Adam had said he could talk to animals, she had assumed that meant cats and dogs, never insects. But Anna was in for a bigger shock.

'Thank you for offering to help,' Adam signalled to the ant, 'but we need to get into a locked cage. It may be too difficult.'

'Nothing is beyond the determination of the Special Ant Service,' Private Mandible signalled back, forgetting for a moment that he'd actually been suspended from the Special Ant Service for being a conscientious objector. 'We have a motto: "He who dares wins."'

'Prove it, then,' signed Anna.

This was her biggest shock: she could understand Private Mandible too! Human sign language and insect language had evolved independently, but by coincidence had developed in such a similar way that a user of one could understand a user of the other.

'Put me into the lock,' said Private Mandible. 'Army ants are the strongest of all ants. I will open it.'

Adam lowered his hand to the padlock and Private Mandible marched straight inside.

'It doesn't matter how strong an ant he is,' Adam informed Anna. 'Locks are made of metal. The mechanism will be too heavy for him.'

There was a metallic click from inside the lock.

'I mean, he can't . . .' Adam began.

There was another click.

'It's impossible . . .'

There was a third click and the padlock dropped open. Private Mandible marched proudly out of the keyhole.

'Mission accomplished,' he announced, and he saluted Adam with his legs.

'I thought you didn't want to be in the army any more,' Adam reminded him.

'Only when the mission involves violence,' Private Mandible said. 'Violence solves nothing. It only leads to more violence. How many more ants have to die before we know too many ants have died?'

His philosophical musing on the senseless waste of insect life was interrupted by the escape of Sniffage. As soon as Anna pulled the padlock off, the spaniel shot out to freedom. He was desperate to bark with joy but somehow he managed to limit himself to a simple quiet gruff of pleasure.

Adam put Private Mandible back in his pocket.

'Let's get out of here,' he said to Anna.

The main gate was at the end of the exercise yard. Once through it, they could disappear into the anonymous streets of Buenos Sueños.

Adam and Anna began to run, but Sniffage didn't follow them.

'Come on, Sniffage,' Adam urged. But the dog wouldn't move. 'What's the matter?'

Sniffage looked sorrowfully around at all the other dogs – their noses pressed up against their cages.

'Yeah! Yeah! I can't leave them!'

'But the wardens could be here any moment,' said Adam. 'We've got to go now or we could be caught.'

'Yeah! Yeah! But we've got to get them out first,' insisted Sniffage. 'I know what it's like in there. No smells. No dead things.'

Adam saw Sniffage was right. Whatever the risk, they had to free the other dogs. He reached into his pocket.

'Private Mandible reporting for duty.'

'We need twenty more padlocks unlocking.'

Private Mandible saluted. 'Take me to them.'

Each lock opened faster than the last. Five, ten, fifteen padlocks were opened, and as soon as Adam and Anna took them off the dog inside the cage slipped out and joined the others in a happy but silent pack, their tails wagging together as they waited for the next of their fellow prisoners to be released.

But now Private Mandible was beginning to tire. There are limits to even an army ant's strength and straining to move the locks' heavy parts was having an effect.

Locks sixteen and seventeen took longer.

Lock eighteen was even slower.

Adam thought Private Mandible had got lost during lock nineteen, but eventually there was a click and another dog was free.

Only one dog remained – a dachshund called Sausage.

'Hey!' There was a shout from the dog warden's office. They had been spotted.

'We've got to go now!' Adam cried.

Private Mandible shook a leg. 'No,' he signalled. 'There is still time. Put me into the lock.'

'But the wardens?' Adam protested.

'Put me in,' insisted Private Mandible. 'An army ant knows that you never leave a comrade behind.'

Adam put him into the lock.

'Get down to the other end of the yard and open the gate into the street,' Adam signalled to Anna.

She nodded. Taking the other dogs with her, she ran towards the gate. Only Adam and Sniffage stayed by the final cage.

Three dog wardens charged out of their office.

'What do you think you're doing?' shouted one angrily.

'Put those dogs back in their cages.'

There was a click. The final padlock fell open.

Sausage the dachshund barked joyfully. He was free. Private Mandible staggered out of the padlock, exhausted.

'Tell General Lepti that I died like a true army ant!' And he collapsed on to Adam's hand. Adam had no time even to worry about Private Mandible. He thrust him into his pocket.

The wardens were running towards them.

'Come on!'

Sniffage and Sausage didn't need to be told. They were already running as fast as they could towards the gate.

There should have been no problem. The dog wardens were fat and out of shape. Adam and Sniffage were easily fast enough to outrun them. But Sausage was a dachshund, and dachshunds have a problem when it comes to speedy escapes.

Little legs.

However fast the determined little dog ran, it was never going to be fast enough.

Ahead of them, Anna swung open the gate. The other dogs rushed through it. Adam and Sniffage would soon be safe too. But the distance was too far for Sausage. With every step, the dog wardens were catching him up.

'Get him,' shouted one warden angrily.

Dogs are pack animals, and pack animals survive by acting and thinking as one. Suddenly a collective thought seemed to flash through the group waiting on the other side of the gate. When they were captured by the dog wardens they had been on their own, outnumbered, cornered and overpowered. But now . . . Now they were the greater in number.

Just as Sausage was about to be caught, the dogs turned round, formed a pack and charged.

'What?' cried one dog warden.

'I don't . . .' began another.

'Nooooo,' shouted the third.

The dog wardens were about to be given a taste of their own medicine.

'Run!'

Adam and Anna watched them turn tail and flee towards their office, pursued by twenty dogs, who were very much enjoying themselves. They barked, they harried, they growled. Even Sausage managed to get in a quick nip before the wardens reached the safety of their office and slammed the door behind them.

Outside, the dogs capered about gleefully. The jailers had become the prisoners.

Adam could not permit himself to join in the celebrations, not when his mother, the Doctor and Calico Jack were still prisoners. But watching the joyful dogs and thinking about what had just happened gave him an idea.

He and Anna had been running from the police. But now they had an army of their own. Maybe they didn't need to run any more.

CHAPTER 27

There were two officers standing outside the police headquarters. Along with uniforms and guns, they wore the earmuffs that seemed to have been added to the uniform of every member of the force. Otherwise the square was empty. The citizens of Buenos Sueños were still being allowed a respite after the enforced 'Hokey Cokey' routine earlier that day. But if the past was any guide, this respite could not last for long.

One policeman yawned. The other scratched his nose. Neither of them particularly enjoyed sentry duty. They would rather be out searching for the escaped conspirators.

And the escaped conspirators were nearer than they could ever have imagined. For Adam, Anna, Sniffage, Sausage and the rest of the pack of dogs had navigated back to the square through the narrow streets. The dogs had led the way, using their sense of smell to guide Adam and Anna safely away from their pursuers. Now, after an order from Adam, they split into two groups: humans on one side of the square, dogs on the other.

Adam nodded at Anna. The two of them ran into the square and tripped over each other. They went down in a heap of arms and legs.

'Come on, Anna!' shouted Adam, making sure the officers caught her name. 'We've got to keep running.'

Anna struggled to her feet clumsily as though she was exhausted.

Outside the police headquarters nobody was yawning or scratching their nose any more.

'It's the conspirators!'

'We must arrest them!'

Neither of the policemen stopped to consider why the conspirators would run back into the main square. They were too busy thinking of the promotions that might come their way when they brought them to Chief of Police Grivas.

They sprinted after them. And it appeared they were in luck. Adam saw them coming, but as he turned to flee he banged into Anna. Once more they fell over in a muddle of arms and legs. The two policemen could almost taste their promotions.

Had they looked behind them, the taste might have changed from sweet to sour in an instant. For the pack of dogs was in pursuit. They were led by Zip the greyhound, and they stretched all the way back to Sausage.

Ahead of the police, Adam tried to pull Anna to her feet. But amazingly (at least to the policemen) he was so desperate to escape that he pulled too hard and he overbalanced again. The policemen couldn't believe how easy this arrest was going to be.

'Surrender in the name of the Crime and Punishment Code of Buenos Sueños!'

Still running, the officers reached for their weapons as, finally, the clumsy conspirators regained their feet.

'You'll never take us alive,' shouted the boy conspirator, shaking his fist theatrically at them.

Normally the policemen would have hesitated before shooting, but these were not normal times. They had just raised their guns to take aim at Adam and Anna, when an army of dogs struck.

'Aiieee!' cried the policemen simultaneously as Zip and Sniffage sunk their teeth into their arms. The guns clattered harmlessly to the floor.

And before they could even twist and turn to try to fight off their assailants, the officers were overwhelmed by the pack and dragged to the floor.

'Help!' shouted the policemen.

But there was nobody in the square to hear their screams.

The dogs knew what they had to do. While Adam and Anna scooped up the guns, they chewed, they bit and they tore. Moments later, the officers were naked apart from their underpants, and as soon as the dogs let them up, they fled into the narrow streets.

Sausage arrived just as they were disappearing.

'Curse these little legs!' he woofed. 'I never get to join in the fun.'

But there was no time to commiserate with Sausage. Adam needed to put the second part of his plan into operation.

'Are we ready?' he asked the dogs.

'Woof!' replied the dogs.

'Let's go then!'

Adam, Anna and the pack of dogs charged towards the police headquarters, followed doggedly by Sausage.

'Only just got here and they run off somewhere else,' he complained to himself, watching the rest of the dogs vanish into the building. 'Story of my life.'

But he didn't stop running.

Surprise is a key element in any attack, and Adam, Anna and the dogs had more than their fair share. Firstly, policemen in a police headquarters do not expect to be attacked. Secondly, they do not expect to be attacked by children. Thirdly, they do not expect to be attacked by dogs. Fourthly, they do not expect children with dogs. All in all, it is safe to say that the policemen were very, very surprised indeed.

The dogs went straight for the policemen's most vulnerable area.

'Arrgghh! My trousers,' cried all three Officer Grivases who were manning the reception.

But their protests were in vain. The sound of shredding trousers echoed through the building.

Meanwhile Adam and Anna rushed behind the main

desk. Even though Private Mandible could work the mechanism in a padlock, Adam guessed that a proper lock with a huge bolt would be too much for him.

'Look for the keys that will open the cells!' Adam reminded Anna.

They ransacked the desk, finding papers, handcuffs and pots of red paint. But no keys.

'Aiieeee!'

The policemen were trying to wrestle themselves free, but as soon as they got one dog off their trousers, another tore at their sleeves. There were ripped clothes everywhere.

'Got it,' said Adam, opening the final drawer and finding two big keys. One was marked 'Cells', the other was marked 'Code'.

Adam grabbed the first. Anna grabbed the second.

'Keep them occupied,' Adam told Sniffage.

The dogs needed no encouragement.

There was only one other door that led out of the lobby. Adam and Anna charged through it. They found themselves in a grey corridor with closed doors on either side. But the door at the end of the corridor was different. It had bars. It could only lead to one place: the cell block.

They hurried through and down a set of stone steps. As they descended they felt the temperature cool. The thick walls of the basement prevented the heat from getting in and the jail was one of the coldest places in Buenos Sueños.

Their arrival caused a great deal of excitement. The

prisoners rushed to the front of their cells just like the dogs had done in the pound.

'Ciao,' shouted one.

'Chico! Chica!' cried another, waving his hands through the bars.

Instinctively, Adam backed away. But Anna showed none of Adam's caution. She had lived in Buenos Sueños all her life and she knew that you didn't need to do much wrong to end up in the cells. She reached out and shook the hand of the prisoner. Adam felt ashamed.

Down the line of cells they went, more hellos, more hands. But no Calico Jack.

'Is there another jail?' Adam signed to Anna.

The dark girl shrugged to show she didn't think so. There were only two more cells to go. The next one didn't hold Calico Jack.

'Hey!' shouted the man inside it, obviously recognising Anna. 'I'm Fidel Guavera, the Mayor's chief political strategist.'

Adam looked at Anna, who nodded. The man was telling the truth.

'Has he sent you to free me?'

Adam vaguely remembered the Mayor complaining about the arrest of his political adviser, but he had no time to think about that now. There was only one more cell to go. It had to hold Calico Jack . . .

And it did. When he saw them, Calico Jack's mouth dropped wide open.

'What are you doing here, young 'un?'

Adam allowed himself a little pause of satisfaction. He no longer felt like the lost young boy Calico Jack had first met on the *Ark of the Parabola*. He'd done a lot of growing up in the past few days.

'We've come to rescue you,' he said proudly.

'Who gave you the right to do that?'

Adam was taken aback. Calico Jack was furious.

'Nobody,' he stammered.

Anna punched Adam on the shoulder.

'What was that for?'

'Don't let him talk to you like that,' she signed.

She's right, thought Adam. *Why should I?* He met Calico Jack's angry glare.

'It was my decision,' he said. 'And maybe if you hadn't got caught so easily, we wouldn't have had to.'

Calico Jack's face was still dark with anger.

'Did you ever wonder why I got caught so easily, young 'un? Calico Jack, a legend among criminals, a man who has spent most of his life escaping the clutches of the world's most sophisticated police forces, caught by that fat fool of a Chief of Police.'

'Why?'

'Because of what you said about the double helix,' his grandfather replied. 'It's been nagging at me like an infected tooth. There's something linking all these things and we need to know what it is. And since we hadn't managed to find out

232

from the outside, I thought we might stand a better chance from the inside.'

A few days ago, Adam might have accepted this explanation and told himself that Calico Jack knew what he was doing. But the new Adam wanted a better answer than that.

'What can you learn stuck in a jail cell?'

'My, my,' said Calico Jack. 'Someone's been learning to talk back. You've got more cheek than the back end of a pig.'

'Don't talk to me about pigs,' said Adam. 'Answer the question.'

Calico Jack reached into his coat and pulled out a key. He waved it in Adam's face.

'I've not been stuck in here,' he told Adam. 'I picked the guard's pocket as they were locking me up. I've been sneaking round the headquarters. I've found out one or two interesting things, let me tell you. And I'd have found out a whole lot more if you hadn't come busting in here with Little Miss Fireball to rescue me.'

Anna deserved Calico Jack's nickname, for her dark eyes were indeed blazing.

'What did you find out?' Adam asked.

'Not as much as I would have liked,' admitted Calico Jack. 'But the most interesting thing happened when a man called Señor Le Blacas arrived.'

'I know him,' said Adam. 'I'm responsible for staining his trousers.'

'He and Chief Grivas seemed to be in cahoots. Le Blacas

was congratulating the Chief on declaring martial law, but the more I listened, the more it sounded like it was his idea in the first place, not the Chief's. If you ask me, our next port of call should be Le Blacas. My guess is, now the Mayor's no longer running the city, he is.'

'But what about —' Adam began.

There was a crash and the door to the cell block smashed open. The three policeman, stripped of all their clothes bar their pants, tumbled down the steps into the room. Nineteen dogs came barking gleefully after them. Seeing their captors so humiliated, the prisoners let forth a great cheer.

'Please,' pleaded the policemen, throwing themselves at the mercy of Adam and Anna, 'lock us up. Throw away the key. Anything, but get these dogs off us, please.'

Calico Jack unlocked his own cell and stepped neatly out.

'You're very lucky,' he informed the officers. 'A cell has just become free. I can highly recommend it: bare cold walls, one lumpy bed and a plague of cockroaches.'

'We'll take it,' shouted the policemen, rushing in.

The prisoners clanked their metal mugs against the bars at the front of their cells, delighted to see the policemen under lock and key. The dogs joined in the celebration with a chorus of joyful woofing. It was almost time to . . .

BANG!

A shot echoed in the cell block.

Standing at the top of the stairs, holding two huge rifles, one in each hand, was Chief of Police Grivas.

CHAPTER 28

'Man, boy, girl or dog, the first to move towards me will be blown to smithereens.'

The rifles were huge, well capable of carrying out the Chief of Police's threat, and he wielded them expertly.

'Now, chicos and chicas,' said Grivas. 'Some people are going back to their cells. And some dogs are going back to the pound.'

'You don't need to do this, Grivas,' said Calico Jack. 'We know it's Señor Le Blacas who is pulling the strings here. Now, if you'd just let us talk to him . . .'

At the mention of Señor Le Blacas, the colour drained from the Chief's face.

'Señor Le Blacas is a friend of Buenos Sueños,' he said. 'He is advising me during this difficult time.'

'He's not advising you,' said Calico Jack. 'He's telling you what to do. I heard him.'

The Chief tightened his fingers around the triggers of the rifles.

'Nobody tells me what to do! Now release those officers and get into that cell,' he shouted. 'Take the dogs in with you. There's no time to take them to the pound. And this time there will be no mistakes. I will station armed guards in front of every cell, with orders to shoot to kill at the slightest hint of an escape attempt.'

With the barrels of the Chief's rifles pointing straight at them, Adam, Anna and Calico Jack began to back towards the last cell. Tails down, the dogs followed them.

'This is terrible,' said Adam. 'If we're all imprisoned, then there's no one left to free my mother and the Doctor and save Buenos Sueños.'

'Faster!' shouted the Chief.

'Can't anybody think of something?' said Adam desperately.

Calico Jack shook his head. Anna shrugged. They were beaten. They unlocked the cell and the policemen sidled out, glancing nervously at the pack of dogs.

'Get upstairs and find new uniforms now,' Chief Grivas yelled. 'And you lot, get inside that cell and shut the door behind you!'

This was it. One by one, they filed reluctantly into the open cell. Adam was the last one in. He prepared to shut the door on hope.

And then he saw something move behind the Chief of Police.

'Hurry up!' Grivas snapped.

Sausage the dachshund!

His little legs had meant he'd taken much longer to get across the square, and then the other dogs had charged off after the policemen and he'd got lost looking for them. But Sausage had learnt one thing in his life. If you had little legs, you had to make up for it with massive determination. He hadn't given up looking for the rest of the pack and now he had found them.

But would he understand what was going on?

'I think your cell door needs oiling,' said Adam, desperately trying to delay things to allow Sausage to understand the situation. 'Listen to that squeak!'

'You'll be squeaking if you don't shut that door,' said the Chief menacingly, aiming his rifles right at Adam.

Meanwhile, behind the Chief of Police, Sausage surveyed the scene in the cell block, noted the sad, lowered tails of his fellow dogs and decided to act. He trotted forwards and sank his teeth as hard as he could into Chief Grivas's calf muscle.

'Aiiieeeeeee!' screamed the Chief of Police.

The surprise attack sent him staggering forward. He teetered for a moment on the edge of the step and then plummeted down the staircase.

BANG! BANG!

The two rifles fell from his hands and immediately discharged themselves, the bullets echoing in the cell block as they ricocheted from wall to wall. Adam and Calico Jack instinctively ducked at the sound. But Anna didn't hear it, and even if she had, the daring girl knew that there was no time to look for shelter. What mattered was to be the first person to pick up the fallen shotguns.

She raced across the cell block. At the same instant that Anna reached one rifle, Chief Grivas stretched out and grabbed the other. A moment later, both of them were pointing guns at one another.

Nobody in the cell block moved.

'Chica, put that gun down!' ordered the Chief of Police.

Anna shook her head.

'It's dangerous. You aren't trained. You might make a terrible mistake.'

Anna shrugged to show that she was prepared to risk an accident.

'Now, now, chica,' smiled Chief Grivas. 'Let's me and you be friends. You put the gun down and I'll let you and your friends go.'

Anna stared unblinkingly at him. His finger tightened on the trigger.

'We've got to break the deadlock somehow, little chica,' he said, 'and I know you don't want to get hurt.'

If he was hoping that fear would break Anna's resolve, he had picked on the wrong girl.

But it wasn't the Chief of Police who broke the deadlock. And it wasn't Anna. Padding down the stairs, unnoticed on his little legs, was Sausage the dachshund.

'I'm going to count to three,' said Grivas. 'One . . . two . . . owwww!'

Sausage sank his teeth into the Chief of Police's other calf muscle. His rifle clattered to the floor and Anna grabbed it.

Adam and Calico Jack charged across the cell block to join her.

'That was brilliant,' said Adam to Sausage.

'Little legs, big heart!' woofed the dog.

'Get into the cell!' Calico Jack ordered the Chief of Police, taking one of the rifles from Anna.

Glaring at them with seething hatred, Chief of Police Grivas backed reluctantly into the empty cell. Calico Jack locked the door behind him.

'So what now?' he said. It was meant to be a rhetorical question – one that he asked with the intention of providing the answer himself. But Adam, filled with a new sense of self-belief, had other ideas. He answered immediately.

'We've got to free the Doctor.'

'What about Señor Le Blacas?' said Calico Jack, a little taken aback. 'He seems to be the one running things. We should try to find him.'

Adam shook his head. 'The Doctor first,' he repeated firmly.

Anna walked over and stood resolutely next to Adam. Then Sniffage went and stood next to him. Then Sausage did the same. At least, Sausage set off to do the same, but all the other dogs overtook him, so in fact he got to stand next to Adam last of all.

'Curse these little legs!' woofed Sausage.

Calico Jack looked at the children and the pack of dogs ranged against him. 'Looks like I'm outvoted,' he said with a rueful smile. 'You're in charge, young 'un.'

They were about to go, when there was a cry from the cell next to Chief Grivas's. It was Fidel Guavera, the Mayor's chief political strategist.

'Hey, amigos,' he cried. 'Don't leave us behind.'

'We've got to go and save Buenos Sueños,' said Adam.

'We can help you if you take us with you.'

Adam didn't know what to do. He knew where he was with strange animals. With strange people it was a different story.

'Rattle your mugs if you'll help,' cried Fidel Guavera.

There was a tremendous crashing as the prisoners bashed their mugs against the bars of their cells.

'I am an official opinion poll collector,' said Fidel Guavera, 'and I conclude that the prisoners are a hundred per cent behind helping you and saving Buenos Sueños.'

Anna pinched Adam.

'You would have been in this jail too if it hadn't been for me,' she signed furiously. 'It's their city. You have to let them save it too.'

Adam knew she was right. He nodded and she rushed to unlock the cell doors.

'If we're going to rescue the Doctor we're going to need everybody,' Adam barked to Sniffage, while the prisoners were being released. 'Take the other dogs and go back to the *Ark of the Parabola* to get the rest of the Arkonauts. Then meet us at the bus stop for Tibidabo!'

The dogs rushed out of the cell block, yapping excitedly. Calico Jack was looking at Adam with a mixture of amusement and amazement.

'It's your show, young 'un,' he said.

Adam realised that everybody was waiting for him to give orders. 'We will take the bus up to Tibidabo and go into the forest and rescue the Doctor,' he announced.

He looked at Anna, Calico Jack and the recently freed prisoners.

'Are you with me?' he called.

'Yes!' they shouted.

Adam issued a rallying cry. 'To the bus stop!'

CHAPTER 29

Bus Pilot Torres almost crashed when he saw the crowd that had assembled by the bus stop. Since the Dreadful Alarm had come to Buenos Sueños, almost nobody travelled anywhere that wasn't necessary.

But today the bus stop was packed. And not only with people. There were animals too.

Torres stopped the bus. The door opened with a whoosh. Adam leapt on board.

'I want tickets for fifteen adults, two children, twenty dogs, a cat, two parrots, a bat, a monkey and a troupe of army ants,' he said.

'Remember to ask for a group discount,' shouted Calico Jack.

But Torres shook his head. 'I am not authorised to carry animals until they have spent six months in quarantine.'

'That's only on planes,' insisted Adam. 'This is a bus.'

Torres grimaced. However, he had to grudgingly admit that Adam had a point.

'Well, they can't travel inside the cabin,' he said. 'They'll have to go in the hold.'

'Where's the hold?' said Adam.

'I haven't got one,' said Torres.

'Where can they go, then?' demanded Adam.

'On the roof?' suggested Calico Jack.

Bus Pilot Torres looked incredulous.

'We will be cruising at over 30,000 feet,' he said.

'No, we won't,' Adam reminded him. 'We'll be cruising at zero feet. All the animals on the roof!' he shouted. 'All the prisoner . . . er . . . er, I mean, all the free friendly nice people who have never been in a prison cell in their lives on the bus.'

The animals either flew up or were helped up on to the roof by the ex-prisoners. Then the people got on to the bus.

'Are any of the animals under twelve years old?' enquired Torres. 'Because if so, they are entitled to a discount.'

'They're all eleven and a half,' Calico Jack jumped in.

'How do you –' Adam began.

'Leave this bit to me,' his grandfather said, pushing Adam to one side. 'I've been negotiating prices since before you were born.'

One and a half minutes later, Calico Jack had convinced the Aerobus driver that, because of the extensive discounts, not only were they all entitled to go free, but Torres, in fact, owed *them* money.

'I don't understand,' said Torres.

'Don't worry about it,' said Calico Jack. 'A free return

journey back down the hill when we've finished and we'll call it quits.'

Torres shut the doors and the fully laden bus began to the steep climb up to Tibidabo.

'We're going to rescue Buenos Sueños!' cheered the prisoners.

Above them on the roof they heard the animals thumping about in excitement.

Only Adam felt apprehensive. He remembered what had happened the last time he had been to Tibidabo. He had gone with the Doctor but he had returned alone. How many of the brave creatures alongside him would be coming back? he wondered.

'What's the matter with you, young 'un?' said Calico Jack. 'You look like you've lost a penny and found out you've wet yourself. Cheer up.'

Adam managed a weak smile. Until the Doctor and his mother were free, and Buenos Sueños saved, he could manage no more than that.

The bus creaked its way round another hairpin bend as it rose towards an encounter with Professor Scabellax.

CHAPTER 30

Adam led the way, leaving Señor Torres at the final bus stop waiting for their return and still trying to puzzle out why he owed Calico Jack money.

Adam suggested that he and Anna go ahead with the animals while Calico Jack stayed a little distance behind with the ex-prisoners. He didn't want them all to see him communicating with the animals. He told Calico Jack he'd send Sniffage as soon as they'd got an idea of the task they faced in trying to get into Scabellax's base and rescue the Doctor and his mother. Calico Jack gave his grandson a nod of approval and immediately took command of the men.

Adam and Anna led the animals in an advance party. Once he was out of earshot, Adam told Sniffage and the dogs to scout the route ahead. The dogs would smell any black-clad guards Scabellax had lying in wait for them long before the guards saw them. Then Adam beckoned to Gogo and Pozzo, who flew down and settled, one on each arm.

'How many parrots does it take to change a light bulb?'

Gogo squawked before Adam had a chance to give them any instructions.

'I don't know,' Adam sighed.

'Not nearly as many as it takes to change a heavy one.'

Adam couldn't help smiling. 'Now I need you to do something for me,' he said sternly.

For once, the parrots decided not to continue their repartee.

'Fly over the wood,' said Adam. 'Then come back and tell me if you see anything unusual.'

'Aye, aye, sir,' said the parrots. And two green blurs disappeared high into the sky.

'I hope you realise,' mewed Malibu, who had been dragged along against his wishes by Sniffage and who was now padding along beside Adam with a distinctly hurt air, 'that some of us are missing winks in order to be here.'

Next to him, Simia snorted. 'Missing winks will be good for you, cat,' she said.

'Do you know how long it has taken me to get into a sleep pattern?' Malibu hissed. 'All this disturbance could send me back to insomnia.' And the cat shuddered as he recalled those dark days.

Adam had to ask. 'You,' he said incredulously, 'suffered from insomnia?'

Malibu nodded. 'Sometimes I'd sleep as few as eighteen hours in a day. It had a terrible effect on my eye–paw co-ordination. I need at least twenty-two to perform at my best – that's what my sleep therapist said.'

Simia was beside herself with anger. 'When there are animals suffering all over the world, you were going to a sleep therapist?'

'If I woke up in time,' the cat replied haughtily.

Adam was glad to see Sniffage charging towards him, a large stick in his mouth and his brown-and-white ears flapping wildly in the breeze. Hopefully his arrival would put an end to the argument.

'Yeah! Yeah!' announced Sniffage, dropping the stick. 'There's some really smelly dead things around here. And lots of sticks. It's great.'

'Sniffage!' said Adam sternly. 'I hope you didn't let yourself get distracted by the dead things and the sticks.'

'Yeah! Yeah! Distracted from what?'

Adam sighed. 'Distracted from finding out how many guards there were outside the wood.'

'Yeah! Yeah!' said Sniffage. 'There's four guards on the edge of the wood. They've got guns but no sticks. And none of them is dead. Yeah!'

'Thank you, Sniffage,' said Adam.

Sausage, who had been scouting with Sniffage but had been delayed in returning on account of his little legs, finally arrived.

'Yeah! Yeah! Look at this stick,' Sniffage said to him. 'Quality workmanship.'

Sausage examined the stick.

'You don't get sticks like that any more,' he agreed.

And both dogs were lost in thought as they remembered being puppies, when sticks were solid and the smells were nastier.

Two green blurs shooting out of the sky signalled the return of the parrots.

'I say, I say, I say,' chirped Gogo. 'What sits in a tree and watches the ground?'

'A parrot with a broken television.'

'No, a guard with a gun.'

'How many did you see?' asked Adam. 'There were four in the trees last time, and they were all deaf.'

The two parrots nodded. 'That would explain why they didn't laugh at our jokes.'

Not necessarily, thought Adam.

Anna had been watching the exchange between Adam and the parrots with increasing agitation. Now she signed to Adam that he needed to hurry up.

'Was there any other sign the guards couldn't hear you?' he asked the parrots.

'They didn't turn round when we squawked right behind them.'

This was good enough for Adam. Gogo and Pozzo had the loudest squawks he'd ever heard. He turned to Anna.

'There are four guards at the edge of the wood and another four in the trees around the clearing where the entrance to Scabellax's base is.

'How do we get past them?' signed Anna.

It was a good question. Adam didn't think they could use the army ants again, because the guards would be expecting . . .

He stopped himself. Of course. Had the guards been defeated by humans, they'd have made sure they were better prepared for another assault by the same method, so the next time they would defeat their enemy. But the guards were overpowered by animals. They would assume that it was just bad luck, that it could never happen again, that lightning wouldn't strike twice – because it would never occur to them that the first attack had been planned. Humans thought that only other humans could plan. Adam knew this wasn't the case. Maybe he could use the guards' arrogance against them.

He put the white box that contained the Special Ant Service on the ground. The troops, led by General Lepti, marched out and formed themselves in serried ranks. Adam wasn't sure, but he thought he remembered the squad being bigger. The General saluted.

'General Lepti,' Adam signalled, 'I need you to take out four guards at the edge of the wood.'

The General scratched his thorax.

'Four,' he repeated.

'Yes,' Adam signalled.

'Hmm.'

Adam couldn't believe it. He had never known the Special Ant Service to pause before embarking on a mission.

'Trouble is,' signalled General Lepti, 'more than half the troops are down with leaf poisoning. Still back at the boat. Down to bare bones here. Skeleton staff. To take out four guards I'd need a minimum of one thousand active ants. Any less and I'd be sending my men to face certain death. No commander can do that.'

'How many ants have you got?' signalled Adam. He couldn't believe that his plan wasn't going to work.

'Nine hundred and ninety-nine precisely,' reported the General.

'Is one more *that* important?' Adam asked.

'It is crucial in order to maintain our attack and defence formations,' said General Lepti.

It was at this moment Private Mandible emerged from Adam's pocket to see what was going on. Adam breathed a sigh of relief and smiled.

'You need one more army ant to carry out the mission,' he told General Lepti. 'You are an army ant,' he told Private Mandible. 'Can you see a solution to the problem here?'

Both ants shook their legs to indicate they didn't. Adam explained.

'Have a damned conchie in my ranks?' General Lepti's legs waved furiously. 'Impossible.'

'Ditch my moral objections to violent solutions which can never work in the longterm and inevitably lead only to further violence?' signalled Private Mandible. 'Never.'

Even with six legs this took quite a lot of time to say.

It was clear that they were at an impasse. Adam could think of no way to break it. However, Anna, who had been following the exchange, had a very simple idea. She approached the Special Ant Service, who were still standing in their serried ranks and picked up an ant at random. She held it out in the palm of her hand for both General Lepti and Private Mandible to see. Then she raised her other hand and indicated that she was about to squash it.

'Stop!' signalled General Lepti and Private Mandible at the same time.

Anna stopped and waited.

'This is blackmail, pure and simple,' the General fulminated. 'You're threatening that if I don't allow Private Mandible to rejoin the SAS, then you will squash one of my own soldiers.'

'And,' added Private Mandible waving his legs extravagantly to show his distress (sadly this kind of exaggerated waving meant nothing to Anna – the subtle nuances of insect communication were lost on her), 'you're saying that if I don't rejoin the SAS and risk taking part in further acts of violence, then I will be partly responsible for the death of a former comrade.'

Anna nodded calmly.

'I . . . I . . . I . . .' General Lepti was lost for legs.

Anna began to lower her hand towards the helpless ant. Army ants are very dangerous when working together, but when one is isolated from his fellow soldiers he is tremendously vulnerable. Her hands got closer and closer together. Any moment now they would clamp shut.

'Stop!' signalled General Lepti and Private Mandible, exposing their thoraxes to indicate surrender. 'We agree!'

Anna placed the soldier ant back with his platoon.

General Lepti decided to welcome his erstwhile comrade back into the platoon in true military fashion.

'Private Mandible,' he commanded furiously, 'I demand to know what you are doing out of the ranks.'

'I –' began Private Mandible.

'Don't answer, you horrible little ant,' interrupted General Lepti. 'Rejoin the platoon immediately. Hop, two, three, four, five, six.'

So Private Mandible became the first ever pacifist army ant to return to active service.

'You wouldn't really have squashed one of the SAS, would you?' Adam asked Anna.

She winked.

Adam decided the wink meant no. It made him feel better. But he didn't know how long the uneasy truce would last. He resolved to get the assault under way immediately.

'General Lepti, commence the attack,' he ordered. 'When you have finished, return to the *Ark of the Parabola* and we will rendezvous with you there.'

'Yessir!' signalled General Lepti. 'Special Ant Service, forward!'

The ants marched off to battle. Adam, Anna, the

Arkonauts and the other dogs sneaked up to the position where, only a few days before, Adam had crouched with the Doctor.

Again the guards were vigilant. Again the guards were armed and dangerous. And again they were no match for the Special Ant Service.

'Aiieeeeee!'

'Owwwww!'

'Yaaaaaaaa!'

'Aiieeeeeee!'

Frantically trying to fight off the army ants, the guards ran back and forth, little realising that they were running into General Lepti's reserves. More and more ants swarmed up their legs and over their bodies. They ran for their lives. The way into the woods was clear.

But Simia was not about to let anybody go in yet.

'If I let a human like you in,' she chattered to Adam, 'you would mess everything up, clumping about on the ground with your oh-so-well-evolved upright walking. This is a job for a creature who had the good sense to stay in the trees. Wait here until I return.'

'But I can't let you go on your own,' Adam protested. 'They've got guns.'

'If you said they had tails I might be nervous,' Simia shot back. 'Tails are useful in the trees. But you humans had to get rid of yours. And as for guns. Tch! I'll have knocked them unconscious before they even know I'm there.'

Without allowing Adam another word, Simia headed towards the wood, clambered expertly up the first tree she came to and disappeared into the canopy.

Adam looked at Anna questioningly. Did she think Simia would be all right? Had he done the right thing in not going with the monkey? The girl shrugged in reply. They would have to wait and see.

Adam looked up at the sky. It felt like the day had lasted for ever, but it was only mid-afternoon. The sun still beat down mercilessly upon them and its heat showed no sign of waning. Knowing that they had to wait, Adam and the other Arkonauts tried to search out some cooling shade, but the power of the Buenos Sueños sun was so strong that they could find very little respite.

So it was to a dry and thirsty group that Simia returned less than half an hour later. The monkey dropped calmly out of a tree and loped leisurely over to Adam.

'Tch Tch!' she said. 'I don't think they'll be doing any more evolving for at least a couple of hours.'

'Excellent.' Adam turned to Sniffage. 'Go and get Calico Jack and the others. We're ready for the final assault.'

CHAPTER 31

The last time Adam had stood where he was now, he had witnessed the Doctor's capture by Professor Scabellax. He remembered that awful feeling of shock and helplessness, and, above all, the loneliness that had engulfed him when he had seen the Doctor disappear into the base of his sworn enemy. But this time the echoes of those feelings were mixed with hope as he watched Calico Jack, who seemed to be getting younger by the minute, scurry back from the hatch that led into Professor Scabellax's base.

'It's not good, I'm afraid, young 'un,' he said.

Crouched next to Adam, Anna also waited for the answer. Next to Anna, Malibu was much less interested and demonstrated this by sleeping. Alongside the cat were Sniffage and Sausage. Simia kept watch in the trees overhead. The other dogs and the prisoners had fanned out around the edge of the circular clearing.

'It's made of unbreakable glass, and there's a guard posted underneath.'

'Do you mean we're going to have to knock?'

'Knock,' sneered Calico Jack. 'Knock, young 'un? That'll give away the element of surprise.'

'I can't think of anything else. Can you?'

Calico Jack had to acknowledge that he couldn't.

They all looked at each other with grim expressions. They had come so far, but it would all be for nothing if they couldn't save the city and rescue Adam's parents. They racked their brains, desperately searching for a solution. While they were doing this, Malibu woke up.

'Hey, did someone die? What's with the long faces?' he mewed.

'Nothing that would bother you,' said Adam, suddenly angry. 'You only worry about yourself and your sleep.'

Malibu was most put out by this.

'I am a very giving cat,' he yowled casually at Adam. 'My therapist said that's why I get so tired.'

'Huh,' said Adam. 'If you're so giving, why don't you give us a hand getting into the base?'

'Why don'tcha just open the door?'

Adam could hardly contain his anger. 'Because it's shut and locked from below. And the glass is the thickest in the world, so we can't break in. That's why we can't just open the door. And you'd have known all that if you hadn't been asleep.'

Malibu was impervious to Adam's anger. 'Did ya say glass?' he said.

Adam nodded angrily. 'You know I did.'

'And does that mean that a guard could look up and out of the base through the door.'

'You know it does.'

'I don't know what all the fuss is about,' purred Malibu. 'This should be sooooo easy.'

'What do you mean, easy?'

'Do you know what my final great role was?'

Adam could feel himself going red. 'I don't want to talk about your stupid film career!'

'I played "limping cat" in the latest Harry Potter movie. The critics said that I brought a previously unseen feline poignancy to the screen.'

'I'm not going to talk to you any more. All you think about is yourself.'

'As Daniel said, "Nobody can resist a cute cat with a limp."'

'I don't –'

'Just be ready, kiddo,' yowled Malibu. 'When I bite the hand that feeds me, it's your signal to go.'

'What do you mean?'

But Malibu wasn't talking any more. Instead, he limped gingerly out from the cover of the trees and dragged himself painfully across the clearing towards the entrance to Scabellax's base. Watching him struggle so convincingly while knowing for a fact there was nothing at all wrong with him, Adam had to admit the cat was good.

But how was being good at limping going to help them get into Scabellax's base?

'What's it doing?' demanded Calico Jack, who had witnessed the exchange between Adam and Malibu but had, of course, understood none of it.

'Er . . . acting,' said Adam.

'Cats can act?'

'Tch!' chattered Simia from her vantage point in the trees just above them. 'That's all they can do.'

Meanwhile, Malibu had reached the entrance to the base. And as he reached it his strength seemed to fail. He collapsed heavily on the thick glass portal. Then he stood up. But his injured leg wouldn't hold him and he sat down with a bump once more.

He paused for a second, trying to recover. And as he did, he looked around him nervously. Anyone watching would have seen an injured cat terrified of being so exposed and vulnerable to predators. And so it seemed with fear spurring him on, Malibu lifted his exhausted frame and, one final time, tried to limp on. But it was to no avail. With a pitiful miaow, he fell heavily back on the portal again.

It was a performance so moving that, despite his previous anger with the cat, Adam half wanted to rush over and help Malibu. But it was a good thing he didn't, because the portal door began to rise. Malibu, seemingly on the verge of death, slipped uncomfortably off it and into the grass. A black-clad guard clambered out of the hatch. In one hand he held a gun. In the other he held a saucer of milk.

'Here, kitty, kitty, kitty,' he said.

Malibu looked frightened. Using all his remaining strength, he stood up and limped pitifully away from the guard.

'He's limping on a different foot,' whispered Calico Jack.

The guard didn't notice.

'Here, kitty, kitty,' he said. 'You don't need to be afraid of me.'

Malibu stopped for a moment and turned back. The cat's eyes were as big as saucers and they seemed on the very verge of trusting the guard. But at the last moment, doubt seemed to enter his mind and he turned away again and continued his pathetic limp towards the edge of the clearing.

'No, no, kitty, don't go,' said the guard, following Malibu slowly, trying desperately not to spook him. He had left the portal door open. 'I've got milk. Nice tasty milk. Make you better. Make you strong.'

Malibu was almost at the edge of the clearing now. Suddenly it appeared that he was swayed by the soothing tone of the guard. He turned round.

'Miaow!'

'Here, kitty, kitty.'

'Miaow!'

This second miaow was so piteous that Adam was tempted to run out and give Malibu some milk himself. The guard shook his head.

'So you won't come to me, will you? You are a difficult cat. Well, then I suppose I must come to you. Now don't be scared.'

The guard tiptoed up to Malibu. He was right on the edge

of the clearing now and so close that Adam decided to stop breathing as a precaution. He hoped Malibu acted soon, because this was not a plan that was feasible in the longterm.

Meanwhile, the guard bent over and set down the saucer of milk. Malibu looked at it for a second and then looked up at the guard.

'Drink the milk, kitty,' he said, pointing at it with his finger.

Finally Malibu seemed to understand. He limped the couple of steps to the saucer.

'Good, kitty, good . . .'

And sank his teeth into the guard's finger.

'Aiiiieeeeee!'

Blood poured out of the wound. The guard reached for his pistol with one hand, while trying to shake himself free of Malibu with the other. But Malibu refused to let go.

'Stupid ungrateful moggy!' shouted the guard. 'Let's see how you like being shot.'

Adam realised he'd been so entranced by Malibu's performance that he'd forgotten to react to the cat's signal. He jumped to his feet, seconds too late. Despite his pain, the guard had still managed to train his gun on Malibu. All that remained was for him to pull the trigger.

A figure leapt out of the branches above Adam.

Simia whizzed through the air, crashed down on the guard's shoulders and immediately clamped her hands over his eyes.

'I'm blind,' shouted the guard, stumbling backwards.

Adam, Anna and Calico Jack charged towards him. Close behind them was Sniffage. A little behind Sniffage was Sausage. They tackled the guard together. He tumbled to the ground and, with an expert blow, Calico Jack left him unconscious.

Simia relaxed her grip on the guard's head.

'Tch!' she chattered. 'Try to be a bit faster next time, humans. All that evolution has really slowed you down.'

At the same time, Malibu let go of the guard's finger.

'That was amazing, Malibu,' said Adam.

But the cat seemed far from happy.

'My greatest ever performance,' he yowled despairingly, 'and not a camera in sight.'

'We've no time for this,' said Calico Jack. 'We've got to get inside the base before another guard finds out that the hatch is open.'

Adam felt a rallying cry was appropriate

'Arkonauts, dogs and ex-convicts,' he cried, 'let us defeat Professor Scabellax!'

From every side of the clearing emerged prisoners and dogs. Behind Adam were Anna, Calico Jack, Sniffage, Malibu, Simia and Sausage. Above them swooped Gogo, Pozzo and Vlad.

They converged upon the hatch, not knowing what lay inside waiting for them.

CHAPTER 32

A dam reached the bottom of the steps and took in the awesome sight. He was on a walkway high above a vast cavern of shining black metal which had been carved out of the mountain. It hummed with activity. Computers and other highly complex machines flashed and flickered as they performed all kinds of diabolical calculations. At the far end, underneath a huge screen, diligently monitoring the readings and printouts, were technicians wearing pristine white lab coats and carrying smaller notepad computers. Patrolling menacingly around them were black-clad guards with guns slung loosely from their waists. But none of these sights held Adam's attention for long. Instead, his eye was drawn to one figure standing rigidly straight and unmoving in this hive of activity.

The Doctor.

His face was stretched into a rictus of agony.

Adam couldn't understand it. There appeared to be nothing surrounding him and none of the guards was paying him any attention, but still he did not move. And yet it seemed as though the effort of staying perfectly still was the cause of his awful discomfort.

Behind him, Anna, Calico Jack, the Arkonauts, the dogs and prisoners were dropping down as silently as possible on to the high walkway.

'Scabellaxians!'

A terrible voice echoed round the chamber. Immediately every guard and every technician stopped what they were doing to listen. Adam tensed. Had they been seen?

'Scabellaxians, I, your leader, Professor Silus Scabellax, address you.'

Desperately, Adam scanned the cavern. Where was Scabellax? Where was . . . There!

A man wearing a neat brown suit, sporting a monocle and holding a gold walking cane stood speaking on a small raised podium. Adam could not see a microphone, but there had to be one somewhere because his voice boomed out across the cavern.

'Scabellaxians, know that the moment we have waited for is upon us. Today we complete the process that will lead us, ultimately, to rule over the entire world. My research into sound enabled me to create the perfect noise which, when played for the right time at the right frequency, eventually destroys the free will of humans. Today, in Buenos Sueños, we will see the culmination of this process for the first time. Soon every city in every country will fall to us. And then, thanks to the information which Doctor Forest is on the verge of providing us with, we will be able to control the animals too. I will be the first leader to have dominion over man and beast! But, fellow Scabellaxians, I will not stop there. After that I go after the plants. Soon every living thing will bow before me. I . . .'

Adam was listening, open-mouthed, to this terrible plan. Scabellax wanted to control the entire world. Every human, every animal, even every plant. He had to be stopped. He had to –

'INTRUDERS!'

Too late did Adam look up. Too late did he notice the little metal ball hovering above him, and inside that little ball, a camera lens. They had been spotted.

WOOWOOWOOWOO

All around him a siren sounded. The cavern flashed red, and then black, red, and then black. Adam cowered back. It was as though the cave itself had suddenly come to life. But there was no point in trying to hide now, for on the screen at the other end of the cavern, blown up to fifty times his normal size, he saw himself.

And so did every black-clad guard in the cavern.

And so did Professor Scabellax. The element of surprise was lost.

'Kill the intruders!' he bellowed. 'Show no mercy!'

WOOWOOWOOWOO

The siren pulsated around them. The walls flashed black

264

and red. Adam looked at the centre of the cavern. Despite everything that was happening, still the Doctor didn't move.

BANG!

The first guard took aim and fired at Adam, the bullet twanging off the metal walkway.

'Attack!' shouted Adam.

There were two sets of stairs that ran down into the main body of the cave. Half the prisoners headed towards one and half to the other, bullets peppering them as they ran.

'Ahhhhhh!'

The first ex-convict was hit. He staggered once, then tumbled off the walkway and plummeted to the ground. His body lay in a heap on the floor. It didn't move again.

The gunfire from the guards was relentless. Two more ex-prisoners were blown from the walkway. Adam and his companions were nothing but moving targets. With no weapons of their own, they had no way of defending themselves. Somehow they had to get down into the main body of the hall and come to grips with Scabellax's forces, hand to hand. But the closer they came to the guards, the greater the chance of being shot. It would take a brave person to be first down the stairs that led from the walkway.

It was Anna.

The dark-haired girl knew no fear. Ignoring the bullets that exploded all around her, ignoring another prisoner who was blown off the walkway behind her, she ran for the black metal stairway. Below, the tramp of the guards echoed as they rushed to take up their positions.

Adam ran after her.

Bullets flew in front of him, behind him, above him. He kept running. His luck couldn't hold. Any moment now one would find its mark. Ahead of him, another ex-prisoner ran out of luck, falling silently from the walkway, flopping dead on the ground below. Adam saw Anna reach the stairs. She took them two at time, but Adam also saw two guards at the bottom with their weapons trained upon her. However fast she moved, the closer she came the easier she was to hit. Adam wondered if his friend was about to die. The guards prepared to pull their triggers. Any . . . moment . . .

Two green blurs flew directly into their faces. Gogo and Pozzo swooped to the rescue.

'Woah!' shouted one guard.

'Arrggh!' shouted the other, as he received a vicious peck in the cheek from Pozzo.

Their guns were a hindrance rather than a help when they tried to deal with the attacking parrots. A bird flapping and fluttering and pecking at your face is best fended off with a hand. The butt of a gun is clumsy and useless. It was almost as though the animals were using the weapons against the men. The guards didn't know whether to drop their guns or not, and this hesitation proved their undoing.

Anna sprang off the stairs alive and well, as did Sniffage and the other dogs (save for Sausage, whose little legs were yet again slowing him down). The guards had been trained to pick off humans, but dogs moved faster and stood lower, and they had proved much more difficult to hit. Every one of them reached the floor of the great cavern alive and ready to bite.

'Kill them,' shouted Scabellax. 'Show no mercy!'

But now his guards were attacked from below by the dogs and from above by Gogo and Pozzo. The parrots were joined by Vlad, who came to life in the dark cavern. While Gogo and Pozzo distracted guards by flapping and pecking at their faces, the vampire bat swooped in behind, silent and unseen, and sank his fangs deep into their necks.

And hanging from the walkway, her arms stronger than any human's, was Simia. The monkey spotted a guard train his gun at Adam. She swung towards him and dropped down. The guard never knew what hit him. His weapon clattered to the floor. Unaware of his narrow escape, Adam dashed towards Anna, who was showing her normal crazy zeal for the fight by grappling with a guard three times her size. Nobody could doubt the strength of the dark girl's heart, but nevertheless she would soon be overpowered.

Adam rushed to her aid but, again, the Arkonauts were there before him. Pozzo flashed into the guard's face. Vlad sank his fangs into his neck. Sniffage bit his calf. And, finally, even Malibu discovered enough energy to spring from the walkway and sink his claws into the guard's back.

All around the cavern, others were suffering the same fate. The animals may not have been trained as a team, but their different methods of attack complemented each other perfectly. If a guard managed to fight off a dog, a parrot or bat flew into his face, giving the dog or monkey or even a human the chance to attack him once more. The guards were bewildered by the numerous types of assault. Their guns felt useless.

'Fight,' ordered Scabellax. 'Fight!'

But all the fight was gone from the guards. They were confused and overwhelmed, and fled down the dark passages leading out of the cavern. The technicians, terrified at seeing the guards so efficiently defeated, did not even attempt to put up a fight. They fled too. Soon the passages echoed to the panicked cries of Scabellax's henchmen.

Only one man remained: Professor Scabellax himself.

He stood by a bank of computer monitors, whose lights flashed red, blue and green as they continued to perform all manner of evil calculations. The Professor watched his own guards crumble under the assault without a flicker of emotion, save perhaps a slight sneer of contempt. He had the air of a man who had seen it all before.

'Congratulations,' his voice boomed around the chamber. 'It appears that you have defeated my foolish guards and scared off my cowardly technicians. You must be very proud of yourselves. What a shame that all your hard work and the loss of so many of your comrades has, nevertheless, turned out to be in vain.'

Sarcasm dripped from every word.

Adam looked around and registered the full sacrifice that had been required to defeat the guards. Apart from himself, Anna, Calico Jack and Fidel, all the ex-prisoners had been shot. Their bodies littered the walkways, the stairwells and the main body of the cave. Their taste of freedom had been brief. They had been mercilessly mowed down. Adam was furious. And he wasn't the only one.

'So we finally come face to face Scabellax,' Calico Jack said coldly. 'I'm waiting to hear you surrender.' He picked up a gun that had been dropped by one of the fleeing guards and walked towards the Professor.

Scabellax smiled.

'That, my dear sir, is the one outcome that I can assure you is *not* going to happen.'

'You think so, do you, Scabellax?' said Calico Jack. 'Well, let's see if me and a few of my animal friends can't change your mind.'

'No.'

But it was not Professor Scabellax who protested, it was Adam. He was looking at the Doctor and he could tell something was very wrong. Even though all the guards had now fled, the Doctor still hadn't moved a millimetre and continued to stand rigid in agony. Adam didn't understand it at all.

'What's the matter, Doctor?' he said. 'We've rescued you. The guards are gone.'

The Doctor didn't move.

'Ah, yes.' Scabellax's voice boomed through the cavern. 'I

think you might have some difficulty chatting with Doctor Forest. You see, he is imprisoned by a rather amusing little device. I'm rather proud of it – the Electronic Self-Generating Lethal-Strength Figure-Hugging Force Field!'

'What are you talking about?' demanded Adam. He wanted more than anything to see the Doctor move again. Looking at him was like looking at a living corpse.

Entirely unruffled, Scabellax leant casually against the bank of computers.

'Please don't speak to me in that way,' he said. 'I do so despise rudeness, especially in the young.'

Adam was at a loss. They had won and yet Professor Scabellax, whom they had defeated, appeared totally unconcerned, whereas the Doctor, who had been rescued, was still trapped. This wasn't how it was supposed to work out at all. With a tremendous effort, Adam controlled himself.

'If you wouldn't mind explaining it to me,' he said to Professor Scabellax, 'I'd be very interested to know more about this force field.'

'You see,' said Professor Scabellax, tapping his cane approvingly, 'politeness costs nothing and gains so much.'

Adam fumed inwardly.

'The Electronic Self-Generating Lethal-Strength Figure-Hugging Force Field is most ingenious,' said Professor Scabellax pompously. 'I invented it . . . Well, when I say *invented* it, I obviously mean I stole the idea from a superb Slovenian physicist who was sadly murdered soon afterwards

– I suppose I'll have to collect the Nobel Prize for him. What happens is that when the subject stands upon the platform, the force field immediately generates around his body shape. Any further movement by the subject will lead to him breaking the force field and receiving a lethal electric shock. The only option, therefore, for the subject who wishes to stay alive is to remain totally still. Any significant movement whatsoever will result in his immediate death. Really very, very clever, wouldn't you agree?'

Adam looked at the Doctor in horror. No wonder he was in agony. How long had he been standing like that, without moving?

'You've got to let the Doctor go,' he said.

'Oh, I don't think that's going to happen,' said Professor Scabellax. 'You see, then you might decide to turn off the Great Booming Sonic Mind-Control Procedure, which is programmed to go off again in . . .' Scabellax glanced at a digital counter on the bank of computers behind him, '. . . exactly eight minutes and thirty-two seconds, and then where would we be? I'm actually rather grateful to you for chasing off my guards and technicians. They'd done all the work I required of them and I only would have had to kill them myself.'

'What is the Great Booming Sonic Mind-Control Procedure?' demanded Adam.

'You would know it as "the Dreadful Alarm",' said Professor Scabellax. 'Not a very scientific name, and one I'm,

frankly, not very happy with. It's very simple. I invented –
oops, there I go again. I *borrowed* the invention from a group
of Finnish scientists who had been working on sound waves
in Helsinki. It appears that if you regularly play a certain
sound at a certain frequency for a certain length of time to
people, then you can destroy their free will for ever, particularly if those people are already under significant duress. It
really is fabulous. I was so impressed with the scientists' work
that I almost didn't kill them.'

'Almost?' said Adam.

'Let's not get too sentimental here,' said Scabellax.

'So that's why you've been trying to prevent the Mayor
from abolishing the Crime and Punishment Code – to soften
up the brains of the citizens so you can use the Dreadful
Alarm to destroy their free will.'

'Ten out of ten,' said Scabellax with an approving tap of
the cane. 'You see, I have known about Buenos Sueños for a
long time. Its idiosyncrasies made it the perfect testing
ground for my research into mind control. Even better still,
two of its stupider citizens – Chief Grivas and Felipe Felipez
– were more than willing to help me achieve my goal.

'A few years ago, I – or should I say, a friend of mine –
convinced Grivas to introduce his zero-tolerance system of
law, which destroyed the lives of the citizens by making them
all criminals in huge debt. So mentally weakened were they by
this regime, I was encouraged to implement the next stage of
my plan: the physical assault on their senses. When elections

were called and the Mayor threatened to abolish the Code as part of his new mandate, my, er, friend gave Felipez the funds to stand against him, together with a guarantee that he would stop the so-called "Dreadful Alarm", providing the Code remained in place. Felipez and Grivas have unwittingly provided the Mayor with enough distractions and obstructions to allow me to see through my experiments with the Great Booming Sonic Mind-Control Procedure, refining and perfecting the technique. It was easy to persuade Grivas to declare martial law as an insurance policy against any attempted meddling by the Mayor when I was so close to success.'

'Anyway, thanks to the rapid progress of my sonic experiment, the outcome of the elections is now utterly irrelevant. The test with the "Hokey Cokey" demonstrated that the citizens have lost their free will, though it is not yet a permanent state. One last extra-special session of the "Dreadful Alarm" should ensure that the effect becomes irreversible.'

'I don't understand,' said Adam.

'Of course you don't,' said the Professor. 'You are a mere boy and cannot think on the grand scale that I do.'

'But what's so important about being powerful in a small city like Buenos Sueños?'

Scabellax sighed. 'You really are a dimwit, aren't you, boy? My experiment was never about ruling Buenos Sueños. I couldn't care less for this isolated little excrescence. It was about ensuring beyond all doubt that my procedure would be one hundred per cent successful, that power gained by the Great Booming Sonic Mind-Control Procedure can never be lost again. I want to show that I can order the citizens to do anything I choose.'

'Why?' said Adam.

'Remember, I am a scientist,' the Professor replied. 'It is not enough that one believes something will work; it must be tested with rigour.'

'I think you're crazy,' said Adam boldly.

'Of course you do,' Scabellax replied. 'And in the centuries to come, who will know of your insignificant little opinion? Nobody. But the words and deeds of Scabellax will last for ever. Then we will know who is crazy and who is nothing.'

The Professor smashed his stick dramatically against the floor as he spoke. After such a speech, Adam half expected fireballs to explode all around him. But in fact there was only a rather tinny echo. Scabellax glanced at the countdown clock. It showed seven minutes and thirty seconds. He chuckled.

'What are you going to do?' Adam asked. 'What is going to happen?'

'Have you ever thought about lemmings?' said Scabellax.

'Lemmings?'

'Fascinating creatures,' the Professor went on. 'For no reason at all they occasionally join together to throw themselves off cliffs and plunge to their deaths. Remarkable.'

'I don't under—'

Adam stopped. He'd just realised what the Professor was getting at. And it was a horrible thought.

Scabellax read the look on Adam's face.

'I see that you appreciate the power of the idea. The sound will be played one final time, louder and more piercing than ever before, and then the citizens of Buenos Sueños will be ordered to gather together in one large group, run down to the harbour and throw themselves into the sea. Drowning themselves is a suitable action with which to test the success of my experiment, because it is unquestionably against their best interests.'

'But . . . but . . . but . . .' Adam protested – he was rendered almost speechless by this monstrous proposal.

'There are no buts,' said Scabellax. 'It is perfect.'

The counter clock clicked down to seven minutes.

'But what about the people?' Adam blurted out.

'They will have died for the greater good of science,' said Scabellax.

'No,' said Adam, realising that reasoning with Scabellax like he was a human being was useless. He had to appeal to his vanity. 'What I mean is, if the citizens are dead, then there'll be nobody for you to have power over.'

Scabellax clicked his fingers dismissively.

'What is one small city?' he said. 'Once I have proved that the Great Booming Sonic Mind-Control Procedure works, I can take over the world. There are more than enough people on the planet for me to control. I can spare one tiny city.'

'But you're not sparing them. You're killing them.'

Scabellax tutted angrily.

'This conversation is rapidly becoming tedious,' he said. 'And I have little time if I am to travel to Buenos Sueños and watch the results of my experiment at first hand.'

Adam couldn't believe that Scabellax, with all his technicians and guards gone, could still seem so confident.

'What if we were to smash every single one of these machines now?' he said.

'You'd probably make a mess,' answered Scabellax calmly.

'But it would stop you, wouldn't it?'

'I'm afraid not. The launch codes have been fed into the computer. Only an expert who has had access to all the preparations and who has a precise knowledge of the initiation sequence could possibly manage it.'

'Someone like you,' suggested Adam.

Scabellax stroked his chin.

'Oh, dear me, no,' he said. 'I, you see, am responsible for the big picture, the overview. The little details I leave to others. I simply give them suitable incentives, like threatening to kill them and everyone they know if they don't do precisely what I require. It seems to do the trick. In truth, I could no more halt the procedure than you could.'

There was something about Scabellax's calmness that convinced Adam he was telling the truth. And he remembered that the Doctor had always said that what had sent

Scabellax mad was his lack of ability as a scientist. He was good, but not quite good enough. Someone else would have to stop this, but who?

'If it would help,' said Scabellax, reading his mind, 'and I do like to be helpful, I will inform you that the only person who could have reversed the procedure was one of the white-coated lab technicians you rather foolishly chased down one of the tunnels. The salvation of Buenos Sueños is no doubt lost deep inside the mountain. Still –' Scabellax glanced at the counter – 'you have five minutes forty-seven seconds to find him. Of course, it is hopeless. But I do find that even when they've been beaten, people do like to keep themselves busy in the final moments before the reality of their defeat becomes clear, so do please amuse yourselves. But, rude as it may be, you will now have to excuse me. I have to witness the destruction of the free will of the people of Buenos Sueños.'

'You're not –'

'Oh,' added Professor Scabellax, almost as an after-thought. 'You may also be interested to know that your mother –'

'Where is she?' interrupted Adam.

'She's quite safe for the time being,' said Scabellax. 'I keep her away from here. I didn't want her seeing things. But as I was saying before you interrupted me, her free will is going too. I had hoped to avoid that, but it has become necessary. For years she has refused my – how shall I put it delicately?

277

– my . . . er . . . *advances*, no matter what I promised. Luxury, wealth – everything you could imagine I offered her, if she would only consent to bestow her love on me. But all she ever said was, "Take me back to my husband and son." And, frankly, her answer has become tiresome. Therefore, I have resolved to remove her free will and her objections all in one.'

Adam felt himself choking with rage. To take his own mother from him for ever? Adam wanted to kill the Professor with his own bare hands.

'So if you'll excuse me . . .'

Adam couldn't believe that this monster actually believed Adam would be willing to let him go.

'You're staying here,' he commanded. 'If we can't stop anything else, then we'll stop this. I'll never let you see my mother again.'

'How very protective you are,' said Scabellax with an indulgent leer. 'But, of course, you are correct. I'm so used to everybody doing exactly what I say, when I say it, that I had completely forgotten that you are in control here. Well, I suppose I'll have to get used to it. I'll just sit down over here and wait to see what else you do.'

Resting heavily on his cane, Scabellax walked over to a chair and sat down.

Adam turned helplessly to Anna and Calico Jack.

'Does anybody remember which tunnels the technicians went down?'

Anna shrugged hopelessly and pointed at all of them.

'I –' began Adam.

BOOM!

There was a loud explosion behind him. Adam turned round to see Professor Scabellax shooting up towards the roof of the cave in his chair.

'An ejector seat!' cried Calico Jack.

And above them, the ceiling was opening.

Professor Scabellax gave a dismissive wave.

'Adieu, my little friend,' he called to Adam. 'I will send your regards to your mother, though of course she won't know who you are.'

'Stop him!' shouted Adam desperately.

But it was a futile cry. Before anybody could react, the ejector seat had shot through the gap in the ceiling. Adam saw that a tiny turbo-powered jetpack was attached to the back of it. Scabellax fired it up as he rose. He would be able to go straight to Buenos Sueños. The ceiling shut smoothly behind him.

The counter was down to three minutes.

'We've got to stop the procedure,' cried Adam.

But how?

Scabellax and the technician were gone. And Scabellax had said that only a scientist who had witnessed the entire process could possibly reverse the procedure. And there were no . . .

'The Doctor!'

The Doctor had been standing in that very room for

Scabellax's amusement the whole time.

'He couldn't possibly remember,' said Calico Jack. 'He's done well simply not to move for three days. Almost anyone else would have buckled and died. He couldn't possibly have memorised the initiation sequence too.'

But Adam knew that if anybody had the willpower and memory to do it, it was his father.

Two and a half minutes.

'We've got to get him out.'

Anna waved her hands helplessly.

'He's stuck behind an Electrical Self-Generating Lethal-Strength Figure-Hugging Force Field. Even if he does know, we can't free him.'

There must be a way, thought Adam. *Think like a scientist.* Was there anything in the name that might give him a hint?

A light bulb went on his head. It gave him an idea.

Electrical.

Perhaps when the Professor said that the force field was self-generating, he meant that its shape was self-generating, not the power that ran it. If that was true, then the electricity had to come from somewhere.

'The plugs! shouted Adam. 'Switch off all the plugs! Now!'

Adam, Anna, Calico Jack, Fidel and the animals rushed to the sides of the cave. Frantically, they switched off any the plugs they could find – some with their fingers, some with their noses, some even with their wings. Fifty plugs were turned off in a minute.

The cave was plunged into darkness.

'Doctor,' cried Adam, 'get off the platform.'

They all waited in dread for the sudden frazzle that would indicate the power source was still present and the Doctor was being electrocuted.

There was a cry.

Adam froze.

'I appear to have fallen over,' said the Doctor. 'Could someone put the lights back on, please?'

He was alive!

Fingers, noses, wings pushed. The cave flickered back into light. Lying on the floor in the centre of the room was the Doctor.

The launch counter clicked below two minutes.

'Doctor!' shouted Adam. 'You're safe!'

Sniffage barked, Malibu miaowed, Simia chattered, Gogo and Pozzo screeched, all in delight.

'There's no time for that,' said the Doctor. 'My legs have failed me – I can't get up. You're going to have to get me to the main computer terminal.'

Adam and the others rushed over to the Doctor, lifted him up and dragged him across the cave. He slumped on the chair.

The counter clicked under one minute.

'Do you remember the initiation sequence?' asked Adam.

The Doctor nodded. He tried to raise his hands to press the keys. But, after the tremendous effort of not moving for three days, his arms had cramped up so severely that, like his legs, they were beyond his control.

The counter clicked under thirty seconds.

'I can't do it,' said the Doctor.

'Tell me,' said Adam.

The Doctor looked at the different coloured keys and closed his eyes and concentrated on reversing it in his mind.

'Blue.'

Adam hit the blue key.

'Green, yellow, yellow, red.'

Adam hit the four keys fast.

Fifteen seconds.

'Blue, green, red, yellow.'

Ten seconds.

Adam's hands flew over the keys.

Nine.

'Er . . .' said the Doctor.

Eight.

'Unfortunately someone crossed my line of sight for the last one.'

Seven.

Silence.

Six.

'You mean . . .'

Five.

'You're going to have to guess, Adam.'

Four.

Adam looked frantically at the four colours.

Three.

One attempt. The lives of everybody depended on him.

Two.

If in doubt, pick your favourite.

One.

Adam hit the red key.

One.

One.

One.

The counter had stopped.

'I would have gone for blue,' said the Doctor.

'I'm more of a green man,' said Calico Jack.

Anna pointed to the yellow.

'No,' said Adam confidently. 'Red is always the right answer.' But his brow told a different story. It was pouring with sweat. He pulled a handkerchief from his pocket to dab it dry.

Around him, the cave erupted in cheers, barks, miaows, chatters and cheeps.

But the Doctor was not cheering. He knew that although Buenos Sueños was safe, his wife was still in danger from Scabellax. When he found out that the Great Booming Sonic Mind-Control Procedure had been switched off, his anger would undoubtedly be terrible, and who knew what awful revenge he would wreak on Adam's mother?

'We've got to get back to the city! We've got to go to the . . .'

Then the Doctor stopped. He realised that they had absolutely no idea where in the city the Professor was hiding. Trying to locate Scabellax without some kind of clue would be like searching for a needle in a barn full of haystacks.

'Where can they be, Adam?'

Adam was caught a little unawares. To be truthful, he had not been thinking about the whereabouts of his mother. Instead, he had become distracted by his handkerchief, which felt coarse on his forehead and didn't seem to be doing a particularly good job of absorbing the sweat on his brow.

He pulled it from his face and looked at it. No wonder it hadn't worked. Instead of a handkerchief, he'd pulled a piece of paper from his pocket – the scrumpled-up register from the Hotel Dormir. It seemed so long ago they had taken it, even though in reality it was just a few days.

And little good it had done them: a list of names of total strangers like . . . Adam glanced down. Well, one of them wasn't a stranger: the man with the coffee on his trousers . . . Adam saw his name on the register.

Señor Xavier Le Blacas.

And next to him his abbreviated signature: *X. Le Blacas*.

Something went click in his mind. The letters seemed to swim in front of him and reform themselves as . . .

'Scabellax. Doctor! I've got it!'

'What?'

'I've found the double helix.'

'What are you talking about, Adam?'

'Scabellax is X. Le Blacas! It's an anagram.'

The Doctor couldn't believe it. 'But Professor Scabellax is clean-shaven and Le Blacas has a beard.'

'A false beard,' said Calico Jack, shocked to realise he had been fooled by the disguise of someone else for once.

'I always told you the answer would be simple,' said the Doctor. 'Just like the double helix.'

'The only problem with simple answers,' said Calico Jack. 'is they don't half leave you feeling stupid.'

Everything had happened so fast since the Doctor's release that it was only now that he realised that he didn't know who Calico Jack was.

'I don't believe I've had the pleasure of meeting you,' he said to the older man. 'Although something about you feels familiar.'

'Doctor,' said Adam excitedly, 'don't you remember? This is –'

'Why should he remember?' interrupted Calico Jack brusquely. 'We've never met before. My name is Calico Jack and Adam here asked me for help, and after I heard his story I was more than happy to oblige.'

'But –' began Adam.

'But nothing,' Calico Jack said, cutting him off again.

'There'll be plenty of time for proper introductions when we've saved your mother.'

Adam got the idea. If the Doctor were to find out that Calico Jack was really his father, it would slow everything down.

He glanced back at the torn piece of hotel register, wondering how he could have missed something so simple as an anagram and a false beard. Then he noticed the name above Scabellax's.

Flores Tily.

Where there was one anagram, there could easily be another. The letters swam before his mind's eye and rearranged themselves as . . .

Lily Forest. His mother.

If she and Scabellax were anywhere, it would be there.

'To the Hotel Dormir!'

CHAPTER 33

Bus Pilot Torres screeched round another hairpin bend.
'Faster,' shouted Adam. 'Can't you go any faster?'

Every moment was precious. By now, Scabellax would know his plan had been foiled.

The next hairpin bend was upon them. Torres had to slow down.

'Come on,' urged Calico Jack. 'You can drive faster than this.'

Torres angrily slammed his foot to the floor and turned the bus at the same time. The road disappeared. The bus flew through the air, bypassing the bend completely.

'That wasn't quite what I had in mind,' admitted Calico Jack.

As it landed with a sickening shudder on the next stretch of straight road, Torres laughed gleefully and accelerated again. The bus flew once more.

Crash. And smashed into the next level of road.

'You're destroying the bus!' cried Adam.

'Who cares?' bellowed Torres ecstatically. 'I'm flying.'

They were going down the mountain faster than the bus had ever done the journey before. But would they – and the bus – be in one piece when they got there? The Arkonauts hung on and waited to find out.

'Ladies and gentlemen,' began Bus Pilot Torres, 'we are now beginning our final descent into Buenos Sueños. Please switch off all electrical devices.'

The bus went off the road for the final time. And this time there was much more of a drop. The road rushed up to greet them.

Craaaaaassshhhhh!

'Ladies and gentlemen, welcome to Buenos Sueños. We trust you had a pleasant journey and we look forward to you travelling with Aerobus again.'

'Not likely,' muttered Calico Jack.

But Adam was already out of his seat and at the driver's side. 'Can you take us to the Hotel Dormir?' he asked.

Bus Pilot Torres nodded before accelerating into the narrow streets of Buenos Sueños, with bits of bus falling off on all sides as he did so.

'Faster,' urged Adam.

No bus had ever navigated the narrow streets of Buenos Sueños before. They were only millimetres wider than the vehicle itself, but Bus Pilot Torres knew no fear. The bus squeaked through entrances, crashed through washing lines, spun at right angles and never hit a thing. Torres brought it to a screeching halt outside the Hotel Dormir.

'Thank you,' said the Doctor. 'You may need a new bus.'

'Maybe next time,' said Torres, 'my bus will have wings!'

The Doctor turned to the rescue team and barked in fluent dog: 'Please can all the dogs, apart from Sniffage, surround the hotel to cut off any of Scabellax's escape routes. Bark twice if you see him.'

The dogs all rushed off to form a cordon round the hotel – all, that is, except Sausage.

'Grrr!' he growled to himself. 'Think I'm not going inside? They've got another think coming.'

Adam, Anna, the Doctor, Calico Jack and the Arkonauts charged off the bus and up the steps to the Hotel Dormir. Sausage followed them as fast as his little legs would allow.

Miguel, the concierge, was standing by the door.

'Stop, please,' he said, seeing Sniffage and Sausage. 'The Hotel Dormir does not welcome dogs.'

His eye fell on Malibu.

'Or cats.'

He saw Simia.

'Or monkeys.'

Gogo and Pozzo swooped past his ears.

'Or parrots.'

Vlad fluttered down on to Miguel's shoulder, his sharp fangs poised to bite.

'Or . . .' The concierge fainted. He had never liked horror films.

The Arkonauts charged into the lobby. Arantcha shot to her feet behind the reception desk.

'What is the meaning of this?' she demanded. 'Do you have a reservation?'

'No,' said the Doctor. 'We've come to visit one of your guests, a certain Professor Scabellax.'

Arantcha was confused. 'We have nobody of that name staying in the hotel.'

'You may know him as Señor Le Blacas.'

Arantcha nodded. 'We have a Señor Le Blacas. But what of this Professor Scabellax?'

'He'll be in the room with him,' Adam assured her.

Arantcha's expression was stern. 'Having guests in the room is strictly against hotel policy. I shall go up to room 101 and tell him personally. After you take your pets out of my lobby.'

'Pets?' said Adam, looking at the Arkonauts. 'I don't see any pets.'

'Those creatures.'

Sniffage, Malibu, Simia, Gogo, Pozzo and Vlad all looked back at her.

'Aren't they pets?' she asked weakly.

'No,' said Adam. 'They're Arkonauts. And they've got a job to do.'

He led the Doctor, Anna, Calico Jack and the Arkonauts up the stairs, two at a time.

'If any of your Arkonauts make a mess on the carpet,' shouted Arantcha after them, 'there'll be a surcharge.'

CHAPTER 34

The door to room 101 was locked.

'Private Mandible can . . .' Adam began. Then he remembered that Private Mandible had rejoined the Special Ant Service and was not currently available to pick locks.

'Anything he can do, young 'un,' said Calico Jack, 'I think I can do better.'

He pulled a tool from his pocket and inserted it in the lock.

'What did you say your name was again?' said the Doctor.

'Calico Jack.'

'Are you sure we haven't met before?'

'Do you want to save your wife or don't you?'

Calico Jack didn't wait for an answer. Instead he curtailed any further questions by swiftly picking the lock and opening the door.

Room 101 was empty.

At least it seemed empty to the humans. But to Sniffage it was full of smells. He jammed his nose to the floor and started sniffing. Moments later, he was following Scabellax's scent to the window.

'Yeah! Yeah! He went this way!'

A fire escape led up to the roof.

'Are you sure, Sniffage?' Adam said.

'I never forget a smell,' barked the spaniel.

Anna was first to leap into action. She ran to the window and clambered out on to the fire escape. The other Arkonauts ran after her. Up the steps they went, as fast as they could, and climbed on to the roof, only to see at the far end . . .

A large yellow hot-air balloon. It was filled with helium and tethered to the ground by a single length of rope. Discarded next to the balloon was Scabellax's jetpack. He could no longer use it because he was taking a passenger.

But not a willing one.

Scabellax was dragging a woman towards the basket. Her arms and legs were tied up. She could only be one person . . .

'Mum!' Adam shouted across the rooftops.

The woman looked round.

'Adam!'

There was joy in her voice but also fear. And the fear was there for good reason. Professor Scabellax turned round too. His face was contorted with rage. He looked ready to kill.

'Stay where you are!' he cried. 'Come any closer and I throw your mother off the building.'

The Arkonauts stopped in their tracks. Scabellax was standing near the edge of the hotel roof, and he wasn't bluffing.

'Give up, Scabellax,' said the Doctor sternly. 'Let my wife go.'

'Give up?' said the Professor mockingly. 'That, Doctor, is the last thing I'm going to do. You may have postponed my conquering of the world but you have not stopped it. I have the knowledge, and you know, as a scientist, Doctor, that once the knowledge exists, then sooner or later it must be used. The unstoppable wheels of progress demand it.'

'Destroying free will . . .' replied the Doctor. 'Controlling people's minds . . . That isn't progress. That is the very opposite of progress.'

'There we will have to agree to differ,' said Scabellax. 'Governments and politicians have been trying to control people's minds and destroy their free will since time began. But they have all failed. Only I have found the secret to success.'

'You could stop this now,' said the Doctor. 'Reject the dark side of science.'

For a moment Scabellax hesitated. Did he remember the young idealist he once was? Was he tempted to try to be that man again? But then his brow blackened.

'I will tell you something, Doctor,' he said. 'Darkness is more powerful than light. In the end we will all be swallowed by it.' And he hoisted Adam's mum into the basket of the balloon.

As though hearing the Professor's words, the burning Buenos Sueños sun tipped below the horizon. Darkness was coming.

'No,' shouted Adam.

'Adam!' his mother cried again.

He couldn't bear to hear her anguish.

'At least let the woman go,' demanded Calico Jack, pointing at Adam. 'Think of this boy without a mother.'

'I will think of it,' answered Scabellax. 'And I will laugh every time that I do. Goodbye.'

He untied the rope and jumped into the basket. The balloon began to rise.

'No!'

'He's getting away!'

The length of rope was uncoiling fast as the balloon climbed steadily into the air.

'Grab the rope!'

But there wasn't enough of it. Already the end of it was being dragged towards the edge of the roof. No human could have got across in time to grab it.

But perhaps a dog could.

With his brown ears flapping wildly, Sniffage charged across the roof, the other Arkonauts sprinting behind him. The balloon got higher and higher, and the trailing rope left the ground. Sniffage jumped and grasped it with his teeth.

Sniffage's weight held the balloon for a crucial few seconds while Anna, Adam, the Doctor and Calico Jack caught up. As soon as they had a grip on it, Sniffage dropped to the ground, exhausted.

'Yeah! Yeah!' he shouted. 'That was as good as chasing a stick.'

Slowly, and with great effort, they began to haul Scabellax's balloon down.

'We've got him, young 'un,' said Calico Jack. 'We've got him.'

But he spoke too soon. A sack fell from above and crashed on to the roof, narrowly missing the Arkonauts. Suddenly the balloon started to tug upwards again.

'He's shedding ballast,' shouted the Doctor.

Another sack crashed to the ground. Now, even lighter, the balloon was too powerful to be pulled down. It was all Adam, Anna, the Doctor and Calico Jack could do to hold it in position. But their strength was not going to last for long. Already their muscles were beginning to weaken.

Professor Scabellax leant over the edge of the basket and leered at them.

'Parting is such sweet sorrow,' he crooned. 'That is, sweet for me and sorrow for you.'

'I can't hold it much longer,' said Adam.

'Tch! Tch!' chattered Simia. 'This is when you really need a monkey.'

'And some parrots,' cheeped Gogo and Pozzo.

'And a vampire bat,' squeaked Vlad.

Malibu sighed.

'And, I suppose, a cat,' he yowled. 'Even though I must warn you, I'm very tired.'

'What are you talking about?' said Adam.

'You humans stick to the simple stuff, like holding a rope,' said Simia. 'Leave the rescue to us.'

'But how . . . ?'

Simia climbed up the Doctor's back and leapt on to the rope.

'Normally I require a stunt cat for all action sequences,' said Malibu, 'but I suppose I'll have to make an exception.'

The cat followed the monkey, climbing up the Doctor's back and leaping on to the rope, which he gripped with his claws. Then he and Simia scrambled up towards the basket. Meanwhile, Gogo and Pozzo flew to one side of the balloon and Vlad to the other. Simia was right – all the humans could do was hold the rope with all their might and watch. Sniffage barked his encouragement.

'You don't think Simia's right about us going down the wrong evolutionary path, do you?' Adam said to the Doctor.

The Doctor grunted.

'What's going on?' shouted Scabellax, seeing the monkey and cat climbing closer. 'Shoo! Get away from my balloon! Shoo! Woooahhh!'

Scabellax never knew what hit him. Two green blurs flew into his face.

Straight afterwards, a pair of sharp South American fangs sank into his neck.

'Arrrrghhh!'

And before he could recover, a monkey was on top of him, pummelling him hard, and a cat's claws were scratching down his face.

'HELP!'

The Professor's voice rang out over the streets of Buenos Sueños. But there was no help to be had. He was forced to throw himself down into the basket, face first, to try to minimise the effect of the scratches and the pummelling.

Down below on the hotel roof the rope holders were weakening. Were it not for Sniffage grabbing on with his teeth again to help Adam, Anna, the Doctor and Calico Jack, they would already have been forced to let go. Even so, their muscles cried out for relief. They couldn't bring the balloon any lower and they wouldn't be able to keep it from flying off for much longer.

'Hurry up!' shouted Adam.

The Arkonauts in the basket of the balloon understood the urgency. So while Simia, Malibu and Vlad kept Scabellax occupied with a painful combination of fists, claws and fangs, Gogo and Pozzo used their sharp beaks to bite through the ropes that bound Adam's mum's hands and feet.

'Why did the road cross the chicken?' Gogo asked her in between bites.

Lily had never encountered parrot comedians.

'Shouldn't it be the chicken crossing the road?' she said.

The parrots gnawed through the first rope and her legs were free.

'We can't hold it much longer,' cried Adam.

The parrots set to work on the rope that tied her hands.

'All right, then,' said Pozzo through a mouthful of rope. 'There were these two parrots who flew into a bar.'

'Really?' said Lily.

'They should have looked where they were going,' said Gogo.

Adam's mum groaned — it had been a long time since she'd heard jokes this bad. But her groan swiftly turned to a sigh of relief. The parrots had chewed through her second rope. She was free.

At least, free in the sense that she could move about. But she was still trapped in a balloon thirty metres above the ground.

The rope was beginning to slip through the fingers of Adam, Anna, the Doctor and Calico Jack as the balloon tugged relentlessly against their ever-weakening arms.

'Don't let go,' cautioned the Doctor. But even as he said it, he felt the rope slipping.

Adam too was struggling. But he thought of his mother and somehow found the will to hold on.

Malibu leapt out of the balloon basket and skittered down the rope, landing safely back on the roof of the Hotel Dormir. Lily's face appeared over the edge of the basket.

So near but so far. How was she to get down? Simia's face

appeared next to hers. The monkey tapped her on the shoulder and pointed to herself.

'If Simia is giving her one of her lectures about why humans should never have come down from the trees . . .' said the Doctor said through gritted teeth.

But that was not what Simia was trying to do. She knew that Adam's mum couldn't communicate with her like Adam and the Doctor, but she could understand enough to follow the monkey's lead. Simia pointed at herself, then at Lily and then she clambered out of the balloon and slid down the rope to safety.

But sliding down a rope was easy for a monkey. It was not easy for a human.

'Come on, Mum,' shouted Adam. 'You can do it!'

Tentatively, Lily straddled a leg over the edge of the basket. Everyone below held their breath.

She leant down for the rope. It was just out of reach. She stretched a little further, but still it dangled centimetres from her grasp. On her third attempt, her fingertips brushed the rope and she grabbed it as the rest of her body tumbled out of the basket. There was a collective gasp from below as the others watched her dangle helplessly for a moment. Then she managed to grab the rope with her feet and wrap her legs around it.

'Slide down!'

Adam's mum closed her eyes and slid. It was not an elegant descent like Simia's. It was slower and clumsier. But now she was twenty metres away, fifteen, ten, five, three.

The watchers' strength gave way. The rope was dragged out of their hands. The balloon began to rise.

'Let go!' shouted Adam.

His mother was confused. She opened her eyes. Why was she going up again?

'Let go!' Adam screamed as loud as he possibly could.

This time the words blasted through the confusion. Lily let go of the rope, dropped through the air and landed in the open arms of her husband.

'Hello,' he said. But his eyes and his smile said much more.

Adam's mum wanted to see someone else too. She dragged herself from her husband's embrace and rushed towards her son.

'Adam!'

'Mum!'

They had the biggest hug in the history of the world.

Everybody cheered.

Simia stopped cheering first.

'Of course,' she chattered drily, 'with a few centuries' evolution you might be able to turn back into monkeys and then the sliding down a rope business wouldn't be such a palaver. There's no harm in you humans admitting you made an evolutionary wrong turn.'

There was a bark from behind them.

Everybody turned round. Sausage had just reached the roof.

'I'm ready to help,' he woofed. 'Where's this Scabellax fella? I'll bite his ankles.'

Adam pointed to the yellow balloon, which was flying away towards the mountains.

Sausage shook his head in disbelief. 'You mean I've missed all the fun?'

Adam nodded.

'Curse these little legs,' said Sausage.

And he was most put out when everybody laughed.

CHAPTER 35

For two nights and three days Buenos Sueños slept. Nothing moved, no shops opened and no children played in the streets. The only sound to be heard was snoring, which drifted from open windows on all sides of the narrow streets. The snores mingled together and the sound swelled until a symphony of sleep rang out through the streets of Buenos Sueños. But loud as it was, it didn't wake anybody up, as the city enjoyed the longest siesta the world has ever known.

And then the party started.

The fiesta began on the third night. The Mayor, newly restored to power, ordered that the terrible loudspeakers used to broadcast the Dreadful Alarm were brought down to the harbour, where it was decreed the celebrations be held. But now, instead of an alarm, they blared out music with an infectious beat which got inside the body of even the stiffest and sternest of men and made their feet stamp and their bodies want to dance.

The celebration parade snaked its way through the narrow white streets and terminated in one great dancing mass on the wharf. Everybody in the city was there in all kinds of outrageous costumes. Models of giants with outsized heads danced behind human castles, eight people high, with waving children on the top. Señor Gozo abandoned his tourist information kiosk and changed his T-shirt to join in. The Bajapuentalists were there, having travelled to the fiesta via every low bridge in the city. Fidel Guavera twirled a rolled-up opinion poll about his head like a cheerleader's baton and Bus Pilot Torres performed a dance which involved a lot of hand flapping. Diego, the spot painter, came too – his dance resembled a rhythmic shrug. Fireworks shot into the sky and exploded in showers of colour. The celebrations would last all night.

The Arkonauts had no distance to travel to join the party as their boat, where they, too, had slept solidly for three days, was moored just along the harbour. Adam watched in disbelief as the Doctor and his mother danced together down the gangplank and into the throng of partygoers. Then his disbelief turned to embarrassment as he noticed that the Doctor, despite being a great scientist, had no sense of rhythm and was the cause of considerable amusement with his jerky robotic movements, which contrasted so strongly with the sinuous dancing of even the oldest Buenos Sueñosian. And talking of old Buenos Sueñosians, Grandma Marquez, free at last from the fear of arrest for the pea-related offence, could be found drinking wine and laughing with her family.

All the Arkonauts joined in. Sniffage and Sausage capered around, barking and sniffing dead things. Simia demonstrated that monkeys could dance better than humans. Even Malibu deigned to swing a paw. And circling around the mast of the *Ark of the Parabola*, watching everybody below, were Gogo, Pozzo and Vlad. Even the Special Ant Service, safe on board the boat, did some ant dancing – though, under the supervision of General Lepti, they were expected to move in strict formation.

Adam was watching the joyous mayhem and tapping his feet to the music, desperately hoping that he hadn't inherited the Doctor's sense of rhythm (his mother, he couldn't help noticing, was a much better dancer), when he felt a hand clap down on his shoulder. He turned round to see Calico Jack.

'Well, young 'un,' said Calico Jack, 'you did it. You rescued everybody and you saved the city.'

'It was Anna as well,' said Adam, unwilling to take all the credit. He was still looking out for the dark-haired girl, hoping she'd show up to the fiesta.

'Aye,' said Calico Jack. 'She's a fine girl, I'll give you that. But you, lad. I have to say I wondered whether you had my blood running through your veins when I first met you.'

'Why?' said Adam.

'No offence, young 'un, but you seemed so proper.'

'You mean honest,' said Adam.

'You're not old enough to tell me what I mean,' Calico Jack replied. 'You needed to loosen up a little if you were going to save a whole city, to bend a few rules. That's all I'm saying. The Doctor might be right about living life by the rules most of the time, but you know what his problem is?'

Adam shook his head.

'He's so busy looking for rules and answers and explanations, he can't see that sometimes there aren't any to be found.'

'What do you do when there aren't any rules?'

Calico Jack's face crinkled into a smile.

'You do what you did, young 'un: you live by your wits and you make 'em up as you go along. That's how you saved this city, and I'm proud of you.'

Adam couldn't help but smile at the praise. Behind him there was whoosh as a firework shot up into the sky. 'Can I ask you something?'

'Course you can, young 'un,' said his grandfather. 'If I can answer it without incriminating myself.'

'Why doesn't the Doctor recognise you? He's seen plenty of pictures of you. He told me.'

Calico Jack nodded. 'I was wondering if you'd get around to that. Thing is, young 'un,' he said with a wink, 'I've been in disguise the whole time. Your grandfather doesn't look like me one bit.'

He patted Adam on the back.

'Remember. Live by your wits when you have to. Now

m going to dance.' And Calico Jack slipped into the crowd.

As he disappeared from view, the Mayor and Anna emerged from the swaying throng and climbed up the gang-plank. Behind them was someone Adam was very surprised to see at the fiesta: Felipe Felipez.

'Hi,' said Adam.

Anna nodded hello.

'Where is the Doctor?' asked the Mayor.

'He's dancing,' said Adam, and he pointed to his parents.

The Mayor followed Adam's finger.

Unfortunately the Doctor was attempting an ambitious twirl at precisely that moment.

'You call that dancing?' said the Mayor incredulously. 'It looks like he's in pain.'

'Quite the opposite,' said Adam. 'I think he might be happy for the first time in ten years.'

'Well,' said the Mayor, 'I won't interrupt him. I just wanted to thank you for saving my city. While the Chief of Police had me held like a prisoner in my own town hall, you and Anna bravely undertook to stop Señor Le Blacas – I mean, Professor Scabellax – from destroying Buenos Sueños. Deputy Mayor Felipez and I wanted to thank you on behalf of all our citizens.'

Adam couldn't believe it.

'Deputy Mayor?'

Felipe Felipez shook his hand. 'Pleased to meet you.'

'But a few days ago you hated him.'

The Mayor laughed. 'You obviously don't unders
politics, chico. Deputy Mayor Felipez and I have always *
a great mutual respect, haven't we, Felipez?'

'Oh yes,' nodded Deputy Mayor Felipez. 'A great mutua
respect.'

'And we both want what's best for Buenos Sueños.'

'Best for Buenos Sueños,' echoed Deputy Mayor Felipez.
'With Mayor Puig as our leader, the city will make great
progress. When the terrible truth about Scabellax was
revealed I immediately withdrew from the election and gave
all my support to Mayor Puig.'

'And,' smiled the Mayor, 'it was coincidentally at that very
moment that I realised the city could not do without a
Deputy Mayor.'

The old Adam would have still been mystified. The new
one understood.

'You did a deal?'

'Of course we didn't!' said the Mayor.

'To think that we would stoop to such squalid behaviour!'
added the Deputy Mayor.

They shook their heads in unison.

'But,' said the Mayor, 'we won't dwell on what you have
just said. Instead we want to thank you once again for saving
Buenos Sueños. We will for ever be in your debt. Tomorrow
we will begin our work to make this city a better place . . .'
The Mayor was distracted from his plans for the future by the
fiesta on the wharf. 'Please excuse me,' he said. 'Someone

. teach your father how to dance before he stamps on
r mother's feet again. The poor lady may sustain some
rmanent injuries if I don't intervene.'

He hurried down the gangplank with Deputy Mayor
Felipez in tow, leaving Adam and Anna alone. With a con-
spiratorial wink Anna reached behind her back, and from
under her jumper she pulled a thick black hardback book.

'What's that?' said Adam.

With a smile Anna showed him the title.

'The Buenos Sueños Crime and Punishment Code!'
Adam couldn't believe it. And then he remembered. 'You
took the key when we were rescuing Calico Jack.'

Anna nodded.

'And you sneaked back to get it today?'

Anna nodded again.

'I can't believe you didn't take me.'

Anna indicated that Adam had been asleep.

'What are you going to do with it?'

Anna shrugged. Adam shrugged back. Anna smiled.
Adam's shrugs were getting to be as good as any Buenos
Sueñosian's.

They looked at the book.

'I don't suppose anybody really needs it, do they?'

Anna shook her head.

Together they took hold of the tome and, on the count
of three, hurled it into the harbour. There was a splash and
then it sank beneath the waves. The city was going to need a

whole new raft of laws in the morning.

And that morning was already dawning. The first rays of sunshine were beginning to light up the harbour and, with them, the great fiesta was coming to an end. As Adam and Anna walked down the gangplank to join their parents, he turned to her.

'Do you think you will stay in Buenos Sueños when you grow up?'

But before Anna could answer, they were interrupted by an all too familiar sound.

PHEEEP! PHEEEEP!

Chief of Police Grivas and the Buenos Sueños Police Force rushed out of the narrow streets of the city, roughly pushing the celebrating citizens aside.

Chief Grivas, his face dark and furious, strode up to the Mayor.

'What have you done with it?' he demanded.

'What are you talking about?'

'The Buenos Sueños Crime and Punishment Code. It's gone. What have you done with it? My officers have been searching for it, but it's as if it's vanished into thin air. I know you've got it. Hand it over.'

The Mayor shook his head. 'I can assure you, Chief, that I have never set eyes upon it. I can't think who could have taken it.'

Anna and Adam exchanged looks.

'But I do know,' continued the Mayor, 'that if the one

copy of the Buenos Sueños Crime and Punishment Code has gone, then all its laws have gone with it and we will have to start again to build a newer, fairer, happier Buenos Sueños.'

'That doesn't sound like the kind of city I'm going to like,' Chief Grivas mumbled doubtfully.

The news spread through the crowd and, realising that the dreaded Buenos Sueños Crime and Punishment Code was behind them, the people became even happier.

'I declare today a public holiday,' shouted the Mayor.

The harbour erupted in glee.

'I'm afraid we can't stay,' Doctor Forest told the Mayor apologetically.

'What?' he cried. 'But you are our guests of honour.'

The Doctor shook his head.

'I am sorry. We must depart immediately. There are more scientific discoveries to make. For ten years I have delayed searching for the fabled blue-eared pygmy goat of Patagonia.'

'The pygmy-eared blue goat of Patagonia?' repeated the Mayor incredulously.

'Don't be ridiculous,' said the Doctor. 'Pygmy-eared blue goats live in Siberia. Everybody knows that.'

'Do they?' said the Mayor.

The Doctor assured him they did. 'Besides,' he said proudly, looking at Lily and Adam, 'my wife, my son and I have a great deal of catching up to do.'

The Mayor smiled. He saw that the Doctor would not

change his mind. He proffered his hand.

'Buenos Sueños will always be in your debt,' he said.

And so, an hour later, the *Ark of the Parabola* pulled up the gangplank, weighed anchor and set sail from the port of Buenos Sueños. An entire city crowded on the harbour to wave farewell. The Arkonauts stood side by side to wave back. Above them, Gogo, Pozzo and Vlad flapped farewell wings.

'Just moving your arms back and forth to say goodbye seems a rather pointless ability to evolve,' chattered Siniia as she watched the harbour recede. 'It would be much better to use your hands for climbing trees, like monkeys.'

'You know,' yowled Malibu, 'I think all this waving might be giving me repetitive strain injury in my paw. I'm going to need many restorative winks.'

'Yeah! Yeah! Has anybody got a stick?' woofed Sniffage. 'I haven't chased a stick in ages.'

There was a bark from behind him. Sniffage whirled his head round, getting his ears tangled in the process.

'Yeah! Yeah! Who's that? I thought I was the only one who barked on this ship.'

Sausage emerged from below deck.

'Where's the land going?' he woofed.

The Doctor and his wife turned round in horror.

'Why didn't you get off the boat?'

Sausage was offended. 'Sniffage said he could smell a dead thing so I went to investigate. It took me some time because I have little legs.'

'Yeah! Yeah!' barked Sniffage, delighted to see his friend still on board. 'Want to be an Arkonaut?'

'Are there sticks?' asked Sausage cautiously.

Sniffage barked yes.

'And smells?'

Sniffage barked yes again.

Sausage woofed back that he wanted to join and the two dogs sniffed each other's bottoms in celebration.

'Look!' said Adam, pointing into the sky.

The Arkonauts looked up. There, just visible against the razor-sharp snow-capped peaks of Los Puntos Afilados, being buffeted back and forth by the strong winds that raged at the top of them, was a yellow balloon.

'Scabellax!' Adam exclaimed. 'Where do you think he's going?'

'Wherever the winds take him,' said the Doctor. 'Perhaps it's fitting that a man who tried to bend nature to his will is now helpless in its power.'

'But what if –' began Adam.

'Today we're not going to worry about Professor Scabellax,' said Adam's mum, putting an arm around him. 'We'll leave him to the elements. They seem to know what they're doing.'

And as if to confirm her words, a giant gust swept the yellow balloon into a menacing black cloud that clung to the tallest peak and out of sight.

The Doctor turned to his wife.

'How does it feel to be part of a family again?' he asked.

She smiled. It felt very good.

'Well, of course, a family plus Calico Jack,' the Doctor added.

'Where *is* he?' said Lily. 'I saw him here just before we set off.'

'Yes, he was . . .' said the Doctor, looking around. 'Ah, there.'

'Where?' Lily couldn't see him on the deck.

'There!' The Doctor pointed back to Buenos Sueños. And there, on the edge of the wharf, watching the ship sail away, was Calico Jack.

'He must have slipped ashore just before we weighed anchor,' the Doctor said. 'Why would he have done that? I had a lot of questions to ask him. I'm still convinced I've seen him somewhere before.'

'Maybe we'll meet him again one day,' said Lily. 'The world is a very strange place and the most surprising things seem to happen in it, don't they, Adam?'

But Adam didn't answer. While everybody else waved to the crowd, he was waving to only one figure, a figure who grew smaller and more distant with every gust of wind that pushed the *Ark* away from Buenos Sueños. Anna. Dark, pretty, mischievous Anna. The only friend he'd ever had. He would miss her.

And now read a quest unlike any quest that's been before...

'Inventive, charming, and very funny'
Observer